What readers are saying about Cinderella Assassin…

"A magical read!" – Sairaika

"I highly recommend reading this book if you like coming of age stories, fairy tales, action, romance, and kick-ass heroines. I can't wait to keep reading this new series." – Essiery's Reviews

"An interesting spin on a classic and timeless tale." – Goodreads Reviewer

Cinderella ASSASSIN

A Glass Slipper Adventure

ALLIE BURTON

Allie Burton
Cinderella Assassin
A Glass Slipper Adventure

Copyright © 2020 by Alice Fairbanks-Burton
All Rights Reserved

ISBN-13: 978-1-951-245-08-5

Join My Newsletter And Receive A Free Book!

Details at: www.allieburton.com

Stay in touch with Allie:

allie@allieburton.com
www.twitter.com/allie_burton
www.facebook.com/AllieBurtonAuthor
www.instagram.com/allieburtonauthor

Chapter 1

The dark and dingy alley was the perfect place for making an illegal deal.

The bright crystal castle sitting high on the nearby mountain prevented the early morning light shimmering through the almost-invisible dome from reaching this drab, grease-filled spot. Adding to the dreariness, the shiny business and residential towers reflected sunlight in the opposite direction. The crowded skywalk didn't travel this way, so people weren't wandering about, and the area had an abandoned feel to it. Rustling and blowing papers, darkness, and despair.

We were isolated here, safe from discovery.

As long as the SCUM—Security Collectors of Unique Magic—didn't show up.

Then I'd be a goner.

For now, however, I was huddling near a trash chute with my best friend, Arbor, nervously waiting for our contact to arrive, I tapped a quick beat on the dirty pavement with my boot-clad toe. In spite of the monotonous-official-perfect-year-round temperature, sweat dribbled down my back.

Arbor, a smoke sprite, buzzed in front of my face. Her short, psychedelic hair stood out like a multi-colored flower in hues of pink and purple. "Don't hum," she hissed. "No one should be relaxed."

Her command had me biting my lower lip, gnawing at its edges. I wasn't relaxed, far from it. My humming was just a distraction from the eerie, quiet surroundings. I didn't like it being so quiet, although at least I didn't have to worry about someone sneaking up on us. I hadn't even realized I'd been humming.

I knew the habit made Arbor nervous, and her being nervous would have her going up in smoke—literally. One of a smoke sprite's idiosyncrasies was showing their emotions by the color of mist they produced.

"Are you sure we can trust the fairy?" I loosened my grip around the delicate, vintage, glass perfume bottle etched with swirling gold designs. If I clutched it too tight, the fragile glass would crack, shattering my chances of fitting in and having a normal life.

Arbor fluttered her tiny wings in front of my face, creating a slight breeze and stirring my whitish-blond hair. "Who *can* you trust completely these days, Elle?"

Her skepticism stabbed my chest. She was right.

I remembered the first time my stepsisters tricked me. They'd convinced me to borrow a necklace from my stepmother's jewelry box saying they needed it to play dress-up with me. I believed them and swiped the necklace, but then the two of them ran off to play together, leaving me out. When they'd fought over the necklace and broken it, they told their mother I'd stolen the piece of jewelry. Which had technically been true, but I was the only who'd gotten in trouble. As punishment, besides all the other chores around the house, I had to give my stepmother foot massages.

Gross.

Arbor was different. I trusted her advice. From the

beginning, when she'd shown up at my house lost and alone six months ago, she'd steered me straight. She'd taught me about the lost art of humming and the sway it held. She'd shared her laughter and friendship, and information about the secret underbelly of the Kingdom of Alandaska, and tales from the fairies. Hailing from the same province as my mother, she *had* to be good.

"Why does this fairy want my mom's old perfume bottle enough that they're willing to pay creds?" I sniffed at the top, taking in the strange rotting vegetable smell and crinkled my nose. "It certainly isn't for the scent."

"The bottle is a fairy artifact." Her luminous mossy-green eyes blinked. She wore a green dress with a purposely made rip in the skirt. Her fingerless gloves made her appear more edgy. "The government is trying to destroy our heritage, one tiny item at a time."

If the SCUM came upon us, I'd be arrested for possessing a fairy item, and the perfume bottle would be destroyed. Humans couldn't use or own majik artifacts, in case they were tempted to access the magic within.

My heart tugged as though I'd be handing over the vital organ along with the bottle. I hated parting with anything that had once belonged to Mom. The small trunk hidden in my attic bedroom held my only reminders of her. A precious and emotional link to the mother I barely remembered. But right now, I couldn't risk being distracted by the past. I needed to focus on my future. I desperately needed the creds the perfume bottle would get so I could buy a dress to wear to the royal ball.

Stupid to risk so much for something so silly, except an appearance at the ball would establish my place in society.

A silhouette emerged at the end of the alley. Holding my breath, I watched the gloom float forward, sticking to the edges of the walls until he reached us. The male fairy cast a taller shadow than me. Too-large pants and jacket swallowed his thin frame. If he was trying to look human, he was failing miserably. Fairies came in different types and sizes just like humans, but it was difficult to hide their shorter stature, pointy ears, and fluttering wings.

"Do you have the item?" His cold, beady eyes raked over me and then narrowed as if spotting something he didn't like.

I ran a finger over the edge of my almost-perfectly-round ears. He wasn't the first to make me feel like I didn't belong, and I was tired of others' biased attitude toward me. "If I didn't, would I be here risking getting caught?"

Caught by the SCUM or my stepmother. Either would have severe consequences.

"Elle, shush." Arbor's tone resembled that of an army sergeant. It must be how she displayed fear—by ordering me around.

I understood her fear. I was terrified. We were in a dark alley, making a shady deal with an illegal fairy for an illicit artifact. But why was Arbor fearful when she used the same tone while teaching me things I didn't want to learn? I got enough bossiness from my stepmom. I didn't need it from my friend.

My hands shook slightly as I held out the atomizer, knowing I was giving away a piece of my mom. A vision flashed through my mind of her squeezing the soft bulb at the top and spraying perfume on each side of her neck. The scent hadn't smelled rotten then, it had smelled beautiful, like her.

"This is it." I forced the words between tight lips.

"How do I know it is what you say it is?" The fairy glowered at Arbor, and her colorful hair spiked higher.

Once more I was being overlooked and belittled. He was buying the bottle from me, not her.

"Because I say so." Her little kid imitation edged with authority.

"Why would I lie?" My muscles tensed tighter. Fairies couldn't lie, but I could. He must not trust me. I realize I appeared younger than my sixteen years and also had plenty of lies spoon fed to me. He didn't know that. "It's my mom's perfume bottle."

"Lily Kunglig?"

Hearing my mother's maiden name again after so long was like a kick to the gut. It shouldn't bother me. She'd died when I was a toddler. "You knew her?"

He snatched the bottle from me and held it up to his eyes. I fisted my hands together, forcing myself not to snag it back. My hands felt empty, and the sensation traveled to my chest. Another memory of my mother slipping away.

This was a bad idea, but it was the only choice I had and the only way to get creds. Creds I desperately needed.

The fairy clutched the bottle to his pointy nose and smiled. The exact opposite reaction I had. Maybe majiks had different smell sensations.

He slipped a plastic cred payment out of his pocket. "I'm not allowed to carry creds in this kingdom anymore."

Bitterness laced his words, as though he remembered better times for majiks, before the regent decided to put an end to magic in favor of technology, something he could control.

"Neither am I." Arbor dove toward the card. With her eight-inch height, even if she was allowed, she wouldn't be able to carry something so large.

My fingers tingled as they closed around the card. The creds were the first step in achieving my goal.

The fairy's gaze narrowed. "The card better not get traced back to me."

"It won't. I'll be spending it today." I had to hurry.

Shopping was at the end of my very long list. Laundry, cooking, cleaning, and helping my stepsisters prepare for the ball, all before I could head to the mall. The creds weren't worth much, but I could find a dress on sale.

Then, when I stepped onto the dance floor at the royal ball, the kids from school would finally accept me as being just like them.

Nothing strange. Nothing unusual. Nothing out of the ordinary.

"Elle, I'm thirsty."

I huffed. The words might not be an order, but my stepsister Ilana's tone said otherwise.

Pinching my lips together, I stopped myself from telling her what she could do with her life quotient drink.

Since returning from the illicit meeting this morning, I'd been running around, doing both my stepsisters' and stepmother's bidding.

Regenerate my skin.

Apply whitening powder to my body.

Electra-wax my nose hairs.

I shivered at the thought of the last one.

Just because I had an old book filled with natural beauty treatments did not mean I wanted to be their esthe-tech. There was enough work to do around the house, and I still needed to get a dress for myself.

Ilana waved her fat fingers as if she expected the straw to reach her lips by magic. "I can't see the glass." Her face was coated in green goo from the facial I'd just applied to her skin, and her eyes were covered by silicon discs. Her blond hair had been pulled back off her face while the deep conditioning worked on the roots.

"Ilana needs her hydration." My stepmother Sybil's lips thinned. She had a green face too, but no silicon discs. She watched every move I made. "Do it, Elle."

Wrapping my fingers around the condensing glass, I wanted to dump the contents of the technological equated health drink onto both of them. However, if I did, I'd be the one cleaning the mess, and then I'd have to start the body treatments over.

Squeezing my fingers tighter, wishing it was Ilana's neck, I put the metal straw to her lips and held the glass while she sipped…

And sipped. And sipped.

I tapped my foot. I only had two hands and couldn't finish my other stepsister's facial while holding the glass. "Done yet?"

"Fine." She spat the straw from her mouth. "As if you can't hold a glass up for a few more seconds. You're so lazy sometimes, Elle."

I'm lazy? My fingers cramped thinking about all the work I'd done. But I wouldn't complain. Not today. Not ever, really. I needed to keep things harmonious in the household.

I set the glass down with a snap and moved over to Ingrid, who was propped up on a chair, half-laying and half-sitting. Taller than the average human girl, her feet dangled off the edge.

We were in the master bedroom, Sybil's domain. She and Ilana lay on the bed, their heads on multiple pillows. The younger stepsister, Ingrid, got stuck with the glido-chair, which didn't have a good view of the small vid screen hanging in the corner.

The master bedroom was so different compared to how it

was before my father died. The old wooden bed with silk curtains circling it had been replaced by a metallic headboard and sleep-sensing mattress and pillows, with the hyperbaric lid hanging over the top ready to enclose the sleeper. The dresser matched the bed with sharp, metallic decorations and a large mirror hanging over the center.

Scooping the green goo out of a bowl, I used a brush to apply the glop to Ingrid's face. Her fair skin was free of beauty marks, making the application easier. She really didn't need any kind of enhancement. She was beautiful inside too, if only she'd let that niceness shine through. Around her sister and mother, she tended to be timid and follow their mean leads.

"This natural rockweed and lichen mask is itchy." She wiggled in the chair and almost dropped her celltab. "Are you sure this is good for my skin, Elle?"

"I wouldn't know. I've never had one." Pampering myself had never been a priority.

I'd found the book of treatments in my mother's trunk when I'd been younger, BDD—Before Dad Died. He'd encouraged me to be friends with my new stepsisters, so I'd pulled out the book and offered to play beauty spa. Sybil had heard about our fun and insisted she be included. She'd loved how her skin looked afterward, and suddenly this became a weekly event. Me giving the three of them treatments.

I'd never complained because I hadn't wanted to disappoint my dad. Now, I didn't have a choice.

Grabbing an old-fashioned emery board, I started filing Ilana's nails.

Sybil studied her own newly filed and painted fingers. "Girls, I know tonight is special."

Ilana sighed. "We're going to meet Prince Zacharye."

Ingrid giggled in a high-pitched, excited squeal. It was how all the girls in school reacted at the mention of the prince's name.

I filed a little rougher, ignoring the instant flush that rose to my skin.

When I'd been younger, I'd been just as silly about the prince. But now I understood the evil changes happening in our kingdom, and how the prince was complicit.

"Ouch." Ilana slapped at my hand.

"Elle's treatments are the best we can do when creds are tight." Sybil redirected a small, electric fan at her face. Tendrils of her graying, red hair blew in the slight wind. "Later this afternoon, when the professional hair and make-up techs arrive, they will make your faces flawless. Not that either of you have flaws."

My mouth dropped open. Cred amounts *cha-chinged* in my head.

Of course, Sybil would spend money on making sure her daughters appeared perfect to impress the prince. But those services weren't cheap. Yet she'd refused to spend creds on buying me a dress.

At least while they're occupied, I'll have time to go to the mall and get dressed for the ball.

"Has it been on long enough?" Ingrid sounded antsy, with her voice rolling up into a whine. She swiped a finger across her cheek, creating a streak.

"Stop. You'll ruin the effects." I did not want to reapply the mask. Time was short.

"Nothing will help Ingrid's ugly features." Ilana crinkled her nose, pretending to smell something bad.

The only thing that smelled bad was her.

"Ilana, stop. Both of you are beautiful, and you both will have a shot at the prince." Sybil spoke as if he was a target or a meal.

Or a meal ticket.

Ingrid sat up, stretched with her long arms to reach toward the bed with a slap trying to smack her sister. She missed, only hitting thin air. Momentum took her forward and she toppled about to fall.

I dropped the emery board and grabbed her arm trying to stop her from hitting the ground. My fingers slid across her moist skin. Darn, the moisturizer I'd applied earlier. Her arm slipped from my grip and her face planted in the carpet, the green goo splattering across the pink threads.

That was going to stain.

Stilling, I waited for Sybil to yell at Ingrid. Silence filled the room. Ingrid stayed rooted to the ground. Sybil's gaze narrowed at her daughters. Ilana smirked.

"Elle hit Ingrid." Ilana's false accusation struck me, especially when she winked at her sister in conspiracy.

Gaping, my gaze swiveled back and forth between the two of them. It had been obvious what had actually happened. I'd tried to save her from falling. Would Ingrid tell the truth?

When the younger sister didn't speak, I spoke for myself. "I did not." I was so tired of taking the blame for things these two did, tired of doing their dirty work, tired of doing all the work around the house and getting no appreciation.

It wouldn't be much longer. A few more months until my Continuum.

"Quit quibbling, Elle." Sybil took the wet towel on the nightstand and wiped off her face. She stared at her daughters, ignoring me. "I expect both of you to be perfectly behaved at the ball."

A slight smile snuck on my face. Maybe Sybil did realize it was her daughters causing the trouble. She knew there was no need to tell me to behave. I always listened and did what I was told, followed the rules and the laws. Well, except for this morning.

"Elle." Sybil's short tone had me rolling my eyes. What now? "Take that junk off Ingrid's face."

The poor girl gripped the edge of the glido-chair and struggled to pull herself up. The silicon discs had fallen off and the green mask had been flattened and dripped in her eyes.

"She's got a few more minutes and I'm filing Ilana's nails at this second." Concentrating, I rounded a corner of her nail.

Tension filled the air.

Slowly, I lifted my head knowing what was coming. I shouldn't have directly contradicted Sybil. It was like waving a red flag in front of a cyborg bull. I'd only stated a fact. They're the ones who wanted to look perfect. The recipe called for a specific amount of time for the mask.

Her nostrils flared and her cheeks puffed up about to explode in a fit. "Take care of her, now." Each word was pronounced with emphasis.

Do this. Do that. My fingers tingled. I clapped the file on the nightstand and fisted my hands to stop the sensation. Standing, I clasped Ingrid's arm and helped her back on the chair, took a wet washcloth out of a small tub filled with water, and wiped the mask off her face.

"You're rubbing off my skin." Ingrid's fair complaint had me easing up to finish cleansing her face.

"There." I held up a hand mirror.

Her skin shined from the deep cleaning. Ingrid was pretty and toning her skin added to her natural beauty. The point of her nose gleamed, and her strawberry blond eyebrows highlighted her eyes.

"Oh wow." She moved the mirror to peer at herself from every angle.

Standing there, I waited for some kind of acknowledgement because this time was different. This wasn't for fun or a school dance. This was for the prince.

"I look great." She turned to smile at her sister and mother, not even recognizing my existence.

The tingling in my fingers progressed up to my hands and wrists. I fisted my hands and took a deep breath.

"Do me! Do me!" Ilana raised her hand up and down imitating a monkey.

"You could use a little more time." Sybil's unusual derogatory tone toward her daughter surprised. She normally fawned over the oldest believing she'd make a marriage match first and save the family. "You want to look your best for the prince. Clean my face."

Letting out a breath, I picked up the wash tub. Careful not to slosh over the edges, I moved slowly around to the other side of the bed. My eyes pricked and I squeezed the lids tight trying to control my unsettled emotions. Why was I surprised Ingrid didn't thank me? Possibly because she was the nicer of the two.

I would not cry in front of them. I would not let them see how their treatment affected me. I would not show weakness.

"Don't dawdle, Elle." Sybil's command jarred.

The water in the bowl sloshed. I'd had to go to the park to collect the natural spring water for the facials. The book was very specific. A twig from a black birch tree floated around the remnants of Ingrid's green goo. The golden berries had to be crushed by hand to make the potion. And a drop from the morning dew had been added. I took care with the recipe because it's what my mother would've done. She'd made specific notes in the margins of the book explaining precisely the best way.

If they hadn't known about the natural recipes, they would've had to spend more creds on a zinc metallic facial mask, nail trimmer and varnisher, and narrow-band light therapy for their hair. Which I didn't believe worked as well.

"Could you walk any slower?" Sybil spoke as if I was a robot servant running low on batteries.

"I don't want the water to spill—"

Ilana's foot kicked out. I crashed into it, pain ratcheting up my leg. Losing my balance, the bowl wobbled in my hands. The water seemed to fizz and bubble. Water splashed over the edge getting my palms wet. My fingers shifted and the bowl slipped from my hands. I tried to grab it, to stop the bowl from falling. Instead, it crashed forward and flipped upside down.

I froze, watching as the water plunged out of the bowl like a waterfall. Cascading forward. All over the bed. All over Sybil. All over everything.

My eyes almost popped. I couldn't believe what I was seeing. The twig flew like an arrow and hit Sybil right between the eyes. The crushed berries and green goo smeared across Sybil's large chest which was bare above the towel wrapped around her body. The blankets and sleep-sensing mattress were soaked. Splashes of the dirty water hit me and Ilana.

Stupid, me. My klutziness had worsened once I'd turned sixteen. Sure, I'd tripped and dropped things before but now my awkwardness had magnified. Heat rushed through my veins and I wanted to disappear.

"Elle!"

I gawked at Sybil. The twig had just missed her eye and could have possibly done serious damage. Then, I stared into her dark pupils. What I saw caused me to tremble.

Fury, rage, a willingness to do violence.

Her nostrils flared cracking the green goo around her nose. Her lips pursed so tight I didn't understand how she breathed through them. Her chin pointed like a knife. "You're a bumbling, blundering, bungling idiot."

I didn't realize she knew so many *B* words. A laugh tickled in my chest. Knowing I was going to get in huge, no *behemoth*, trouble, I clamped my mouth shut. But I couldn't help seeing the funny side. If I didn't laugh at times like this, I'd be crying.

"You're ignorant and lazy." Sybil snatched the twig from her skin and a spot of blood formed.

My cheeks puffed, torn between fear and humor. But if I laughed, I'd be in even more trouble. Not wanting to look at her anymore in case I couldn't control my chuckle, I glanced toward the window.

Arbor fluttered outside. I don't know how long she'd been peeking in, but she held her stomach with both hands emphasizing a big, belly laugh. I knew she was laughing with me, not at me.

There was no laughing inside the bedroom. Everyone else had gone still. Ilana lay on the bed, smirking, knowing this was her fault and that she wouldn't get blamed. Ingrid had slipped off the chair and onto the floor. Maybe she was trying to hide a chuckle, too.

Sybil took the edge of her soaking wet towel and wiped the mask off her face flicking the green goo onto the carpet. "If you ever accomplish Continuum—"

"When." There'd be no *if*.

I had to advance through my Continuum. I had to get out of this place and be recognized as an adult. I had to graduate from technical school and get a job in order to claim my inheritance and be officially accepted into human society. The first step was attending the royal ball.

Continuum was similar to a *Quinceanera* or a Bat Mitzvah, except it wasn't religious and I didn't have to wear a white dress like functions in the past. It was an official ceremony where I would be recognized as a Beta in adulthood. A human Beta adult. And then approved for college.

"If," Sybil snarled, "you accomplish Continuum and then

attend college and officially take your place in society, you'll be an embarrassment to my family. Ruin my daughters' prospects."

"Not if I advance through Continuum first." Ilana stood, shaking off what water had landed on her. She was in the same grade as me, but a few months older. Her Continuum would be earlier than mine.

Originally, I believed this was good. By going second, I wouldn't take the spotlight away from her. But what if Sybil tried to stop me?

Ingrid flailed her hands as if wanting to point at me, but not wanting to. "You are an embarrassment, Elle. Look at what you wear all the time."

So much for her being the nicer one. The insults dug deeper and hurt longer coming from Ingrid. When we were alone, she usually expressed sympathy.

Absorbing the pain, I glanced at my reflection in the mirror. Damp from the spill, my hair hung limply around my face. My dusky skin tone desperately needed a whitening powder and dark shadows sullied my green eyes. The oversized T-shirt hung loosely covering my non-existent figure. And, my jeans had rips and holes not because of an ancient fashion trend but because I'd worn the same pair over and over again for years.

Firming my lips, I glared at my reflection. This was the poor and needy and ugly me they saw, not the me I wanted to become. I'd go to the ball, accomplish Continuum, attend tech college, and be welcomed into the human world. "I'm going to achieve Continuum."

Sybil tucked the soaking wet towel tighter around her body. "To be accepted for Continuum your credentials must be impeccable including from your guardian. One more slip…"

The dangling intimidation made my blood run cold. If I failed, if I didn't achieve Continuum and move forward with my life, she couldn't keep me here as her slave forever, could she?

Chapter 2

Finally, I made it to the mall with only a couple of hours before the rented transportation pod whisked me, my stepsisters, and stepmom to the royal ball. What a pain they were. *Ellery, do this. Ellery, do that.* It was as if they didn't have two completely functioning hands of their own.

I was here now. I had creds. And…oh no…

"Hide. SCUM entering the mall." I directed the frantic whisper at Arbor, who quickly dove beneath my oversized T-shirt. I shouldn't have brought my smoke sprite friend on this errand. She would be recognized instantly as a majik, questioned, and possibly imprisoned for no reason whatsoever.

That's how SCUM operated.

Because they were scum. A group of humans charged with collecting fairytale creatures who broke the law. And what they could and couldn't do—the specific laws for majiks—were changing daily and much stricter than human laws. I mean, I know what they taught in high school, but all majiks weren't bad and all didn't abuse their powers.

Some couldn't even *control* their magic.

The glitzy modern mall couldn't outlaw sprites or dwarves or ogres or fairies. But the government made it difficult with curfews and restrictions. And, the clerks could be hostile. Those working in expensive stores didn't welcome majiks believing they would taint the products. Salespeople didn't want to be tricked or enchanted.

Arbor had begged to come, and I'd needed an opinion I could trust. Plus, she'd set up the meeting with the fairy this morning. I couldn't leave her out now.

With trembling knees and sparking fingers, I stood near the LED light fountain wiping my hands on my pants and biting my lip, trying not to appear suspicious. Which probably made me look more suspicious. Two clandestine meetings in one day.

Give me a little free time and I go crazy.

"Elle, what're we going to do?" Arbor fluttered, the tickling sensation of her vapor almost made me giggle, except this was no laughing situation.

"Stay quiet." An impossibility for my small friend.

"Where are the SCUM now? What're they doing? Why are they here?" Each question pitched higher in her squeaky voice.

The guards marched toward the fountain, their dark uniforms glowing with neon stripes. Their sinister faces were shadowed by the large bills of their hats. The stomping of their black boots on the shiny mall floor reminded me of gigantic robots squashing Will o' the Wisps. Shoppers made way for the SCUM using their hover shoes to make graceful exits. My stepmother said she couldn't afford to buy me hover shoes, although both of my stepsisters owned several pairs.

My stomach jittered like a lightning bug creating flashes of heat. Standing in the middle of the courtyard, I couldn't see anywhere to hide. I could run, but they'd wonder why and apprehend me. The laws about majiks constantly changed, and the SCUM had ultimate power.

Better to play innocent. I was nervous for more than just my sprite friend.

"Be quiet and don't move." I spoke without shifting my lips, keeping my gaze on the approaching guards.

"What're you staring at?" A SCUM with four glaring neon stripes announcing his high rank stopped only a few feet in front of me. His threatening tone caused my body to freeze, and fear raced through my impure veins.

His uniformed cronies stood behind him, a big, unpassable wall.

"No…nothing. Nothing." Peering down so I wasn't staring any longer, I shook my head. Frisking me would get us both handcuffed.

"What's your name?" His stinging-aggressive tone jerked me to alertness.

My stepmother would kill me if I got arrested. "Ellery Milford. My friends call me Elle." The SCUM didn't care. They weren't my friends and never would be.

Maybe I should've used my father's earl rank. A lower stature on the royalty scale, but it might have influence over the SCUM. Even with him gone, my stepmother used the title of lady. I wasn't eligible yet. With my too big T-shirt, dirty jeans, and boots, the SCUM probably wouldn't believe my claim.

His gaze raked up and down my body. The spot where Arbor hid grew colder as the sprite's smoke condensed to ice. Did the SCUM get a kick out of scaring people? In school, I was taught to respect authority and the government, although I had to wonder why the SCUM, and the teachers, acted so intimidating.

Or maybe it was my constant fear of discovery.

The guard continued to study me as if he knew I was inferior. When his lips moved his bushy mustache resembled a snake crawling on his face. "What's your business at the mall?"

My muscles loosened a bit. If I was going to the ball it meant I couldn't be a majik. "I'm shopping for a dress for the royal ball."

"Cutting it a little close, aren't you? The ball is tonight." His glare slashed through me as though he could read my mind.

I hoped they hadn't obtained that particular skill. If they did, I could kiss my life goodbye. "Yes, I know."

How could I not know? How could anyone in the kingdom not know? This was Prince Zacharye's Presentation Ball. His official Continuum, and the first step in taking over the ruling of the country from his uncle, Regent Theobald.

The other guards chuckled. Not a friendly chuckle, a making-fun snicker. A kind of chortle I was used to at school. I'd built-up my defenses for being teased, but not interrogation.

Ooh, I had another skill. Not magic. Something Arbor had taught me how to harness. Glancing behind me, I considered the only natural thing nearby—the water spurting from the fountain. Everything else in the mall was electronic, concrete, or man-made. Focusing on the water, I put my lips together and hummed.

Every one of the four guards' shoulders became less starchy. Their facial muscles softened, and their pupils lost the ferocious intensity.

The main guard's head lolled. "What're you doing?"

Alarm bells rang in my head and combined with the humming. "Um, hummmmmmming." I stretched the word into song. "I hummmmm whennnnn I'mmm nervous."

Some old saying said music tamed the beast. Humming tamed the human.

He tilted his head the other way, swaying with the music. "Get along then."

I fumbled a step back. I couldn't turn around for fear they might see the bulge at my back. Ask more questions. Arrest both Arbor and me.

Dismissing me, the SCUM headed for the food court with its sleek wall of vendo-cafes. People lined up waiting to electronically order the micro-delicacies. The five-star cuisine popped out tray after tray, and the scent of seasoned meat and cinnamon rolls wafted in my direction making my belly churn.

A close call. Too close.

"The SCUM left."

"Phew. That was scary." Arbor reformed beneath my shirt. "I thought we both were goners."

"Stay hidden longer. I want to get away from them."

Strolling backwards, I took one careful step at a time. I didn't want to fall and attract more attention. I wasn't known for being the most graceful. Especially since the mishaps started. Shoppers stopped with their heavy bags to gape at my strange walking-backwards behavior. Probably wondering what crazy Alandaska-net stunt I participated in.

I wish. A fad would be accepted. A majik not so much.

"It's clear, Arbor. You can come out." I hoped no one else would create a stir about her presence. An uppity store clerk, a mean-spirited lady, a kid who enjoyed bullying.

With a flutter of her wings, Arbor flew from under my shirt. "Why do SCUM have the authority to harass?"

"The guards can stop and question anyone."

Majiks feared playing outside and strolling the skywalk. How fair was that?

"I'm tired of hiding all the time. In the alley. At your house." Her multi-colored hair spiked out in sharp edges. Not the kind of hair that blended.

"You're only hiding from the SCUM." As long as fairytale creatures didn't use their magic and followed the laws, they were supposedly safe from persecution. Humans couldn't report majiks just for existing. At least not yet.

"Even a hint of suspicion and I'd be led away in magnetized hand-bracelets." She held out both her arms with her wrists bent. "I've learned—all majiks have learned—it's better to avoid the guards in case their power-hungry tendencies decide to come down on someone innocent."

Majiks were scared. I understood. After being arrested, they received a trial presided over by the regent, then they were sent out of the kingdom. No one ever heard from them again.

"The government's goal is to even things out between humans and majiks." I'd learned that in class. Didn't mean I agreed with the statement, but I kept my opinions to myself. "For example, if fairytale creatures used magic to do better on a test at school they would be cheating."

"Which is why majiks can no longer attend human schools." Her dig struck me.

Fair to some, is unfair to others.

Arbor flew beside my ear, trying to take cover in my shoulder-length white-blond hair. "I wish I could be like you Elle, and not have to cower."

"Believe me, I'm cowering." I'd been shaking in my beat-up boots. For years.

My stepmother and stepsisters knew my secret.

The glare from the li-fi and laser lighting hit my eyes and I blinked. The glitzy mall shined bright hiding the flaws beneath. Displays in the store windows morphed from one outrageous outfit to the next and rotating lights flashed from the stores luring customers. Using holograms, shoppers tried on the latest fashions without taking off a single garment.

"You're going to the royal ball." The longing in my friend's voice scaled to notes of anxiety and excitement which echoed inside me. "Like every human in the kingdom. There'll be exotic food, dancing, and cute guys. Ooh, you could meet Prince Zacharye."

Picking up my pace, I scanned the heavily decorated displays. My only goal was to show my classmates I attended the ball. I didn't care about meeting guys, and certainly not the prince, or so I told myself. What was important was everyone from school would be there. I needed to be there, too. "Not if I can't find a dress."

Last minute shopping was not my thing. Any kind of shopping was not my thing. My stepmother didn't give me an allowance and didn't pay for the work I did around the house. Her payment came in silence.

I never bought new things. That was okay. I cherished old things. Sniffing at the white shirt, I swore I could smell the spicy scent of Dad's cologne. The blood in my veins slowed and a sharp prick hit my eyes. He'd worn this type of shirt when we'd played in the yard, kicking a ball or tossing a flutter-disc. I sniffed again realizing smelling Dad's cologne was a ridiculous fantasy because he's been gone for four years and this shirt had been washed hundreds of times. I should know because I'm the one who did the laundry.

This shirt was one of the few things I had left of his. My stepmother had kept his things, including our ancestral home, until I was of legal age. *Once you're responsible*—she'd repeated a million times, she'd give everything back to me.

"Why don't you use your…" Arbor wiggled her tiny fingers. "For a dress."

My heart drubbed, and I scanned the area to make sure no one overheard. "Shh! Do you want to get caught?"

"You'll never get caught. Look at you."

Ignoring the envious tone, I glanced in a gleaming store window. Yeah, I was so glamorous. My hair hadn't seen a comb all day and there was a black smudge on my freckled nose from cleaning. Even with my family's title I wasn't part of the top echelon of society or the cliques at school. Being at the top of the social circle wasn't important though. My only goal was fitting in, flying under the radar, and living my life as human.

"Not worth the risk." I scrubbed hard at my nose with my fingertips until the smudge was erased. I hated looking like a slave. "If I don't go to the ball the kids from school will notice. I'll stand out more than I ever did." They might even think I was a zauber.

My cheeks burned for thinking the word even if it was what many humans called majiks. Even teachers.

The true-blue dress in a window caught my attention stopping my thoughts. Stopping everything. The blue color fell between sky and navy. The folds of the skirt billowed out in layers. The tight-shaped bodice glittered with rhinestones.

My breath snagged. "This is the most amazing dress *ev-ah.*"

"This is one of the most expensive stores *ev-ah.*" Arbor copied my excited tone except sarcasm wove through her words.

Ogling the dress, *my dress,* I imagined myself twirling at the ball. The way the folds of the gown would swirl around my feet. The way the bodice would hug my upper body trying to showcase my small breasts. I would shine and for once everyone would stare for a good reason. Not because I'd done something klutzy, like tripping or having another kind of mishap. I could still hear my classmates laughing when I'd accidentally started a small fire at school.

A teeny, tiny fire in Augmented Reality class when I'd

pointed at a trigger picture of a fairy campfire and it had exploded into life. I mean, not the actual campfire. The computer I was working on malfunctioned and caught fire. But my classmates had seen what I'd been researching, and I'd been mortified. I was already an outcast. Can you imagine the uproar when they found out I was interested in fairies?

The giggles grew louder.

The laughing wasn't my memory. Olivia and Jade, the most popular girls in my grade, strolled out of the store carrying designer-shopping bags, the fancy logos projecting from inside the parcels. The store wasn't too expensive for them.

I wanted to run around the corner or make myself disappear. There wasn't time. At least Arbor had the sense to hide behind my back.

"Ellery, are you thinking of buying the blue dress in the window?" Olivia tossed her curly black hair over her shoulder in a practiced, offhand gesture. Her lips curled in a disbelieving sneer.

Warmth suffused my cheeks. She must've seen my longing. They didn't need to know I couldn't afford the outfit. "Possibly. For the ball. I haven't holographed the dress on yet."

Stepping farther away and in front of Arbor, I tried to keep her hidden. I wasn't trying to protect her. The opposite, really. I was trying to protect myself and the last remnants of my reputation. It was tarnished enough without being caught by the popular girls with a smoke sprite at my side. Humans did not befriend or hang out with smoke sprites—or any magical creature for that matter. It was an us-versus-them world.

Jade shook her multiple bags emphasizing the amount of shopping she'd done. Her short, brown hair puffed out with the action. "Thinking about what you normally wear to school—" She ran a hand along the edge of her flipped up tube skirt. "—I'm stunned you have the creds to pay for the dress."

Olivia smirked, and an evil glint surfaced in her eyes. "Maybe we should alert mall security."

"Or the SCUM." Jade typed something on her ever-present celltab.

"No." My cheeks burned hotter scorching my entire face. She knew one of my stepsisters and I was sure they talked about me and the work I did around the house. They saw what I wore to school every day. Hand-me-downs and rags.

Arbor flew in front of me and raised her fist at the girls. "Hey! Watch what you're saying, you red-lipsticked wormhole."

I grabbed her body and clutched her in my hand trying to stop the outburst. The girls would gossip about a smoke sprite defending me.

"Are you going to have your *friend* use her magic to help pay for the dress?" Olivia's chortle pricked, and any hopes I'd had about flying under the radar went up in smoke similar to how Arbor sometimes did.

"Oh, the sprite's not with me. We're looking in the same window at the same dress." The falsehood flew out of my mouth before I fully thought the statement through. A lump plopped in my stomach knowing I'd wounded my best friend.

Arbor's tiny mouth rounded into an *O* obviously hurt I'd lied about our relationship. "Yeah, I was thinking *I* might wear the dress to the royal ball."

I froze. Not only wouldn't she fit into a single puffy sleeve, she wouldn't be invited to the palace.

My classmates' expressions registered shock, and then disdain. The smirks on both of their faces twisted into a mean pout.

"Funny." Except Jade didn't sound amused. "As if they'd allow a smoke sprite into the royal palace. Or any zauber."

The statement was true. In school we learned about the superiority of humans, how the majiks were dark and untrustworthy. Since Regent Theobald began his rule, he'd introduced the Majik Registration and Protection Act, which didn't protect the majiks at all.

Arbor went stiff as a twig and steam poured from her body. A jolt went through me and I wanted to defend my friend. Yet, I didn't.

How could I? I was supposed to believe in human superiority. I was trying to blend in and couldn't make a scene. Only a few months before Continuum, and I'd be free to take back my life. Still not free to speak my mind though. Never would be.

"Only through the back entrance of the palace." The back entrance is where the SCUM took the majik prisoners. An entrance without an exit.

Olivia's snarky gleeful tone revealed she'd be happy if Arbor was caught.

Jade waved her hand at the dress in the window. "You do know that dress is a Lavender original. It costs a fortune."

I swallowed hard. The limited cred payment in my jeans pocket cut through the worn material. I didn't have a bank debit chip. I couldn't afford the dress. I didn't know if I could afford any dress at this expensive mall. I'd been hoping to find a clearance sale.

I wasn't about to admit it. "I haven't made a decision."

"The ball is tonight. Better decide fast." Olivia's breezy voice almost blew me over. "And look, the guards are coming this way just in time."

Giggling without a care in the world, the two girls moved on.

I fisted my hand and walked in the other direction. Away from my classmates. Away from the SCUM. "Let's get out of here. This was a mistake."

My mother's trunk had clothes inside. Maybe I could make one of her old outfits work and ignore the pain that would come with wearing something of hers. I hauled out of the mall and took a breath of fresh air.

"Uh, Elle." Arbor's tone scratched. "Let me go."

Stiffening, I realized I still crushed my friend in my hand. Her body, and her spirit when I hadn't stuck up for her. Feeling even worse, I opened my fist letting her fly out. I slumped against a bench directly outside the mall. Podships flew above stirring up the wind. The dirt from the small garden around the bench wafted by my nose filling it with the musty scent of earth. The hologram in the shop window morphed to the Lavender dress, taunting me.

The girls would never let this encounter go. They knew about my household situation. They already made fun of me. They'd repeat the story of how a smoke sprite came to my defense.

My gut churned because I hadn't done the same for Arbor. I'd been embarrassed about my poverty, my clothes, and my friend. And only one of those things I could deny. If I didn't attend the ball, the taunts would worsen. And if they ever found out the truth…

If they found out the truth it wouldn't matter because I would no longer be allowed to attend school.

"Don't listen to those girls." Arbor's expression went fierce.

I hung my head. I should've stuck up for her. "I'm sor—"

"Don't worry. We'll find you a dress." She fluttered her wings.

"Why don't you whip up a dress for yourself?" The snide question came from thin air.

Air that glimmered and shot with static electricity. The glimmering formed into an ellipse and took a more solid form. The shape of my fairy godmother, Gardenia.

Internally, I groaned. This was all I needed.

Her majestic wings spread wide with a slight back and forth flutter. The maneuver kept her pointed cloth shoes from touching the ground making her taller than me. I was short for a human and tall for a fairy—guaranteeing I didn't fit in anywhere.

The skirt of Gardenia's glowing silver dress came to several pointy ends. Her long, white hair flowed around her face as if a gentle wind was constantly blowing. She appeared regal and way too magical.

Glancing around, I searched for the SCUM hoping they didn't head out of the building. I did not want to get arrested for hanging around with majiks, especially one I didn't even like. I stood in case I had to run. "What're you doing here?"

Gardenia was a fugitive. Wanted by the SCUM and the regent. My stepmother had repeated rumors about my fairy godmother but didn't tell me the details. Only warned me away.

Arbor hovered trying to distract the interfering fairy. "If you were a good fairy godmother, you'd make Elle a dress."

"I am a good fairy godmother." Gardenia's soft expression displayed patience, and yet the glint in her glowing eyes hinted at determination.

My muscles tensed at her claim. "Some fairy godmother."

The woman had been absent from my life until my sixteenth birthday. I hadn't even known she existed. If she'd been a good fairy godmother, she would've saved me from my stepmother long ago, not shown up a couple of months ago trying to recruit me for an underground majik warrior academy.

"Your stepmother will never let you go to the ball, Ellery." Gardenia flicked her fingers in a careless way. Doing magic near a crowded mall didn't worry her.

"My stepmother promised." Even as I spoke, I remembered other broken promises.

Arbor fluttered her wings catching some of my hair. She was nervous.

Gardenia held out a slender hand with too long fingers. "I'll make you a bet."

Wasn't there some saying about bets and majiks? Zaubers used con-artist tactics and deceit to achieve their goals according to my teachers. Fairies couldn't lie, but they could twist the truth.

"If your stepmother allows you to go to the ball, I'll never bother you again." Gardenia's expression didn't change. "If you don't attend, you will be expected to do me a favor."

I couldn't read her expression, but I knew what she wanted. "I'm not going to your stupid fairy academy."

The academy would be worse than human school. Live-in dormitories, classroom work, fairy magic training, and self-defense, battle methods and strategies. Basically, a military camp. I'd be like the SCUM I abhorred.

"If you were trained, you could make a dress in no time. No bets necessary." She snapped her fingers and sparks shot from her hands. "You. Are. A. Fairy."

Each word spiked through me, a threat and a promise.

Chapter 3

"Half-fairy," I whispered, and checked to see if anyone was near enough to hear.

Fear spiraled inside pulling my muscles taut. I didn't want to be acknowledged as a majik. Only my family and Arbor knew.

Arbor's smoke changed to a sickly yellow. She understood my stress.

I paced behind some tall bushes not wanting people going in and out of the mall to see our strange trio. Arbor and Gardenia followed.

"You will have full fairy magic, Ellery. Fairy heritage takes precedence over human ancestry." Gardenia's superior tone ground against my frayed nerves. Her philosophy was the exact opposite of my teachers.

I'd always known I was half-fairy. My father hadn't kept the secret from me, and unfortunately, he hadn't kept the secret from his second wife, either. Since Dad died, the woman had used the knowledge against me. And yet, until recently I'd had no powers to use against her or my mean stepsisters. My magic hadn't manifested until I'd turned sixteen. My fairy godmother had surprised me on the same day by introducing herself and insisting I leave with her to join the mysterious fairy academy.

Why would I go with someone I'd just met? Why would I give up my chance at being recognized as a full human with all my rights? Why would I leave my ancestral home where my father had been born and my parents had been happy? Besides, my magic didn't work very well. Things happened when I wasn't trying, and the few times I'd tried to do magic? Everything got screwed up. Because I was half-human, I'd never make a good fairy.

Gardenia had been shocked when I'd said no to her request. Angry, even. Over the last few months, she'd pestered me to attend. Always appearing at inconvenient moments.

Like now.

Sucking in a couple of seething breaths, I refused to be bullied. "I don't want to be trained."

I didn't want to be a fairy. *A zauber.* A creature humans feared and ridiculed. A majik with regulations and restrictions placed around their necks resembling a noose.

"The favor I ask isn't regarding the academy, I promise." Gardenia's tone jeered. She believed I wouldn't agree. That I didn't have the guts. "Do we have a bet?"

Arbor's expression didn't give a hint to what she was thinking.

With no help from my friend, options see-sawed back and forth. I couldn't let my fairy godmother think she had the upper hand. I'd find a dress on my own and I'd go to the ball. "What do I get *when* I win?"

"A wish."

Magic was illegal, and I didn't want to get caught. A wish wasn't good enough. I started to shake my head.

"And I will never pester you again about joining the academy."

"No more harassment and no more popping in whenever you want?"

A normal human life with no interference from my fairy godmother. No fear of her suddenly materializing. No fear of being tempted by the magic inside of me. And one wish, I could use to evict my stepmother and sisters when the time was appropriate.

Her nose twitched. "Correct."

One less risk of being caught by the SCUM. I only had a few months left to be extra careful. "Okay."

I put my hand in hers and an electrical current passed from her to me. I didn't want even this simple connection.

"A battle is brewing, and we'll need everyone on our side." Gardenia's expression hardened. Her gaze narrowed and glinted like diamonds.

The agreement had been made. I'd never need to see her again once I succeeded in attending the ball. Pressing my feet into the dirt, I let the scent comfort me. "I'm not fighting, so there's no need to train."

The smoke sprite became a wispy billow.

"Training is your birthright." Her voice strengthened and the air around her trembled.

Arbor trembled.

I refused to show fear. "My home is my birthright. Being human is my birthright. Well, half-birthright." The house had been in my father's family for generations, ever since Concealment Day when our little kingdom had hidden itself from the world. "And once I advance to technical school there will be no question about my human ancestry."

"You haven't advanced yet."

I was done with threats from women trying to control my future. First my stepmother, and now my fairy godmother. I had my own plan.

Determination solidified in my bones. "I will soon, don't worry."

Gardenia smirked, and her pupils glittered. "I never worry because you won't win our wager."

Her confidence shredded my already frayed nerves. What did my fairy godmother know that I didn't?

Turns out Gardenia knew plenty more than me. Which I'd realized on my sixteenth birthday and should've swayed me not to make the bet. That day, I'd woken up to Arbor's greeting of *happy birthday* spelled out in smoke. The best start to my birthday since Dad died.

"Thanks, Arbor."

"Do you feel different?" Her odd question should've clued me in.

"Older?" Not really. I felt the same. A bit more loved because of our new friendship.

Arbor had arrived in the backyard a couple of months ago. She'd made me laugh and we'd become instant, although secret friends. She'd run away from her sprite home, which I empathized with and dreamed about. Except I wanted my stepfamily to do the running.

After dressing and doing my morning chores, which I didn't get out of even though it was my birthday, I headed out the door for school.

Arbor flew out the small attic window potentially exposing herself. "Have a nice day."

"Thanks?" I glanced at the front of the house worried one of my stepsisters might see her. Ilana and Ingrid left later because they both owned hover shoes and could get to school quicker.

Arbor normally stayed hidden until everyone left the house. "Are you feeling okay?"

"Yes." I knew no one at school would tell me happy birthday, and my stepmother never gave me gifts. It would be a regular day except for Arbor's good wishes. And another day closer to my freedom. "Why?"

"Just wondering." Her smoke changed to red. "Be careful."

Ha! I was careful every day. I had to be with my secret.

Once there, Jade shoved a piece of paper in my hand. "Join the movement."

As if I'd be interested in a club or concert or some other foolish school event. I wasn't interested, and I wouldn't be welcomed. My stepsisters had made sure of that by spreading false rumors, knowing the biggest negative about me they couldn't share.

The bright orange flyer flipped, and I caught the words *zauber* and *criminals*. My muscles tightened, and I flattened my lips into a grimace.

Don't let the zaubers catch you off guard. Join Prince Zacharye's Youth Brigade and help the Security Collectors of Unique Magic catch the criminals in our midst.

I crumpled the paper in my hand and my short nails dug into my skin. The prince was building his own army. An army of students who'd been indoctrinated to believe majiks were bad. I understood their fears. Majiks had powers that could be used to the detriment of humans. And yet, humans ruled the country. They had an army, now two, and they had control of the government.

Everyone had power except me.

Fisting my hand tighter and crumpling the paper more, I blew out a slow breath trying to control the antagonism stirring inside. Being half-fairy, I was fearful for my life and had none of the magical benefits. I took another breath, this one hotter and madder. My stepmother took advantage of me because of my secret, I was hated by the other kids because of my stepsisters, and I was terrified of discovery.

Always terrified.

The stirring whipped into an angry foam in my stomach. The paper almost returned to the original pulp with the force of my crushing fingers.

"Join the movement," Jade called to another student.

If lots of students joined the brigade there would be spies in every classroom, every hallway, every bathroom stall. I wished those flyers would disappear.

Jade tumbled to the floor. The flyers flew in the air.

I held in a gasp.

The doors burst open and a strong gust buffeted the hallway sweeping the orange flyers up in the wind, swirling them in a tornado, and carrying them back outside. An unnatural gale.

My eyes opened wide following the paper path. The flyers hadn't disappeared, but they were gone. Like I'd wanted. Like I'd wished.

Like I'd made happen?

That's when I knew something had changed. *I* had changed. And hiding my newly emerging powers was going to make life more dangerous. Especially powers I couldn't control.

"Are you going to be okay?" Arbor's question brought me back to my current problem.

I needed to find a dress for the ball.

"I'll be fine." I kneeled by the old wooden chest in my attic bedroom bracing myself. Carvings of a forest seemed alive on the lid with fairies flying, elves hunting, and a troll hiding behind a realistic rock. The love-hate relationship I had with my mother's things rustled in my lungs. The reason I'd taken so long to decide on selling the perfume bottle.

I flipped open the lid. Mustiness mixed with my mom's flowery perfume stung my nose and eyes. Sniffling, I swiped at my face trying to get ahold of the emotions. Mine and my mother's. Even though I didn't remember much of my mom, I missed her. With my father I had memories I could pull out for consolation and encouragement. With Mom I had nothing but a feeling.

Comfort and closeness. Light and love. Sparks and specialness.

Arbor fluttered around the cramped attic-turned-bedroom, leaving a trail of smoke. Boxes of old stuff, broken furniture, and my bed had been shoved into the eight-by-ten-foot space. I could barely stand in the low-ceilinged room and I was short. The one positive thing was with the long electronic ladder leading up here my stepsisters rarely intruded on my privacy.

I forced myself to peer inside the chest knowing with each item I touched, an emotion would assault. Not my feelings. My mother's.

Another part of my fairy curse.

A part training would help control, or so Arbor said.

She'd explained the difference between fairy magic and the bond fairies had with nature. The humming to calm, causing flowers to dance, and this connection I made through my mom's things was an instinctive fairy kinship with the earth and other fairies.

Too bad she hadn't been my friend four years ago when my father had died. I'd taken the electronic ladder to the attic, a room barely used, to escape my stepmother's hysterics. I'd opened Mom's old trunk, and perfume had wafted out releasing a wave of comfort. I'd wanted to wrap myself up in the warmth, so I picked up a wool scarf decorated with butterflies and flowers. I shivered. The last time my mom had worn the scarf she'd not been cold, but afraid.

I used the tips of my fingers to push a photo album and a journal toward the side of the chest. The fewer things I touched the less of my mom's emotions I'd experience. A long chain with an amulet slid between folded clothes. Another item I wouldn't worry about. I was searching for a dress. Any kind of a dress at this point. The ball would start in a couple of hours.

A floral print caught my attention. The cotton fabric was frayed and not as elegant as I'd want for the ball. But a dress was a dress. I couldn't be picky.

Rubbing my fingers together, I pinched the fabric and tugged it out of the trunk. The soft cotton soothed my nerves before I became flushed. A happy-satisfied-cocooning love threatened to suffocate me. The emotion was so unfamiliar. I sucked down air through my throat which had closed like a dented metal straw.

"Elle, what's wrong?" Arbor's concern loosened the hold.

I sucked again this time breaking free of the latent emotions in the fabric.

"Nothing. Nothing." I shook my head not wanting to explain how the contrast between Mom's happiness and my current situation had nearly broken me. My eyes burned. If both my parents had been alive my life would be different.

Focusing on what life could've been wasn't going to help my situation. I'd made a bet and I needed to focus on getting a dress, getting to the ball, of taking my place in human society. Every girl of eligible age would get to dance with Prince Zacharye, and I planned to be waiting in line with the other girls from school. Not because I wanted to dance with some spoiled prince who cared more about himself than half the population, meaning the majiks, but because people would see me there and assume I was human.

"What do you think of this?" Standing, I held the flowered dress in front of me.

The hem came to my knees. The waistline seemed too narrow. And the un-fashionable sleeves signaled the decade the dress had been created. I'd look foolish wearing this to a royal ball, even so I'd be there. And not naked.

Arbor buzzed around the dress. "Appears a little small."

My shoulders slumped, and I tossed the dress to the floor. That had been my original assessment. I'd been hoping I was wrong. "What am I going to do?"

"What about an elongator spell?" My friend held up a small portion of the dress barely lifting it off the ground. Even though she acted tough, physical strength was not one of her qualities.

The idea tempted. "My magic misfires when I try, and even when I don't."

I cringed, remembering the other day at school when I'd tried to help a guy being punished by a bully. Instead, I'd created fear in all the students.

"Your magic doesn't work because you're not trained." Arbor sounded like my fairy godmother.

Huffing, I was tired of defending my ambitions. "I don't want to be trained. I want to be human."

"Why?" Her hurt tone dug into my chest. She pursed her lips looking mutinous. "Is there something wrong with being majik?"

I opened my mouth and slammed it shut. Arbor was a majik. She didn't hear what the teachers taught or understand how Regent Theobald and Prince Zacharye really felt about fairytale creatures. I did. If I could get away with being human, why wouldn't I try?

My dad was human. I wanted to be like him. Human, respected, allowed to live a life. I knew nothing about being a fairy and didn't want to learn. Mom had died when I was a toddler and Dad had never told me about her family or her history.

Still, Arbor was my only friend in the world, and I didn't want to hurt her. "Of course, there's nothing wrong with being majik."

My teachers taught majiks took advantage of humans with their powers. They'd trick you and cheat every chance they got. The homeland rules were so majiks couldn't relocate out of their natural habitat and into the city. The laws controlled their movements and the immediate arrest of anyone using unsanctioned magic commenced.

The regent did this to make the kingdom a fairer realm. Not a fairytale realm.

My father believed fairness needed to be for all citizens. He loved my mother even though she was fairy, and still he kept it secret. He loved me. I agreed with my dad, except if I spoke out, they might realize I sympathized with majiks. Then, what would happen?

"No majiks are invited to this high and mighty ball." Arbor used a snippy tone mimicking my stepmother. "I don't understand why you think it's so important to attend."

So many reasons. "Because everyone is going."

"I'm not going."

"Everyone else."

My stepsisters dressed in their bedrooms right now. The professional hair and make-up people were probably finishing up, and they'd be stepping into their three-dimensional clothing printers for their gowns.

Brand new gowns.

My stepmother had bought each of them a new dress printing pattern for their clothing printers. They'd gotten new shoes, too. Sybil had gotten a new dress printing pattern too, even though she was too old to dance with the prince.

With advanced technology like the clothing printers, humans didn't need magic. No wonder majiks were mistreated and relegated to a lesser role. Technology was taking over our kingdom.

"Those girls from your school are going. The ones who made fun of you at the mall. Made fun of *me*." Arbor's smoke morphed dark red. She hadn't liked Olivia and Jade.

I didn't like them much either, but they ruled the school. If they'd known Arbor was my best friend, I never would've lived it down and I did not need more negative attention. Only a few months left, and I'd advance through Continuum and move to the relegated technical college. Jade and Olivia wouldn't be there, and neither would my stepsisters because they'd go to university. The thought had become my mantra.

"I just need to go." My voice quivered. This was important, and Arbor didn't understand. Maybe because she didn't know the human rules, the steps to adulthood, and acceptance. Or maybe because she was a smoke sprite she couldn't understand. "Don't forget I made a wager with Gardenia."

Arbor flew higher with the dress. "Elongater spell. Try it."

Even though she didn't understand me, she supported me. That's what friends did, human or majik.

Blowing out, I tried to get rid of my nerves. I wiggled each of my trembling fingers in a warmup exercise as if I knew what I was doing. A wand would be helpful. Except a fairy needed training before receiving a wand.

I could do this. I had to do this.

Flicking my wrist, I pointed at the old dress. I squinted and glared willing the material to grow longer, the waist to increase, and the entire design to become more modern. It's what I wished for anyhow.

The hem dropped, uneven in places. I quirked my head. Maybe I could pin the longer sections. The waist grew and grew and grew. Too big for my measurements. The design didn't change. I moaned. At least the dress hadn't exploded.

"That was pretty good." Arbor's attempt at being upbeat failed.

"It's ugly."

"We might be able to fix the dress now that you can actually fit inside. Try it on." Her wings fluttered as if getting excited my magic actually worked.

What if the dress shrunk while I was wearing it?

I took off my T-shirt and jeans and slipped on the dress. The material smelled musty. At least my mother's emotions had faded. Standing in front of the mirror, I swirled the uneven dress back and forth. The longer sides of the lopsided hem dragged on the floor while the shorter points came to mid-calf. Surely, I'd trip. I wasn't the most coordinated.

My blunt-cut bangs hung over my green eyes. The white-blond strands blended into brighter silver at the ends—a hint of my fairy blood. I trimmed the silver ends every other day. My pointy chin and large cheeks could be considered heart shaped. My pale skin caught my attention. The light shower of freckles seemed to dance, and my cheeks shimmered. "I look...I look..."

"You look like your mom." Arbor's awe made me dizzy.

I didn't want to resemble my mom. "Mom was a fairy."

Standing five feet three inches, according to Dad, I was tall compared to my mother. Same green eyes, and freckles. That's where the resemblance always ended in the past. I'd never glowed before. I didn't even realize my mom had glowed.

"Am I glowing because I did magic?" If so, why couldn't the SCUM catch any fairy using their powers?

"You really don't know anything, do you? About your mother's family?"

I knew glowing in the midst of the current government chaos would not be good.

"You've taken on your mother's emotions from the dress." The smoke sprite darted around my head in circles.

Blood drained from my brain, making me dizzier. I bent down and put my old boots back on trying to return to normal. At least the too-long dress would cover the only pair of shoes I owned.

"Your mom was beautiful." Arbor plucked at my hair. "I remember when she visited Fae Forest."

My body jittered with the information. I didn't know my mom had visited her homeland after marrying. "You've met her?"

A noise caught my attention and I peeked out the window. "The transport pod is here. What am I going to do about this dress?"

"I'll be right back." Arbor buzzed out of the room and was back in seconds with a long, black ribbon streaming behind her. She whizzed around my waist and used the ribbon to tie a bow. "I can't do anything about the length, but at least this will hold the dress up."

"Look at my hair!"

"I can fix it." She flew to the back of my head and yanked. "Ouch!"

"Stand still." Flying around, she tugged and pulled and twisted the strands.

I'd probably end up resembling a ball of string a cat had played with. Imagining the knots I'd have to detangle, I scowled. "Are you sure?"

"Ta da!" She flew in front of my face and held out her tiny hands.

Leaning back, I admired the hairdo. A thick braid pulled the strands back from my face and hid the silver tips. A few wispy strands snuck out adding a softness to the style.

"Wow! My hair looks great. I didn't know you could style hair."

"And no magic." She brushed her hands together.

"Thank you, Arbor. You should've been my fairy godmother."

"I'm better." She stuck up her tiny hand and I used my pinky to slap it. "I'm your best friend."

"Gotta go." Unable to contain my giddy excitement, I rushed out of the room. I was going to win the bet with Gardenia and go to the ball.

I raced down the electronic ladder leading from the attic to the second floor. The flat black boots were good for going fast, much easier than the high heels everyone else would be wearing.

The ultra-modern décor on the second floor clashed with my father's ancestral portraits in gilt frames. My stepmother Sybil told people they were her relatives, which was ridiculous. She was only trying to increase her standing with the nobility. My dad had been a respected member of the court until he'd withdrawn upon his marriage to my mother. I had to wonder if he was trying to hide what she was.

Running past my old bedroom, I glanced through the open doorway. The room was a disaster with shoes and material and jewelry spread across the floor. No wonder Ilana had needed her own space. She and Ingrid had shared a room while my father was alive.

The carpeted floor swallowed the noise of my hurrying steps. Sybil had re-carpeted the entire house in the ghastly chartreuse color.

Pivoting at the metal bannister, I headed down the wide,

clear steps leading to the main living area. I couldn't stop the internal squeal. I'd win a wish and never be visited by my fairy godmother again. Catching a glimpse of my odd dress, my squeal skid to a stop at the landing and I peered over the balustrade.

The pink carpeting continued throughout the main room. The gigantic vid screen sat above the fluorescent flame fireplace where my parents' wedding photo used to take the place of honor. Now, it held a portrait of Sybil and her two daughters. The chrome and acrylic furniture aligned in too-straight angles. And Sybil had recently purchased the most hideous pumpkin-colored chair.

My stepmother and stepsisters headed toward the open front door. Their hair was coiffed in similar updos with feathers and jewels sticking out.

"Wait for me!" I continued my flight down the stairs.

The three of them turned toward me. Their expressions went from surprise to shock to amusement.

Ilana lifted her yellow silk skirt displaying the matching high-heeled pumps. The beauty mark above her lip distorted when she smirked. "What are you wearing?"

The distaste in her tone caused me to survey the dress wondering if it had re-shrunk. It hadn't. Even though the gown wasn't the most beautiful or stylish, it would get me in the palace.

"Who did your hair?" Ingrid patted her red locks before squinting at the ever-present celltab in her hand. She sounded more surprised than cruel. "Where are your eyelashes and lip cover?"

I patted my own hair. Both Arbor and I had thought it beautiful. I didn't own make-up. Forcing my chin to a proud angle, I knew I wasn't glamorous. That's not what mattered.

Sybil took a dramatic step toward me causing her breasts to almost burst from the tight bodice of her purple gown. Her lips pinched, and her gaze narrowed into a glare of disapproval. "Where do you think you're going looking *so* ridiculous?"

Chapter 4

The shock of the question slapped. I was going to the ball, of course. Then, the word *ridiculous* slapped my other cheek. My face burned with the insult. Sybil had no right to criticize my mom's dress.

"I'm going to the ball." I tried to sound confident even though a slight tremble edged my voice. It didn't matter that the dress was ugly. I stuck my chin up. What mattered was to be included, and to prove to Gardenia I was attending.

Ilana guffawed in a cruel, high-pitched sound. The yellow feather in her hair wiggled with the movement of her body.

Ingrid joined in with a shakier and more unsure giggle. Her baby pink dress and feathers matched the flush of her cheeks.

Sybil's expression didn't change. "You are?"

"You said if I finished my chores and had a gown I could go." I tugged at my flopping collar.

Fairy godmother's warning shrilled in my head.

My stepmother stalked around, inspecting me. She hadn't expected me to get a dress. I could tell by the sharp gleam in her eyes. Her gaze raked sending shivers across my body.

Like a BarbBob Doll, I forced myself to stand still and not express anxiety.

Sybil stopped in front of me and ran a final survey from my booted feet barely covered by the too-long material, the sagging waistline at the middle, and the wide sleeves from another decade. Her nose crinkled. "Your gown is not fit for the royal ball."

The burning in my cheeks dropped to my midsection, churning with each word she spat.

She'd gone back on her word before. Yet, this time I thought things would be different because there'd been a royal decree that girls above the age of sixteen must attend.

Wiping my damp hands down the skirt of the dress, I tried to reign in my antagonism. Getting my stepmother mad would get me nowhere. "It was the best I could do with no creds."

"You will disgrace the entire family." She spoke down at me as she always did, believing she was superior.

My shoulders straightened and I stuck my nose higher. I was the one with the noble Milford blood. Those ancestors hanging on the wall were related to me. My fairy blood might be considered lower quality, but my father's Milford heritage gave me a very indirect line to the throne. Pinching my lips, I forced myself to stay quiet.

She twisted toward her daughters waiting at the open door. "What do you girls think?"

I scowled at Ilana and Ingrid. Their gowns must've cost a fortune. The fine silk and detailed lace. The sewn-on jewels. The layer upon layer of flounces. If they'd donated one flounce each, I could've made a simple yet elegant dress. My blood pressure rose. It was my father's money they were spending. My inheritance. I tapped my boot on the floor and repeated the mantra.

A few more months and I'd be free.

Ilana's colorful-shadowed eyes widened in a false expression of surprise. "That's my ribbon!" She dashed toward me and tugged at the bow holding the dress up around my waist. The ribbon tore, and she tossed the pieces to the ground. "Mother! She ruined my ribbon."

I didn't have time to react. One second, I was standing there in a passable dress, and now I wore a flowered sack. Without the ribbon, the dress was too long and had no shape. Even the sleeves slipped off, baring my shoulders.

Sybil's expression flashed with glee, before flattening her smile into a frown. "Stealing Ilana's ribbon?"

I couldn't defend myself. I had no idea where Arbor had gotten the ribbon, and I wouldn't squeal on my friend. Better to take the lumps than involve her. Who knew what punishment my stepmother would give to a smoke sprite who shouldn't even be in the house?

"I don't know where it came from." Weak excuse, I know.

"Lying." Sybil's second accusation blasted me.

I was a liar. My entire life was a lie. I was a half-fairy pretending to be human. Attending school with humans, living in a noble human household, planning to achieve Continuum and attend technical college.

"Now, you're definitely not going to the ball." Sybil patted the poof of her hair finding justification for breaking her promise.

Because my father hadn't registered me as majik, people thought I was human. "I'm of eligible age to attend. I'm expected to attend."

"You are." She slinked toward the sideboard and waved her hand for the top drawer to open.

Every drawer and cabinet in the house were equipped with a skin print sensor. Sybil had access to all of them. I only had access to the ones I needed for cleaning supplies.

"If I don't go people will notice. Our neighbors will notice."

It was one of the reasons she let me go to school. I hoped adopting the same philosophy would work now.

She rummaged in the drawer. Grinning, she took out what appeared to be a fairy wand, only it was slightly thicker. A red electronic light sat at the tip. She whipped it toward me.

I jerked back. "What's that?"

Her smug expression told me I wasn't going to enjoy the answer. "Magic detector."

I'd heard of the equipment, knew they employed some at school when kids got in trouble, but never had been subjected to a search. I'd never feared the detectors before because I'd only recently received my magic.

"You know I don't use magic. I don't know *how* to use magic." I scrubbed every surface of the kitchen and bathrooms. I cooked every meal. If I knew how to use my magic, would I do each and every chore by hand?

She came closer and held up the detector.

My gaze darted to my dress. I gulped. Except by accident, I'd never used magic until today.

Maybe the spell I'd used to fix the dress wasn't strong enough to be detected. If I had used stronger magic, the dress would look a lot better. Surely, I wouldn't get caught for this one indiscretion. I held my breath.

Beep. Beep. The detector swept from the neckline to my waist.

So far so good.

Beep. Beep. The detector swung low on the skirt.

Beeeeeep. Whir-whir-whir-whir.

A siren. The irritating noise scraped against the inside of my skull. The one time I use magic on purpose, the one time it actually worked, and I got caught.

Sybil's expression brightened. "You used magic to make this…dress."

"A little. To make it longer." I needed to explain. "I wasn't trying to get away with anything. It was the only way—"

"The palace magic detectors are stronger than this one." She tapped the detector against her thigh. "You'll get caught. You can't go."

I couldn't *not* go. I'd worked so hard to get my chores done. I'd told Olivia and Jade I'd be there. Come Monday if I didn't go the kids would make fun of me more than usual. And I had a bet with my fairy godmother. "I'll find another gown. One that will fit without a spell."

"Mother." Ilana waved at the transport pod waiting by the open door. "We're going to be late."

The girl couldn't wait five minutes for me to change. I didn't care if the dress was pretty or even fit. Anything would do. "I could wear one of Ilana's or Ingrid's old dresses."

Even one of the sleek, short dresses they wore to school. The ones with the built-in calculators hidden from the teachers.

"Not mine." Ilana pulled back her shoulders and glared down her nose.

I regarded Ingrid and put my hands together in an old-fashioned prayer position. "Please."

"I…I…" She gaped back and forth from me to her mother.

I saw the niceness, or Ilana would say weakness, in Ingrid's eyes. Hope squirmed. Please, please, please.

Sybil's gaze narrowed at her youngest daughter and me. "I was told the palace employs zauber detectors at the entrance."

I flinched at the cruel word, especially since she used it to describe me.

Majik detectors weren't about magic being used like Sybil's detector or the ones at school. The palace's type of detector signaled when a fairytale creature tried to enter the royal hall. Alarms, louder than the beeping I just heard, would warn everyone in the palace and the vicinity a majik was present. The palace guards, and the SCUM, would surround the poor majik. There'd be no questions or trial. The majik would be thrown into the infamous palace dungeon.

I shuddered. "My half-human blood should get me past those detectors."

"Will it?" Sybil pinched her lips, causing the bright red of her lip color to crack.

"Unless she used the servants' entrance." Ingrid played with a feather sticking out of her hair. She'd been unwittingly helpful.

"Yes. I could use—"

"Impossible." Sybil cut off hope at my knees. "We couldn't explain Ellery's need to use the side entrance, *the servants' entrance*, even in a not-so-nice dress. She wouldn't slip in unnoticed."

"Or the back entrance." Ilana visibly shivered.

The back entrance was where they took the majik prisoners.

Each slight poked and prodded. The teasing would get worse in class. *Poke*. The embarrassment of not attending the ball, being the only girl at school not there. *Poke*. Gardenia would gloat and pester me and demand a favor. *Poke*.

The unfairness had me tossing my normal restraint to the curb. "Why do you even keep me around?"

I slapped a hand over my mouth. Sybil kept me here to be her slave. If she kicked me out of the house, there was nothing I could do. I'd get kicked out of school and never advance. Never take my place in society. It didn't matter why she kept me around, I needed to stay strong for a few more months.

Her thick eyebrows flew into a defensive arch. "Good question. Something I'll be reevaluating this weekend."

The threat sent a chill down my spine. A false threat. I did the work around the house. Since father died the finances had been getting worse. I didn't know the details because Sybil didn't share, but she'd gone from extravagant everything with the remodel of the house and hosting lavish dinner parties, to firing the rest of the staff and scrimping creds. She complained about everything from the cost of the upkeep of the house, to paying for cleaning supplies. The pantry was always empty. She'd never get rid of me. Was she going to have her darling daughters clean the toilets?

She strutted toward the door signaling the girls to continue forward.

They were leaving without me. Leaving me behind. Which wasn't anything unusual.

Tonight, I thought would be different. I'd bragged to my fairy godmother about being allowed to go. "Won't anyone notice I'm not there?"

The other noble households knew me, had known my father. Surely, my stepmother's pride would force her to take me.

"Why would they?" She tutted. "And if they do, I'll explain you're sick."

"I'm not sick." I never got sick. "I want people to see me there. To dance with the prince as expected."

I didn't stalk Prince Zacharye like most of the girls and hadn't seen a recent vid of him during the year he'd been away. I didn't care what the neighbors thought, and my pride about being there with all the other kids from school had slipped in importance. Mostly, I needed to prove to my fairy godmother that she was wrong and win the bet. I wanted her to stop bothering me about fairy academy, and my fairy heritage. I would never acknowledge the half-fairy blood inside me.

"Do you really think Prince Zacharye would dance with you?" Sybil's laughter vibrated spiteful and mean.

My stepsisters joined in. The mingling of my stepmother's low laugh combined with Ilana and Ingrid's higher, more jealous giggles scratched through my ears and mixed in my mind in an off-key music track. The noise spun around and around in my head and ignited my anger. A rush of power charged through me and sparks shot from my fingertips.

I curled my hands into fists trying to control the uncurbed magic, wanting to prove to them I wasn't different. I might have fairy in my blood, but I looked and acted like them.

Well, not *like* them. I wouldn't want to be anything like my cruel stepmother and stepsisters.

"Imagine the prince dancing with a half-fairy," Ilana squealed louder.

I tensed hoping the pod driver or anyone nearby wouldn't hear. The door was open, and the streets were quiet.

"Now, now girls." Sybil shushed both girls. "We mustn't tell on Ellery. Not unless she does something really stupid."

I hung my head. Guess I could use the sick excuse at school, hamming it up by adding a cough.

But Gardenia would know, and she'd be back.

"I've left a list of chores to keep you occupied tonight." Sybil stood outside the door and pointed a finger. "Make sure you get everything completed."

So much for being sick. She didn't want my secret out because she'd lose her slave. That's what my fairy godmother had once called me. And she'd be right.

Imagined metal shackles circled my throat and choked. From the doorway, I watched the three of them get in the transport pod. They were all smiles, while I was distraught.

No ball. No fun. No winning the bet.

My eyes burned, and I dashed my hand at my face. I wouldn't let them see me cry. My father never made me feel bad about being half fairy. Only since he'd died, and I'd become Sybil's ward, had I felt the sting of being different. Inferior.

Other transport pods headed in the same direction, toward the palace. Toward a night of dancing and food and laughter.

"It's only a ball." I slammed the door closed with a bang.

Arbor flew down from the upper balcony. She puffed up her hair to resemble Sybil's and pointed her finger. "Make sure you get everything completed."

I couldn't stop my harsh chortle. Arbor sounded exactly like my stepmother. She must've heard everything. "Too bad with your identical voice you couldn't give me permission to attend the ball."

The laughter distracted. I didn't want to think about my stepsisters' arrival at the palace, at the sights they'd see, at dancing with the prince. Dancing with anyone. Being seen and being accepted.

Arbor lost the bouffant and flew in front of my face. "We can have our own ball right here."

My friend was trying to cheer me up. I didn't want to be. I wanted to sulk and revel in my hurt. "There's no prince."

"You can pretend." She tugged my fingers.

"I really don't care about dancing with the prince." My heart protested, and I pulled my hand away. "I'd dance with anyone, but there's no one to dance with here."

"What am I? A foul ogre?" Increasing the smoke surrounding her, she stretched the smoky fog to about the size of a teenage guy.

Shaking my head, I couldn't help a short smile. I needed to make the best of things. I had the house to myself for the entire evening. Sure, there were chores to be done. I had time. I had an excuse set for school. At least I appeared human and would achieve Continuum soon. And my best friend was trying to make me feel better.

"There's no music," I grumped.

"Try your powers." Arbor nudged me with her smoke. "The more you practice, the more control you'll have."

Rebellion sparked and tingled. I was being punished for being majik, why not use what little power I had? Concentrating, I focused on the music vid and waved my hand. Music blasted from the hidden surround speakers in the room.

I raised my hands in success. My magic had worked the way I wanted.

"Yay!" Arbor celebrated by rocking her smoky hips. "Dance with me."

Dancing with my best friend was better than a prince anyhow. I put my hand on the place in the fog where a guy's shoulder would be and pretended to hold a hand. Arbor's smoke and I twirled around the living room.

The movement and the music had my taut muscles relaxing. I deserved a few moments of fun. We swirled faster, giggling. Already I was happier. "We need more."

"Don't get carried away, Elle." The note of caution spurred me on.

Normally, I was cautious. Arbor was the adventurous and risk-taking one. I'd already gotten caught trying out my first intentional magic ever. The elongator spell had prevented me from going to the ball. No one was here to see my weak attempts.

I threw caution away. "Laser fireworks." I pointed at the ceiling.

Streaks of colored light rained down on us.

I couldn't believe I'd pulled off more magic. Fun and colorful magic. It wasn't anything I'd learned or practiced. I'd focused on what I wanted, and made it happen. Who needed fairy training at an academy?

The front door slammed open.

Freezing, I knew I'd be in so much trouble from my stepmother.

"By order of the SCUM," a harsh voice demanded from the open doorway, and not my stepmother's. "You are under arrest."

Chapter 5

I froze, and my muscles grew rigid like stone.

Arbor's smoke shriveled leaving me dancing alone. Her tiny body fluttered in one place, her wings agitated back and forth and back and forth showing her…well, agitation.

Slowly, I put down my hands and angled toward the open doorway. Three uniformed guards filled the space. Each held a majik stun gun. Their stern expressions told me they'd witnessed my magic.

Fireworks. I'm such an idiot.

My heart throbbed so loud I'm sure the SCUM heard. The over-rapid beats resembled an out-of-control rock drum. After all my pretending, I'd been caught because of a stupid mistake.

I stepped in front of Arbor—because going from a large smoke form to her regular body type wasn't an infraction just biology—standing as tall as possible.

"This is a private residence. You have no legal right to come inside." I copied Sybil's disdainful tone.

"I have a key." A skinny guard with two stripes on his uniform held up an electronic card attached to a chain.

"Why do you have a key to my house?" Was this some new technology the SCUM had access to that opened private residences?

"Your house?" The guard's face reddened. A threat threaded through his tone. "This is Lady Milford's house. And she only has two daughters and you're not one of them."

Choking, I cleared the lump in my throat. I wasn't Sybil's daughter, but she didn't even acknowledge my existence out in the city or the fact I'd own this home someday.

Arbor's wings thumped faster imitating a hummingbird. The other two guards glanced back and forth as if watching an esports match.

The guard with the key pointed. "Arrest these trespassers."

Holding up my hands, I tried to ward them off. "I'm not a trespasser. I live here." I held out my wrist with the embedded identity chip. The chip holding my personal information, except the one big lie. "Scan me. I'm Lady Milford's stepdaughter."

A guard with four stripes on his shoulder nodded at the youngest guard. "Patterson, check."

Patterson unclipped a scanner from his belt and approached. He slid the device across my wrist and his sweaty scent stung my nose. "Ellery Milford. Human. She checks out."

Still didn't explain why the one man had a key. Or from their perspective, why Arbor was in the house. The SCUM would demand to know that next. They could arrest her for just being present, didn't matter if she was welcome here or not.

The best defense was a good offense. "Where did you get the key?"

"Sybil and I are dating." The supposed-boyfriend's cheeks reddened with bright splotches. "I wanted to see her dressed up for the ball."

My stomach churned at the expression of devotion on his face. I didn't know anything about this relationship. Did her daughters? "Well, you're too late. She already left. Please leave."

"I have every right to be here. I have a key." He held the card higher.

The guard in charge grimaced. He probably didn't want to hear the details of this relationship, either. "It's the night of the royal ball and we have special patrols. If we suspect anything suspicious, we're allowed to investigate even homes. Special orders."

"You can enter a private residence?" What other rights were being broken in name of law and order?

"We're expecting trouble from terrorists," Patterson said.

Terrorists? Breath whooshed out of my chest.

"That's confidential." In-charge-guard scowled causing his facial hair to twitch.

Patterson must've spoken out of turn.

I glanced at Arbor and back at the trio of guards. I'd never heard of terrorists in Alandaska. "I'm not a terrorist. I'm only a teenage girl who is too sick," *cough,* "to go to the ball."

The head guard's gaze travelled the length of the room. The mishmash of twenty-second century technology, nineteenth century antiques, and my stepmother's awful decorating taste probably made him gag. "Use of unsanctioned magic is illegal."

I fought to breathe. Maybe it was time to magically disappear. If my magic worked…and if that wouldn't bring me more scrutiny. I needed to play it cool.

"Ackerman, spray the vicinity," in-charge guard ordered Sybil's boyfriend.

He stomped forward pulling a hose connected to a tank that was strapped to his back. He pumped a fine mist into the air. The mist fell similar to soft snow covering every piece of furniture, and me and Arbor.

More mess to clean up. Although not my biggest problem. I was going to be arrested for doing magic and be called out for being majik. While Arbor wasn't registered to this home and had run away from her homeland.

The music screeched to a halt.

Arbor shook spreading the mist across my shoulder. No smoke came from her tiny body as if she'd been snuffed out.

My scalp prickled. "What was that?"

The boyfriend sprayed more mist into the room. His smirk seemed to be chiseled into his face. He enjoyed his job. "Magic Blocking Fixatif."

They'd blocked my magic. Even if I knew how, I couldn't use powers to escape.

"It was only fireworks." I'd beg if they'd let it go. A majik doing unapproved magic would face a courtroom ruled by the regent, and most likely prison. There wasn't much sympathy. The rumors of what happened were much worse. Everyone was found guilty. "Nothing harming anyone. I didn't realize…"

Patterson took out a coin-shaped object. He tapped on it and it popped open to reveal a small wire trap made with neon electronics. The eight-inch wire box had crisscrossing lines forming a tight mesh and glared in a hideous electric green color. I wasn't sure what the device was. Another way to curtail magic?

Wearing special gloves, he lunged toward me.

My heart drummed again, slower and louder and more ominous. I took a step back tripping on a low table and bumping into Arbor. This was it. All my plans had gone awry. My stepmother would get my house if I was sentenced to prison.

"Wait!" I stuck my hands up and quickly put them to my sides. I didn't want them to think I was attempting magic. "The Milford name, my father's name, is noble. You can't arrest me."

Ignoring my plea, the young guard's hand snaked out toward my shoulder.

Panic paralyzed my body, while whatever device they'd used to block my magic set off another type of paralysis in my mind. I hadn't had my magic long, and it hadn't been very useful up to this point, still I missed its existence.

His hand strayed past me.

Luck was finally on my side. Maybe I could get away. I could run. Arbor could fly. Maybe they wouldn't chase us since the magic had been simple and they were too worried about terrorists to bother with a smoke sprite and one runaway, half-fairy girl.

Patterson grabbed Arbor in mid-air and her tiny body froze as if she'd been shoved in cryonics fluid. Her wings lost their flutter. Her pupils lost their light.

He shoved her in the small cage and her tiny body lay on the bottom unmoving. Her mouth pursed in a permanent open position.

My eyes widened taking in the action. I couldn't run without my friend.

He secured the cage, and the other two guards relaxed their shoulders pointing the weapons down. What was going on?

"As a favor to Lady Milford we won't arrest you for hanging out with a zauber." Ackerman pounded on the cage with his fist.

Arbor's tiny body jostled, and I jumped at the cruel action and words. She appeared stunned and woozy.

"Is she okay?" I rushed the cage.

Patterson yanked the cage higher keeping it away from me. "The gloves only stun for a second."

"Hey!" Arbor struggled to stand. She pounded on the neon wires and was thrown to the metal ground of the cage.

"See?" Patterson smirked. "She'll learn not to touch the wires."

Her body flopped and jerked appearing to be electrocuted. Her hair, which normally poked in stylish tufts, stuck straight up. Her tiny, round eyes struck with an odd gleam.

I gulped. At a loss, I couldn't make sense of anything. "What's going on?"

"Use of unsanctioned magic is illegal. You're old enough to know that." The head guard wrote on a sophisticated celltab. "I'll need to contact Lady Milford about this majik hanging around her house."

I bit my lip. "Lady Milford doesn't know about the smoke sprite." If I was going to take a fall, I might as well take the fall for everything.

He perused the boyfriend. "You're lucky I'm in a good mood, and Lady Milford has a connection here."

"I'll make sure to tell Sybil personally what her ungrateful stepdaughter has been up to."

My abs clenched imagining Sybil's reaction. Not that it mattered. I'd be in prison once they unloaded a bigger cage for me. My poor friend had been caught in my mess. Arbor kneeled in the small cage with her hands fisted around the non-electrified bars. Her gleaming gaze burned through me.

"Arbor did nothing wrong. I let her stay here. You should let her go."

"As I said, even harmless magic is illegal. Only majiks working for the government are allowed to use their powers." The head guard went into lecture mode. "The sprite should know better."

Shaking my head back and forth, I finally put things together. The SCUM believed Arbor had done magic. It wasn't about her unregistered presence. She was taking the blame for both of us. My stomach muscles tightened, and my pulse throbbed. I hadn't stood up for her at the mall and needed to prove my friendship.

"It was me!" I grabbed the mesh to stop them from taking Arbor. A mild shock went through and I could only imagine how strong the sensation felt to a small sprite. "Let her go."

Patterson's lips twisted in an ironic and disbelieving smirk. "Yeah, right. You're human."

All the oxygen evacuated my lungs. I'd always worried about being recognized as a majik, and now that I was confessing, they didn't believe me. "No. It was me. I did the spell."

Arbor lay on the bottom of the cage. Her eyes were open. She seemed more shocked at my admittance.

"We'll send a communication to Lady Milford letting her know we've arrested the sprite on the property." The head guard scribbled on the celltab and then tucked it into his uniform pocket. "There will be an inquiry to assess any further blame and infractions of the law."

His droning on about laws and infractions were only flies buzzing. I wanted to swat them away. The SCUM believed my only indiscretion was hanging out with a zauber. They believed Arbor had done the magic. Smoke sprites didn't have those kinds of powers. Shouldn't they know the skills of the people they arrested?

I didn't care what Sybil thought. I cared what Arbor thought. And she believed I was a terrible friend, a traitor, and a liar. I couldn't lie about this. I felt as if the dirt outside had coated my skin with filth. I couldn't live knowing I'd let her take the fall for something I'd done. I had to prove my guilt and worry about the consequences later. The SCUM would release her and arrest me. I had to hope my family name would make my punishment less severe. I had to believe my stepmother would negotiate to keep me as her servant.

"It was me." Putting more conviction into my voice, I jostled the cage trying to get Arbor's attention. "Tell them, Arbor." My screech should've penetrated their psyches.

She sat up. "No."

"No? What do you mean, no?" My fingers dug around the wire bars again refusing to let the guard take her away. "Arbor! Tell them!"

She crossed her thin arms and glared. Her purple eyebrows arched in a stubborn and fierce expression.

Pain seared across my chest. I couldn't let her sacrifice herself. She'd been trying to cheer me up. I'd gone over the top with the fireworks, too mad to care.

Ackerman scuttled toward the door.

"Watch. I can do magic." I let go of the cage and waved my fingers at the robo-vac in the corner. "Sweep."

Nothing happened.

The guards' chuckles scraped against my desperation.

The boyfriend tucked his gun into his belt showing he didn't think I was a threat. "If you paid your electricity bills the vac would work." He must know about our financial situation and thought the robo-vac wasn't connected.

My insides heated. Sybil must be close to him if she'd confided the information.

The head guard exchanged a look with the young guard holding the cage. "Even if we believed you—"

"Which we don't." Patterson rattled the cage.

Arbor jostled about trying to use her feet sand hands to keep her balance.

I lurched toward her wanting their mistreatment to stop,

knowing it had only begun. The state media spoke of fair trials, yet I'd never seen a vid of a single one. Convicted majiks were sent out of the country. If that was so, wouldn't the outside world know about our little kingdom? Learn our secrets? Pull us into their perpetual world wars?

Since Concealment Day, the then-king of Alandaska had decided our natural resources couldn't be depleted by another war. Prince Zacharye's great grandfather had worked with the majiks to conceal the kingdom. Majiks had been allies and some of our best scientists. Interesting the textbooks didn't say much about the majiks' involvement in the development of our independence.

"The Magic Blocking Fixatif won't wear off for an hour," Ackerman explained. "Makes it safer for us to protect the kingdom."

"My magic's not working because you sprayed the mist. Give me time." Pushing down my panic, I focused on the robo-vac again. Still nothing. *Stupid vac system.* "I swear. It was me doing magic."

"We don't have time for this. It's a busy night between the extra security at the palace and the unsupervised majiks in town." The head guard jerked his chin in a *let's move* motion.

"One down and hundreds more to go." The boyfriend's grin expressed how he anticipated the confrontations.

Special orders. Secret patrols. Terrorists. Each word planted deep in my conscience. I knew things changed every day, situations for the majiks worsened. They were losing their rights. What was happening to my world?

The head guard hastened out the door.

"I'm telling the truth. I'm a majik. A fairy." Each admission dragged out of my mouth leaving a sour taste. This was the first time I'd admitted to being a fairy without a qualifier. One last desperate attempt to convince them of the truth.

"Nothing you can say or do is going to save this creature. She's a smoke sprite and we witnessed her doing magic." Patterson's no-chance tone said he'd witnessed this many times before.

Majiks were arrested all the time, for real crimes or supposed crimes. The number of missing majiks had quadrupled. Reports of disappearances, and not magical ones, multiplied every single day.

I grasped the edge of the door frame. "What's going to happen to her? When is her trial?"

Maybe as a human coming to her defense, I'd be more believable.

Again the laughter, crueler and sharper this time. Sharp enough to cut. Cut me down and make me useless. I grabbed the guard holding the cage. "I'm serious. I know you can't give me an exact date, but she'll have a trial, right?"

I'd show up and defend her. If I had to, I'd do magic to prove I should be the one arrested. I'd do anything I could to save my best friend.

The boyfriend whipped the stun gun from the holster at his waist. "Let go of the cage."

By his fierce tone and deadly-serious expression I knew a misting spray wouldn't come out of the shaft of this weapon. I let go and took a quivering step back. Getting killed wouldn't help either of us.

"Listen, kid." The head guard stood on the front step. "This is a closed case. Three of us witnessed her magic."

"As a teen, she'll be thrown into the auraguillotine machine." Patterson's mouth shaped into a fanatical grin.

The guard in command whipped around. The boyfriend's mouth dropped open. Another slip by the youngster.

I shivered. "What kind of machine?"

"Stop." Both men glared at Patterson. "She'll be taken to prison and shipped out of the kingdom."

Shipped out. Gone. Forever. My best friend.

"But—"

Ackerman gave a final glance around the once-elegant home of the noble family of Milford. "You shouldn't be friends with a zauber, anyhow. Sybil wouldn't approve."

I flinched at the insulting slur. One I'd heard plenty of times, had used in my head, and never reacted so strongly. Because it referred to me, too.

There had to be something I could do. Some excuse or even a bribe. The only creds I had was the one simple plastic card, not enough to make anyone look the other way. I couldn't use what little magic I knew. So, no magic and no money.

"Bye Elle." Arbor sounded so solemn and quiet. Not like my spirited friend.

My pulse quieted into a sad song.

The boyfriend's lips contorted into a sarcastic curl. "The conversation I'll have with Sybil will be very interesting."

My lungs darkened suffocating me from the inside. The guards weren't going to believe me. I wasn't going to save her. My friend was doomed.

And it was my fault.

Arbor twisted in the cage and gave me a salute "Have a nice *human* life."

The single word tore into me. Even though I denied it, she knew I thought humans were superior. Didn't mean I thought less of her. And I had no way to prove how much she meant to me.

The guards marched toward the transport pod with the swirling red and blue lights. Patterson shoved the cage into the back, jostling Arbor. They got in the pod and flew away.

Arbor was gone. Arrested. Ex-patriated.

I slouched onto the table unable to support myself. Would I ever see her again?

The black cloud inside me grew wider, ready to swallow me in its bleak despair. Struggling back to my feet, I slammed the door again. In a daze, I wandered past the vid screen where Arbor had once pretended to be part of a movie playing out characters in their exact voices. I punched a decorative pillow Arbor had used as a bed when no one else was around. Stopping in front of the flameless fireplace, I sank onto the fake brick surrounding the hearth.

The two of us had loved sitting by the electronic fire talking. Arbor told the funniest stories always making me laugh. She'd been the bright spot in my life. I fought the tears burning in my eyes. Crying would do no good. I didn't deserve the relief of tears.

Static electricity shot out from nowhere, shocking my skin. The space in front of me glimmered.

Gardenia.

I dropped my head lower. I couldn't deal with my fairy godmother right now.

She wore the same dress as earlier today. The silver strands of her hair were swept up into an elegant bun. Her wings fluttered and folded behind her back becoming one with her outfit. My wings hadn't manifested yet and I didn't know when, or if, they ever would. I'd have to find a clever way to hide them.

Fisting my hands, I held in a scream. "What're you doing here?"

Gardenia pursed her purple lips. "I heard about your friend's arrest."

My eyebrows flew up into an arch. "How?"

"We fairies have our own communication system. Something you would know if you trained." She drew out the last few words and each one was a light jab.

Standing, I crossed my arms. My fingers pinched my skin trying to control my mad. "I'm not training."

"It's your heritage. Your birthright. Your rightful place." Her wings whipped stirring the air in the house.

"My rightful place?" The unshed tears scalded, traveled down my throat, and ignited. If Gardenia had never taunted me this afternoon, I wouldn't have tried doing magic on the dress. I wouldn't have gotten caught by my stepmother and I wouldn't have been reckless when they'd left for the ball. The SCUM wouldn't have blamed my best friend and arrested her. "Magic is the reason Arbor is gone. I never should've used my fairy powers. I was showing off."

"Magic is part of who you are, Ellery."

"*Half* of who I am. A half I will never use again." My fingertips sparked and I fisted my hands and crossed my arms. "I'm done."

I'd persuade Sybil to help save Arbor, even if I had to threaten to go on strike.

Gardenia wagged a long, thin finger. "Quit whining and do something to help."

Power thrummed through me in a tidal wave. I couldn't believe my fairy godmother would take advantage of me at my weakest point. "I won't train to be a fairy warrior."

"I meant," Gardenia's tone softened and became more compassionate, "do something to help your friend."

Her suggestion connected in my mind. I paused. I wanted to help my friend. But why did Gardenia want to help me when I'd opposed her at every chance? "What?"

"Go to the ball."

My chortle came out harsh. I no longer cared about going to the ball. Not after losing my best friend. "How's that going to help Arbor?"

"The ball is in the palace and your friend is being held—"

"In the palace," I screeched. If I could get inside, and sneak into the dungeon, and find her, and get her out, I could save her. Each thought spurred me higher. How? Everything plummeted into a pit in my stomach. "I can't go to the ball." I tugged at the floral disaster draping my body. "I have no dress. No transportation. No invitation. And no way to get past the majik sensors."

"I can help." Gardenia snapped her fingers.

"You can?" I could save my friend.

Her eyes glinted, and her lips lifted in an all-knowing smile. "What are fairy godmothers for?"

She was right. This *is* what fairy godmothers were for. To help out. To grant wishes. Lightness filled my chest like puffy dandelion seeds "Let's do it."

Gardenia's wings fluttered, and she stroked her chin with those unusually long fingers. "There's only one thing. You need to do something for me."

Chapter 6

A trick. Just like a fairy.

Gardenia wanted me to do something for her. I could totally guess what *that* was. And here my hopes had gotten so high.

"I'm not enrolling in your stupid fairy school. I should've known you'd have conditions." I hunched my shoulders.

"And I should've known you'd be ungrateful." Her voice thundered, and I took a step back. "Similar to how you are ungrateful for your friend's sacrifice."

Her comeback was a dagger to the heart. Guilt seeped around the internal wound.

"I'm not ungrateful." I heaved a shaky sigh. "I tried to convince the SCUM I was the one who'd done the magic. I tried to take Arbor's place."

Gardenia's gaze bored into me for minutes, or so it seemed. Her wings fluttered, and she sniffed. "My condition has nothing to do with fairy academy."

"It doesn't?"

"No, it doesn't." She managed to sound insulted and superior at the same time. "Besides, since you didn't go to the ball you already owe me a favor. We had a bet. More than a bet."

I remembered the sizzle of our handshake. "What do you want then?" I couldn't think of anything she'd need from me.

"It doesn't matter. You probably couldn't pull it off." She twirled away, leaving.

My nerves stretched tight. "Pull off what?"

"Never mind," she sang the dismissal.

"You were going to help me go to the ball. The dress. The transport. The invitation." The way past the magical sensors. How else was I going to save my friend?

"If I did, I'd lose the bet we made this afternoon."

"Forget the bet from this afternoon. You won, and I owe you." Losing didn't matter and having my friends see me at the ball didn't matter. "Saving Arbor is more important."

Gardenia tapped her long finger against her chin. Her gaze narrowed, and she studied me as if deciding whether I was worthy. "I might be able to help. In exchange for an additional favor. And not fairy academy." She emphasized the last point, knowing it would be a deal breaker.

I stomped across the pink carpet toward her. "Is that how fairy godmothers work? I have to pay for a wish?"

Fairy godmothers were similar to mobster godfathers.

"What you're asking is quite risky and will only save one majik." Her superior-knowing tone chafed. "My goals are loftier. I can't risk getting caught."

"Because you're a wanted fairy." I taunted using my stepmother's words.

Gardenia's laugh trickled like a stream. "The things they *don't* teach you at the human school."

I didn't want a lecture about how fairy academy was superior.

"I'd be taking a risk by going to the ball against my stepmother's wishes, being half-majik, and trying to rescue

Arbor." What danger would my fairy godmother be in by using a little magic to get me in the palace?

"No. No." Gardenia's forehead wrinkled. "I will take my magic and leave. And you can go on with your human life."

Human.

The word pummeled. Arbor had said the exact same thing. I missed her already and she'd only been gone minutes. I didn't want her to suffer. Or be deported. Or die. I had to take this chance to save my friend.

"I'll do it!" I screamed the words trying to counteract the tension inside of me. "I'll do whatever you want if you help me."

Gardenia whipped out a wand and pointed it at my heart. "Do you promise, Ellery?"

Her solemn tone told me this moment was important. No sarcasm or persuasion. A straight question needing a straight answer.

"Yes." There was no other answer I could give. She'd said it didn't involve the academy and fairies couldn't lie. Any other task I'd do if she would help me save Arbor.

"Wonderful." Gardenia's shoulders relaxed and she smiled. "Let's start with what you're wearing."

I really didn't care about a dress anymore. To think hours ago it was my only goal. "Whatever works."

She tapped her chin with her long fingers. "How about the dress designed by Lavender you admired in the store window?"

Waving her wand, Gardenia looped the small stick up and down. Silvery glimmers shot out from the wand and fell around me. The floral bag disappeared, and I was clothed in the elegant blue dress.

I glanced at myself and couldn't stop my big smile. It was beautiful. How did she conjure it?

"The SCUM sprayed Magic Blocking Fixatif when they arrested Arbor." I patted the fluffy folds of the dress. "How does your magic still work?"

"I'm too powerful for those pathetic humans to contain my magic." The boast was followed by a superior snicker. "You could be, too."

I didn't want to hear more fairy propaganda. The government and school gave me enough bull.

Shuffling to the large decorative mirror, I surveyed myself through the gilt frame. Sybil had dug the mirror from out of the attic, *my bedroom now*, and hung it on the wall right after her marriage to my father. I should've known by her taking careless possession of my mother's valuable things and discarding the rest we'd never get along.

"What do you think of the dress?" Gardenia floated behind me.

Just as I'd imagined at the mall, the dress hugged my slight curves showing them in the best light. The waist cinched in tight and the skirt flowed like a fountain. It was wonderful and made me feel beautiful. Imagining Olivia and Jade's expressions if I wore this to the ball brought a smile to my face.

I shook my head. At one time this gown had been my dream. "I don't want to stand out if I'm going to be sneaking around the palace."

A Lavender original would stand out.

"Smart." Gardenia nodded approvingly and looped her wand again.

The blue dress disappeared to be replaced with a mermaid-style dress in pink. This would be similar to trying clothing on by hologram. I'd never had that experience because I only received hand-me-downs from my stepsisters.

I twirled around in front of the mirror. The color of the

material matched the ugly carpet. Stretching out my knees, I couldn't move much. "This dress is too tight. If I need to run, I won't be able to."

She looped her wand again. The pink dress was gone to be replaced by a black pantsuit.

Ducking down to check out the stretch-ability, I studied my backside in the mirror. Definitely could move with the loose-fitting pants with wide bells. Though the ruffled blouse was too foo-foo and the jacket glittered.

She beamed. "Elegant enough to go unnoticed, and yet serviceable."

"*Ug* and *lee*." Not only did I resemble a matron, I'd be noticed for being hideous.

"If you need to run…" Her hint I might need to make a quick getaway resembled my earlier comment.

I sucked in a nervous breath. I had to remember I wasn't a normal girl from the kingdom going to the ball. This wasn't about finding the perfect color to complement my skin or a dress highlighting my feminine attributes. The dress was a costume to get me inside the palace. I needed to blend and roam freely. I was on a mission to save my majik friend.

"I've got an idea." I told Gardenia what I had in mind.

She waved her wand and the pantsuit was transformed. "Voila!"

The forest green dress brought out the color of my eyes. That wasn't important. The bodice fit and wasn't constricting. The long folds of the skirt had slits. If I needed to make a dangerous escape I wouldn't be encumbered. I poked my leg out revealing built-in shorts. "And the skirt can be detached and put back on?"

"Like this." She pulled back the skirt revealing the magno-electric attachments. Then, she wrapped the skirt back around my waist. "And like this."

"Perfect." I studied myself in the mirror. I didn't look half bad. Not as beautiful as Olivia and Jade. Yet, so much better than wearing the floral concoction I'd created. "What about my hair? It's a bird's nest."

Between my stepsister attacking me to take her ribbon and my upset about Arbor being arrested, the strands now stuck up in a mess. I grimaced. My hair was never stylish.

"Simple enough." Gardenia waved her wand in an interlocking pattern.

My hair was pulled tight, twisted and knotted. The flyaway strands tucked in a braid resembling a crown on my head. The length in the back was curled into an upward flip. She waved the wand in front of my face. Lip cover, extendo eyelashes, and blush caressed my cheeks.

Nodding, I assessed myself. Definitely passable.

She opened her hand and presented me with a perfect replication of the royal ball invitation. I'd caught a glimpse of the Milford family invitation Sybil had tucked into one of her drawers. The invitation hadn't come across the vid screen or people's personal celltabs. It had copied the elegant paper from the seventeenth century with basically unreadable calligraphy. A more modern translation had been attached.

"What about transportation?" I'd appear odd if I walked or took the skyway. "I'll already be arriving late."

"Fashionably late." She roamed around the front living space. She wouldn't find a transport pod here. Only needing-to-be-updated electronics and hideous furniture.

Gardenia stopped in front of the pumpkin chair. The arms rose high rounding the edges like a ball. The chair was too big to sit in and be comfortable. I always believed the green around the edges would sprout into leaves and strangle me.

Waving her wand, the chair's legs rounded, turning into wheels and rolling the chair toward the front door. With a wave from Gardenia, the front door opened, and the chair propelled outside. She floated after the chair.

My mouth dropped open. If my magic worked that well, I'd be more tempted to claim my fairy heritage.

I followed out the door. "Sybil is going to kill me for ruining her new chair."

Of course, I'd be blamed. It would be worse for me though if I told her my fairy godmother had magically transformed the piece of furniture.

Stepping outside, I checked to see if anyone was watching. I'd already gotten caught once tonight. The high front garden walls hid us from prying neighbors. The clear night sky showcased the stars through the invisible arched dome.

Using her wand, Gardenia tapped the hunchback chair three times.

The chair grew larger, expanding from inside as if a gigantic kernel of corn had popped. The arms and winged back stretched in several places. The orange material shaped and grew into a small, sleek transport pod. Dark windows materialized, and lines formed a door. The material morphed to metal with a snap of Gardenia's fingers.

"The transport pod will only stay in its current form until midnight." She waved her wand and the door lifted with a whoosh.

I peeked inside to find a bench seat and data center. "Why?"

"You'd know why if you'd been trained." Her frustration curdled in her voice and her sudden irritation jerked me out of the fascination with the chair-turned-transport.

I thought we were past lecturing about what she thinks I should be doing. Arching a brow, I waited.

"Several reasons." She sighed. "My magic is strong, but the palace employs magic blocking misters. I won't be close enough to maintain the illusion. And I can only give you so much of my energy."

I swirled the bottom of my dress. "What about my gown? Will it disappear at midnight too?" I didn't want to end up naked at the ball. Talk about being conspicuous.

Her joyful laughter made me think if we'd met earlier. we might've gotten along. "The dress is real. As is your hair. And this clutch purse."

The bag was the size of about two of my hands decorated with colorful beads shaped into flowers and leaves. The thickness only an inch.

My fingers itched to hold it. "I'm not going to worry about freshening my face or hair."

"This isn't a personal clutch, Ellery." Gardenia snapped it open, reached inside, and withdrew a glass-cut perfume bottle similar to my mother's. The one I'd traded for the creds card. "This bag is a fairy carryall. *And I mean, all.* It's bottomless."

"It has a bottom."

She handed me the perfume bottle and I held it to my nose to take a sniff.

"Don't!" She grabbed my wrist and pulled the bottle away. "It's a potent sleeping potion."

My gaze narrowed. Is that why the fairy was willing to trade for my mom's bottle? Had it also contained a magic potion? I wanted to smack my forehead. *If I'd been trained, I'd have known,* Gardenia spoke in my head and I tried to shake it out. I didn't want to be drawn to fairy ways. This was a one-night stand to help my friend. Then, I'd return to my regularly scheduled human life.

She pulled out a yellow tube. "This holds a magic ointment for wounds." She put the tube in and took out a white box. "And this is a first aid kit for human and majik."

My mouth dropped open. I peered in the clutch and only saw normal items a girl would carry, lipstick, comb, and mirror. "How do all those things fit?"

"It resembles a normal purse with normal items inside. With your fairy blood, you can access whatever you need. It's a Necessary Bag."

My stomach jiggled. "How will I ever get past the detectors at the palace with these magical items?"

The clutch, the dress, and my very own fairy blood would betray me.

"That's what the shoes are for." She held out her hands and two glass-heeled shoes appeared.

The clear shoes sparkled in the light. Two-inch heels led to a slender sloping arch. A decorative green jewel topped off near the toes.

"I enjoy shoes as much as the next girl but how are high heels going to help?" I'd decided on the dress based on practicality. I couldn't run in high heels.

"These shoes are made with Elfin glass and they aren't only high heels." She pinched the gemstone and the heels lowered. The shoes became flats. "The shoes will be acceptable at the ball, and when you go to find Arbor you can make them more comfortable."

I'd known this would be a dangerous quest. Getting past the sensors at the palace, searching for Arbor. If I got caught, I'd be arrested or worse. I might need to run, but Arbor was worth it. "Clever."

Gardenia's arched eyebrows asked what else would be expected. Wearing no make-up from what I could tell, she had a natural beauty. Rosy cheeks, pink lips, white-flawless skin smelling of flowers and cut grass. "The shoes also have deflection technology. Magic and majik."

"So, the SCUM won't detect I'm half-majik." Nodding, I

let confidence seep into my skin. This deal was definitely in my favor.

"Or the magical items in your possession." She snapped her fingers and another item appeared in the palm of her hand.

A knife.

I flinched and my skin prickled.

"This is the Dagger of Justice. It weighs the guilt of the intended target." She reached up toward my head. "You will wear it as a hair ornament."

The sharp steel point glinted. The ruby-encrusted handle reminded me of blood. Blood I might make flow.

"W-what do I need a dagger for?"

"To complete your end of the *Binding Promise*." Her pupils flashed with a winning gleam, yet her expression stayed deadly serious.

The words *Binding Promise* sizzled between us having a life of its own.

My muscles tensed and the hairs at the back of my neck stuck up. This wasn't like the bet we'd made earlier today. How bad could my end of the promise be if it didn't include fairy academy? But if it wasn't bad, why would I need a dagger? I should've asked before I'd agreed, except I hadn't been thinking because of my guilt about Arbor.

My throat tightened. "What do you want me to do with the dagger?"

Gardenia's lips lifted in a slight smile. "Assassinate Prince Zacharye."

Chapter 7

K*ill the prince?*
The single thought circled around my brain getting tighter and tighter, cutting off my circulation, and sending shafts of pain across my forehead. "Are you crazy?"

The prince was my age and the girls at school swooned whenever they saw his image on a vid screen. If he was related to Regent Theobald, then his view of majiks was skewed and I didn't want anything to do with Prince Zacharye even if he was the cutest male in the kingdom.

But kill him? I shook my head making myself dizzy.

Gardenia's eyebrows rose in a superior way. She didn't say anything.

Wiggling my shoulders, I held my hand against my chest. The same spot she'd pointed the wand when I'd agreed. "I can't kill anyone. Especially the prince."

That would be a crime against cuteness and a crime against the state.

Her gaze narrowed, and she pointed one of those strangely, long fingers. "You made a Binding Promise, Ellery."

Inch by inch jagged lines etched into my brain. "No. I didn't know…didn't understand."

I'd realized the moment was significant, just not how significant. Binding? What did that even mean?

"When I pointed the wand at your heart and you promised with no coercion from me, it bound you to your word. Fairies can't lie. And they can't break a Binding Promise." Gardenia tucked her finger into the fist of her hand. "If you'd been trained as a fairy, you'd have recognized a Binding Promise."

The taunt packed a wallop about my choices.

Since I was only half-fairy, I could lie. Could I break a Binding Promise?

My mind searched for anything I'd heard about fairies and promises. I came up blank. I'd learned nothing about Binding Promises when we'd studied fairies in class, and Arbor had never mentioned it. I had to know, even though I'd promised myself not to learn more about my fairy half. "What is a Binding Promise? How does it work?"

Gardenia fiddled with the four-leaf clover necklace around her neck. "Well, the Binding Promise is a magical contract between two fairies where a deal is agreed upon and each of the parties must execute."

"Execute?" I gulped. Sounded a lot like assassinate. "What will happen? Will it force me to kill the prince?"

"Well, um…the Binding Promise," she fiddled with the necklace again, "in this case will recognize your target and take control of your actions. You'll have no choice. You'll have to complete the task."

My blood pressure rose, and I snorted loudly. I might not understand fairy promises, but I understood politics. This promise was going to force me to murder creating a national incident. "Why would you even want to kill the prince? He has no authority."

The gate was open, and a few transport pods zoomed by

the lane. Few people walked and if they did, they wore hover shoes and moved too fast to eavesdrop.

"He will soon. He's now of age at sixteen That's what this ball is celebrating." She made it sound as if the entire event was nonsense. Except nothing she said was non-sensical. She was completely serious.

I had to make her see reason. "The ball is so Prince Zacharye can meet the girls of the kingdom."

"Perfect excuse for you to meet him. And assassinate him."

"I'm not a normal girl. I'm half-fairy." Exasperation came out on a loud sigh.

"Finally, you admit you are fairy." Her amusement grated.

"This is ridiculous. I can't kill the prince. I can't kill anyone." My belly threatened to spew. To stick a dagger into a person. Hear the squelch of skin and muscle and blood. I wasn't a killer.

Her lips pinched and turned blue. "The Kingdom of Alandaska has changed during the last decade. The majiks, who once owned this land and shared with humans, have been shuttled aside. Prejudice against our kind has become rampant and infiltrated the law of the land. Atrocities have been occurring and the human world either doesn't know or doesn't care. This must be stopped."

None of this had affected me so far. I'd heard more horror stories since Arbor had become my friend. The disappearance of fairies, the bigotry at the mall and the market, the general fear of majiks to be out in public in case the SCUM arrested them for no reason.

"That's his uncle, Regent Theobald's doing. Not the prince." I defended the prince only because I didn't want to kill him. "Prince Zacharye is innocent."

"As is your friend, Arbor."

My throat thickened cutting off my oxygen. *My fault, my*

fault, my fault seesawed in and out of my ears. I'd do anything to save my friend.

"The prince has gone along with the regent's policies. Do you think he will change the laws when he becomes ruler? When the regent is by his side, whispering the decisions in his ear? Telling him what to do?" Gardenia lifted her pointy nose. "I think not."

I'd learned in school how the prince apprenticed with the regent since the age of two, learning how to rule fair and justly. But if he was being trained by a regent who wasn't fair and just, what exactly was he learning? Probably nothing favorable for majiks.

A worm wiggled inside me. "Why don't *you* assassinate the regent? It's his policies you're against."

"I'm against?" Her cheeks colored a bright red. "Everyone who has any sense, human or majik, should be against these bad policies for the kingdom."

"So kill Regent Theobald."

"We've tried and failed." She slashed with her hand causing a gleam of glitter to spray through the air. "This action will prove to the regent that he and his cronies are not untouchable. That they can't do as they please. That they can't get away with murder."

"Killing the prince is murder."

"He's a stupid, vain kid who has been absent for the last year doing nothing to stop his uncle and his actions." She glanced at the sky as if searching for assistance explaining her warped motivation.

"He's been on secondment learning every aspect of the kingdom." That's what the official news vids said.

She brought her gaze back down and pierced me. "The political assassination of Prince Zacharye will make a strong statement at the beginning of a revolution."

Whoa. Revolution to overthrow the government?

The glitter seeped into my lungs, floating through my midsection, swishing around and churning. Twice tonight I'd been shocked by terms. First, terrorists and now, revolution.

"I don't know how to assassinate anyone." Using a different word didn't make it more palatable. Murder was murder.

"Something must be done to spark the revolution. The prince's assassination will be a clear signal to humans and majiks change is coming." Her dark tone spoke of dark times.

Shivering, I tried to bring the conversation back to my needs. "If I get caught, I can't save Arbor."

If the prince was killed, the palace guards would go on high alert. We'd never get away.

"Save Arbor first. You might need her help. Then return to the ball and kill the prince." Gardenia's vehemence became a brick wall I couldn't climb over.

That didn't stop me from trying, and I threw out any weak excuse. "I don't even know what the prince looks like." Desperation clawed at my throat making my voice go higher.

She waved her fingers and an image of a clean-cut guy with short blond hair and pale face wearing an ostentatious uniform emerged in the space in front of us. Sashes, medals, jeweled collar and crown. "May I present Prince Zacharye." Her formal tone was at odds with her request.

I took a cursory glance. The same image I'd seen on multiple vids and hanging in girls' lockers at school. The same image I'd seen in my dreams. "It's not a very good image."

"Find the handsome young man surrounded by young ladies competing for his attention at the ball." She sounded so cynical. As if the royal family was of no consequence.

Her disrespect was opposite of how I was raised. Between Dad's deference to royalty because of his noble birth and the teacher's training about being loyal to the crown, I believed the royal family had an unalienable right to rule. But because of the fear I faced every day and the loathing of the SCUM, I understood change was needed.

But assassination? By me?

Short, shallow breaths puffed out of my chest. I'd made this Binding Promise without knowing the task or understanding the commitment. I didn't have the heart, or the non-heart, to complete. "I repeat. I don't want, and don't know how to kill."

Her eyes lit up with what seemed to be malicious glee. "I can help you."

Sure, now she wanted to help. As a fairy, she had spells and magical items at her disposal I didn't even know existed. "What do you mean?"

"You have your bag of goodies, a Binding Promise that won't let you fail your task once you meet the prince, and a dagger making the final decision. If you can't find Arbor, I'll send assistance."

Gardenia was willing to break out a smoke sprite of no consequence to start her revolution. What was really going on in the kingdom and what did my tiny life have to do with a war?

The ride to the palace was short. Too short.

I wanted to linger in this in-between land of innocent teen and assassin.

While trying to remember everything Gardenia had said, I'd gotten into the transport pod in a daze. The protocols of the palace, the layout of the ball, and the stiff smile of Prince Zacharye. I patted the bag on the seat beside me. Between the long shimmery dress and the updo hair and the dagger stuck in my hair braid, everything felt out of place. I felt out of place. As if something had taken control of my body.

Which was possible if the Binding Promise took charge.

Taking a deep gulp, I tried to settle my nerves by talking to myself. "I might not know how the Binding Promise works, but if I never meet Prince Zacharye, I can't assassinate him."

That was my plan. Not a great plan. A plan all the same. Find the prison and save Arbor, and then leave the palace before ever running into the prince. I'd deal with Gardenia's anger later.

If my plan didn't work, I'd be riding in style to my own execution.

The magical transport pod was the height of luxury. Nicer than the rental transport my stepmother and stepsisters took to the ball. The chair-turned-transport had better and more efficient lighting than the original item. Cushioned seats, eco-emissions, and driverless interface with a locked in destination. I couldn't veer from course if I wanted.

Because if I killed the prince, how could I escape? I don't think my fairy godmother had fully thought out her scheme. As a fairy warrior, why would she send an inexperienced teen who didn't even know how to access her magic? Now that I had time to think about it, the entire scenario didn't make sense.

But it was too late to question.

Glancing out the window, I stared at the sights. I didn't visit the technology area of the city surrounding the palace very often. Dozens of skyscrapers climbed toward the top of the dome. The companies that had created the myriad of technological innovations used in the kingdom including the Magic Blocking Fixatif and various majik detectors. I furrowed my brow wondering what other *advancements* they'd made.

Neon vid screens flashed product advertisements. Everything from cyborg components to the latest fizzy drink. Transport pods zoomed in and out and around the buildings. Tubes shooting people from one skywalk to the next spread blazing streaks across the dark sky.

When I was younger, I'd traveled by tube with my dad to the outer ring where we'd hiked into a forest for a picnic close to my mom's natural homeland. I remember stroking the petals of an unusual flower, releasing the violet pollen, and watching it spread.

Sniffling, I twisted my head to face forward. The mountain range rose from behind the castle. Dark and foreboding. The dome trapped in a mystical fog that shielded the castle as it came closer and closer.

My stomach muscles tightened. I was almost there.

I clicked the glass heels together. The clinking didn't settle my doubts. The encapsulated elf jamming system better block the magical sensors or I was doomed.

Everything about my outfit was magical. From the dress to the hair accessories with its tip sharp enough to penetrate deep into someone's skin, to every object magically stowed in the purse. And I had to remember how to use each and every item. While avoiding my stepmother and stepsisters and the prince.

Sure, this would be easy. My own sarcasm strangled me.

The transport came to a stop and I peered out the window. The palace's glass spires rose high into the sky. Metal antennas stuck out of the spires giving the castle a tipsy birthday cake appearance. An enormous disc hovered above the castle like a crown. The gleaming metalloid gleamed in the moonlight. The disc kept the kingdom a secret from the outside world.

I'd seen the palace from a distance with the spires and mysterious hovering disc. I'd never been this close. Never noticed the intricate metal stylings combined with old-world architecture. Never saw the solid rock foundation the glass and metal building was built upon. Never realized the reason the castle seemed so high in the sky was because of the mountain of earth beneath the walls.

Wide marble steps led from the base to the main doors. A red runner ran the length of the steps from the top to the old-fashioned port cochere where the transport pods alighted with their guests. Gargoyles carved from stone stood sentry near the top of the stairs in front of the main door where only a couple of people awaited entrance.

The transport door lifted upwards on silent hinges and a liveried palace cyborg servant held out a metal hand to help me exit.

With trembling legs, I stepped onto a long red carpet. I kept my head down and focused on putting one foot in front of the other. I probably resembled a newborn giraffe I'd studied in biology class. Wobbly and unconfident, as if I was about to topple.

"Do you have your invitation, miss?" The servant still held my arm leading me toward the entry.

My stomach jittered even with no food inside. I was so late and clearly didn't belong in these heels or this dress. "Um, yes. Sorry."

Fumbling in the clutch, I willed nothing magical to fall out. I only needed the invitation.

The paper slipped into my hand and I pulled it out and held it up. "Here's the invitation."

"Show it to the guard at the doorway near security."

The red carpet was empty because of my late arrival. The entire kingdom had been excited about the ball and most wanted to soak up every minute. I had been excited too, until I'd been given my killing task. At the top of the grand staircase leading to the thick wooden doors stood a glass-fronted machine. It was a clear cubicle with metal rimmed edges, and it was lined with the same gleaming metalloid of the castle's hovering ring. Weapons or majik check?

The few people at the entrance waited patiently, probably because there were at least a dozen human guards standing nearby carrying guns. I stumbled, and the cyborg kept me upright.

Focus.

The attendees wore a mixture of the latest metallic fashion technology with old world costumes. Hair piled high with feathers and jewels similar to my stepsisters. Long dresses and electron skirts with flashing neon colors. Men wore suits with tails coming to a point. Trim on the pants blinked in the colors of the kingdom.

As I started up the stairs, several guards whirled toward me. I ducked my head. Nerves notched up and down my spine. I needed to be unnoticeable. I needed to blend.

Climbing each step, I tried to control my quaking knees and quivering hands. A buzzing caught my ear and I glanced up. A beam of light swooshed from the eyes of the stone gargoyle. Camera, magical sensor, or both? My pulse raced. I could be apprehended for a number of crimes, and future crimes. My gaze darted around searching for an escape if I was recognized as a majik before getting into the ball.

Except there was nowhere to go, no way to leave without being noticed and gunned down.

I mixed in with the few people waiting for the final defense of security. My green dress blended in with the ultra-bright colors and sparkling material of the latecomers. I didn't stand out in a good way or a bad way.

Which was reassuring, and yet so many things could go wrong.

I minced forward toward the security cubicle. Only three people ahead of me. I let out a shaky wheeze.

The man wearing a suit made entirely of neon lights stepped into the cubicle. The skin on his face was darker than most.

Alandaska had an unwritten code. The paler your skin, the higher up in society you must be. Farm workers and laborers had tanner skin from working outside and cast as undesirables. Although not as undesirable as majiks.

A shrill alarm blasted. Bright lights swept an arc near the security cubicle.

Jumping back, I pitched on my toes. Every nerve screamed to run. They'd caught me with early detectors. The one beaming from the gargoyle or some other hidden equipment. I hadn't even gotten past the first line of security.

"Don't move," a voice blared over the loudspeaker.

Several clicking noises banged. Guards lifted their weapons and pointed. Getting ready to kill.

I froze. Magic sparked in my fingers ready to come to my defense. I squeezed my hands into fists trying to hide my powers. I scanned back and forth between the sweeping lights and the bottom of the stairs.

Guards blocked the exit. More guards surrounded the cubicle. Surrounded the man standing inside. His glamor disappeared, and I could see a tiny body with large, pointy ears. The oversized head had rows of jagged teeth and beady red eyes below lizard-like ridges. The dapper suit he'd been wearing puddled around his small frame.

A gremlin.

Creatures so mean and nasty most other majiks avoided them.

The guards stuck a weapon in the gremlin's face. A magnetic cuff was slipped around his tiny wrists. A guard clicked on his weapon and a taser of light shot out connecting with the now exposed majik.

"Ahhhhhh!" The gremlin crumpled to the ground. His ears became woodened, and his red eyes lost their glow.

The guards shoved the few of us in line further back, jostling me and causing me to lose my balance. I stuck my arms out to regain control of my feet in heels. One of the guards grabbed the gremlin's ears and dragged him around toward the back of the palace.

My entire body rattled with aftershocks. That could've been me. Still could be me.

"Everyone back in line," the one guard pushed the man in front.

My belly jolted. I studied the arch while the line reformed. Two people to go. Would I be tasered next?

"Step this way." A guard pointed at me and indicated the security cubicle. "Stand underneath while we scan your DNA make-up."

Forcing my trembling knees forward, I hoped the elfin shoes would protect me and conceal my DNA as my fairy godmother had promised. I inched forward.

"Step all the way inside." The guard indicated a line on the ground in the center of the scanning machine.

I did not want to end up like the gremlin. Yet, I couldn't run. Gardenia's protection better work. I surveyed the shoes and stepped onto the line. I couldn't fail before I began. Think of Arbor.

Think of the prince.

I lurched. No, don't think of the prince.

My body heated and sweat formed on my brow. An invisible rope tightened around my lungs and I found it hard to breathe. One thing at a time. Get into the palace. Slip away and find Arbor. And if I never saw the prince, I wouldn't have to fulfill the Binding Promise.

The glass doors of the cubicle swished around me. Surrounded me. I couldn't get out if I wanted. Pursing my lips, I tried to let out long, slow puffs. Tried to calm my frantically beating heart. If my DNA didn't give me away, my physical reaction might.

Green, orange, and red lights flared around shooting out from the walls of the cubicle. Scanning, searching, being intrusive. This wasn't a simple security scan. This machine scoured my blood, determining if I was human, and therefore worthy enough to enter through the palace front doors.

I bristled. Who'd decided majiks shouldn't enter the palace? At one time, majiks ruled the land of what was now Alandaska. They'd counseled the human rulers of the kingdom. Helped them achieve the goal of hiding the country from the rest of the world. Used their magic to protect all citizens.

Now, majiks weren't allowed in the front entrance as my stepsister had teased.

Would the guards discover my true identity? What about the magical dress and shoes? The weight of each thought wrapped around my ankles and anchored me in place. What about my weapon?

The lights switched off and a disembodied voice said, "All clear."

My shoulders slumped, and I wanted to melt into the ground with weakness. I hadn't realized how stiff I'd been holding my body.

"Move forward." A guard waved.

I hurried out of the cubicle's scanning area, wanting as much distance as possible. Gardenia had said there would be other magical detectors throughout the palace so I could never take off the shoes, but the most thorough test was the cubicle I'd just endured. If I could pass that test, I could pass any test. I stood straighter ready to face my mission.

My mission. Not Gardenia's.

Two cyborg servants opened the front double doors to the palace. I rushed through and made my way across the foyer to lean against a balcony overlooking the festivities.

And my jaw dropped.

The size of the ballroom was massive. An entire skyscraper could fit inside. Rows of Roman-inspired columns went from the marble floor to the frescoed ceiling. The images on the ceiling depicted a human king greeting majiks of every kind, even a gremlin like the one arrested. The artwork must be historic because that exact situation would never happen under Regent Theobald's reign.

Two large stages situated at opposite ends of the room. The first held several ornate chairs with a canopy overhead. Must be where the regent and prince sat. I would avoid that end of the room. The other platform held dozens of musicians wearing identical suits. They played various instruments from the historic viola to the electroencephalophone.

A third stage had been erected in the middle of the ballroom. I didn't understand the purpose. A large blue pad covered the stage resembling a sports arena except with no computers or vid screens. Neon electric wires crisscrossed around the edge and top of the structure, similar to the cage Arbor had been shoved in when the SCUM had taken her away. A large, dark tunnel led underground somewhere.

Hundreds of people swirled around the strange stage in the traditional dance of the kingdom. Thousands of people strolled and milled the edge of the dance floor, sampling appetizers passed by cyborg waiters, talking amongst groups of people, scanning their celltabs, raising glasses, and laughing.

A gaggle of brightly dressed girls lingered by the throne chairs, probably waiting for the entrance of the prince. They wanted their chance to dance with Prince Zacharye and the possibility of making an impression.

I'd make an impression. A bad one. A murderous one.

But not if I avoided him.

Enough gawking. Time to go.

Gathering my courage, I pulled back my shoulders and went down the steps to the full ballroom. I planned to stick to the edges, avoiding anyone who might recognize me. Especially my stepmother. With a thousand people, the chances were slim if I hid behind columns and headed toward the prison right away.

A tittering group of women wearing similar ornate dresses flashing in varying bold colors passed and I ducked behind a sleek, wide, marble column.

"I heard it was a troll who will fight in the arena," a woman tittered.

"I've never seen a troll in person." A second woman wearing a headpiece with glowing gems sounded disgusted as if the troll they spoke of was a curiosity, and not a living being.

"Who cares as long as the fight is exciting."

"And the troll ends up dead."

Their uncaringness sent a shaft through my center. The troll might not be human, but he was a living creature. And why would a troll fight in the middle of a ball? Why were humans so mean? I was almost human, and I cared about Arbor, cared about people and majiks and creatures.

"Exactly," the first woman agreed. "One less zauber in the kingdom is always a good thing."

"Why mess around with games? All zaubers should be executed."

"Maybe when Prince Zacharye rules."

"One can only hope."

I sucked in air and backed further away from the cruel women and right into something warm and solid and smelling of subtle sandalwood.

Someone.

"Okay. You found me." The disappointment in the male tone had me swiveling around and scowling.

I was used to guys making fun of me or ignoring me. His clear disdain ruffled my pride, especially since I hadn't been searching for anyone. Only avoiding several. "I wasn't looking."

His shiny black shoes glared even from the darkened corner he lurked in. His pants covered long legs and were made from the finest cloth. The threads glimmered with a special light. The jacket, over a matching vest, defined his slim waist and broad shoulders. He was tall, especially compared to my small. His vivid silver eyes reminded me of the lake in the forest near my mother's home.

My fingers sparked, and I had an urge to touch him. I fisted my hands together. I couldn't have a magical misfire at a royal ball meant only for humans. "I meant, I wasn't looking for you. For anyone."

His simple, wide-brimmed hat shadowed a tanned face and covered most of his shoulder-length, jet-black hair. The lighter tips curled at the end as if only the ends had been bleached by the sun. He had high cheekbones a girl would die for, and yet they were completely masculine on him. A red scar marred his hairline and forehead giving him a roguish quality. By the reddish color, the scar was recent.

"*Everyone's* looking for me." He had an ego the size of this palace.

"Must be nice to be wanted."

No one wanted me. Not my stepmother and stepsisters. Not the kids at school. Not the bigoted kingdom of Alandaska.

"Not so much, sometimes." His forlorn voice contrasted with his rich-boy clothes. "Did you ever want to run away and be free?"

My gaze darted around hoping we weren't heard. He sounded like Gardenia with talk of freedom and feeling imprisoned. This guy didn't understand real imprisonment.

"No?" He answered for me. "Since I can't be free, I might as well start the show." He gave me a slight bow in a courtly manner. "May I have this dance?"

Chapter 8

The question came out of nowhere and wove in a whirlwind through my ribs. I couldn't be distracted by a cute guy, even if he was the first to ever pay attention.

"What? No." I forced my mouth shut before I told him to go stuff himself, too. Being rude wouldn't fit in at a royal ball. Or maybe it would. Except I didn't want to be anything like the women who'd laughed about executing zaubers. "No, thank you."

This guy was another guest at the ball. One who probably lacked dance partners because the girls waited for the prince to arrive. Which was probably unusual for him with his trim, athletic-build and gorgeous face. His dark skin made his cherry lips more prominent and I wondered what they'd taste like. Whoa. He wouldn't remember me two seconds from now.

"Why not? You could guide me onto the dance floor." His lips tilted up in a knowing way.

As if he knew more than I, which I didn't doubt. I felt like that a lot lately.

My eyes stretched. "Dance? Me?" And what did he mean by guide? Couldn't he find the dance floor on his own?

He grinned and the light in his gaze scorched. It wasn't a mean-making-fun smirk, but a kind, teasing smile. A kind of grin I'd never had centered on me. "You are attending a ball. And that's what people do at balls. Dance."

I arched a brow, trying to appear as amused. "Do they?"

"That's what I've been told." His eyes glinted, and between the gaze and the smile and the way both warmed my insides, I was falling under his spell.

Except he wasn't a majik. There was nothing magical about him. And I didn't have time for romance.

"I wouldn't know. This is my first ball." The honest statement slid off my tongue. It felt good to be truthful. "And I'm completely out of my element."

"I understand the sentiment." His mouth positioned into a serious frown. "I hate these events."

So he'd attended royal events before. He looked about my age. Maybe he was a friend of the prince. I froze. I couldn't become friends with a friend of someone I was supposed to assassinate. Although this guy might know his way around the palace.

Hmm. Maybe I could pick his brain.

Ingrid swished by in her pink dress. She scanned the people as she paraded, taking in everyone. She stopped to talk to the group of women I'd been avoiding.

Using the guy to block me from view, I shrunk my shoulders trying to become smaller than I already was. I couldn't leave with my stepsister so close. She'd see me and tattle.

Considering the guy beside me, I needed to figure out what to do and if he could help. I needed to converse, maybe flirt. "What is this arena fighting I've heard people talking about?"

Something hard reflected in his gaze and his expression

starched. Then, he placed a loose, casual smirk on that didn't seem natural. "The regent's favorite sport where they force a majik to fight against a dragon."

Bile curdled in my belly. How could anyone call the disgusting cruelty a sport?

By his flat tone and un-emotional words, I couldn't tell what he thought about the arena fighting. Best to change topics so I didn't scare him off. I needed him to block my stepsister's view and I needed information.

"Do you visit the royal palace often?"

"I never visit the palace." His lips pursed into a sneer.

Trying to be discreet, I peeked at Ingrid. She stared in my direction and I quickly turned around, ducking my head.

The guy ducked his head and faced away from Ingrid, too. Why was he avoiding my stepsister? Did they know each other? He bowed his head. "*Please*, dance with me."

My fingers sparked at his request. A cute guy had twice asked me to dance. I wanted to jump for joy and brag to Olivia and Jade who had written me off as a loser. Except my magic was trying to make itself known and fear of discovery shunted any happiness. I curled my fingers into fists trying to control the power even though my fingers flickered, and my legs twitched to move to music with him. Dancing would be dangerous. The chance of discovery was too great.

And what if while dancing I ran into Prince Zacharye?

The sharp point of the dagger nudged in my hair. My scalp prickled. The weapon wanted to find the prince. Taking a couple of deep breaths, I tried to make my voice stress-free. "I prefer to watch from the sidelines."

"Me, too." He grimaced, displaying cute dimples in both cheeks. "Unfortunately, I don't have a choice."

I understood not having choices. "It appears we are at an impasse. You must dance, and I must not."

He grabbed hold of my fisted hand and uncurled my fingers. The sparks morphed from magical to a shimmering heat. His caress ignited a different kind of power. "I can teach you how to dance."

I ripped my hand from his. "Who said I didn't know how?"

"Then, let's dance." His wide eyes told me he'd never had to work so hard for a girl and my heart swelled.

"Unfortunately," I repeated the word he'd used earlier in the same uptight tone. "I can't right now. There's something I need to do."

"What's more important than dancing at the ball? With me? At the prince's coming out ball." The cute, pleading-puppy eyes returned.

My knees weakened. I couldn't give in. First, there was my mission. Second, I couldn't be noticed by my stepmother or stepsisters. And third, I couldn't take the chance that I might dance close to the prince. His earlier request had hinted at protection, but protection from whom? Was he hiding?

Something we had in common.

I forced a laugh, trying to sound casual. "Are you so sure of yourself? Now, if you were the prince…"

Something dark flashed across his face. "You'd dance with me if I was the prince, not if I was a commoner?"

"The exact opposite." I internally kicked myself for speaking the truth again. I would love to dance with him and stay far away from the prince. It didn't matter what I wanted. Ingrid was strolling away, and time was wasting. My ride only lasted until midnight. "I need to go."

He pressed his fingers on my bare arm and the contact branded. "Why?"

"I'm…um, meeting someone."

His lips flattened into a line.

The crowd closed around Ingrid and I saw my chance. Except I didn't know which way to go. I turned to him hoping he'd know. "Can you tell me where the kitchens are located?"

"You're meeting someone in the kitchens?"

My head hurt from the truth slipping out and the new lies told to cover. Lifting my nose in the air imitating my stepmother, I tried to sound snotty. "I want to see how the other half lives."

"You mean the cyborgs or the zaubers?" His tone hardened as if he hated majiks, yet the harshness was laced with something else. Curiosity, perhaps?

I couldn't have him curious about me, so I picked the most boring reason. "School project." If I act like I hated majiks no one will suspect me of helping one. Or being one. "It's a ridiculous project. Why would I want to learn about *them*?"

"Why, indeed?" Had his voice gone colder? "Skirt around the fighting stage and go past the tunnel. There's a small hallway with two doors. Go through there."

He spoke fast as if he wanted to be rid of me.

Smashing my lips, I held in the hurt. I slung my bag over my head and shoulder and started to saunter away. My sluggish legs wanted to reverse and see him one last time. Would he be staring at me?

It didn't matter. I shook off the sensation. A cute guy was the least of my worries. I needed to find Arbor.

Wending between the marble pillars, I kept my gaze on my goal. I wove between people with the most elaborate outfits. A man wore a psychedelic pleated robe with live birds chained to the collar. *So, cruel.* A woman wore a leather leopard print body suit with spikes sticking out of the top. *Who would want to dance with her?* A girl wore impossibly high platform shoes with live butterflies captured in the heels. *I wanted to set them free.*

People wearing techno clothes with touches of nature

resembled this kingdom—mountains and forests with a technological center.

A throaty, trilled giggle tugged at my ear and scraped along my spine. Dread dripped through me.

Sybil.

Nerves skittered across my skin.

I ducked behind a cyborg passing appetizers to wait for my stepmother to move away. Time was going too fast. An internal clock ticked pounding an unnatural rhythm. I needed to find Arbor before I bumped into the prince, and all before midnight. The ball would end, and Sybil would leave promptly. I had to get home first and make up an excuse for Sybil's boyfriend's tattle.

The fighting arena loomed large, shadowing my hiding spot. People surrounded the cage giving the cloyed air a suffocating scent. The carnival atmosphere tittered with gossip and harsh laughter.

"Elle? Is that you?" The disbelief in the girl's tone had me shifting to stone.

Earlier, I'd wanted the girls from school to see me at the ball. Not anymore.

"What're you doing?" Olivia's question was filled with disgust.

I faced my nemesis, ignoring her second question. "Imagine running into you here."

"Why wouldn't you? Everyone's at the ball." She appraised me and must've concluded I was totally stupid because she took a bite of the bioluminescent squid appetizer she held in a napkin.

"Yes, but the event is so big." And my luck had me running into her, my stepmother, and the cutest guy I'd ever seen. A slow pull had me remembering him asking me to dance. Too bad I'd never see him again.

"Not that big. I've been to other events at the palace." Jade bounced beside the other girl, the hem of her red gown skimming the floor. "My father gets invited all the time."

Maybe she could guide me to the kitchens. Except she knew there was no homework assignment.

"Aren't you lucky?" Olivia's tone filled with prissiness. She always wanted to be the center of attention proven by her peach-colored hair piece that towered over most people's heads.

Jade studied the ground while the awkwardness stretched between the two.

None of my business if the two best friends didn't get along. "Well, nice seeing you."

Bells clanged. The murmur of the crowd rose and fell again. This was the distraction I needed to make my way to the kitchen.

"The fighting is about to start." Olivia clapped her hands together in a fast, excited action.

My gut clenched. To pit a majik against a dragon. Sure, majiks had powers, but not all of them were strong. Some of their magic wasn't powerful enough to defeat a fire-breathing dragon. I couldn't worry about what was happening to this one majik though, I had a friend to save.

"I need to go to the bathroom." Jade held her midsection. She must feel sick, too.

Not everyone wanted to witness the event.

"You're so squeamish." Olivia chortled in a mean-derogatory way. "Regent Theobald wants everyone to watch. The reason the fighting stage is in the center of the ballroom."

"I don't enjoy violence." Jade's voice trembled.

Olivia patted her styled hair. "They're only zaubers. Who cares if they die?"

My insides dropped to the marble floor. "Die?"

Jade crumpled her gown between her fingers. "It's usually an ogre or a troll who's been sent to prison."

"Ugly, disgusting kinds of majiks." Olivia swiveled her dress.

"For now." Jade went quiet. "I've heard rumors about other kinds…"

My heart squeezed. What if they put smoke sprites in the fighting arena? What if Arbor—

"It's not really a fair fight." Maybe Olivia didn't hate majiks. "Zaubers can use magic. They have an unfair advantage."

My jaw dropped. That was ridiculous. Majiks didn't have an advantage. We'd learned in class ogres and trolls only had magic connected to a possession or nature. Nothing to fight off a hungry, wild, angry dragon.

"The electroid wires are being turned on. Please don't touch the electrified wires," a disembodied voice spoke over the crowd. "In the first match, we have a troll against a Wyvern dragon."

A cheer erupted. The excited applause thundered in my head and struck like lightning behind my temple. The crowd was bloodthirsty, and the Wyvern dragon was known to be fierce and unforgiving.

"I'm going to the bathroom." Jade lifted her long skirt and hurried away.

I wanted to follow or head in the opposite direction toward the kitchens.

Olivia grabbed my arm. "Let's get closer."

My entire body stiffened. I'd dreamed of a moment where the most popular girl in school asked me to do something with her. And now, I couldn't go. I didn't want to watch the fight and I had to take advantage of this opportunity to go to the kitchens and find my way into the dungeon.

"I can't. I'm supposed to meet my stepmother." I slipped my arm out of her grasp.

She gave me the oddest look, knowing my stepmother would never want my company. I didn't care what she thought. I'd wasted too much time.

Slinking away, I didn't even think about my social status. Nothing was more important than saving Arbor, especially if there was a chance she'd end up in a battle against a dragon.

People surged toward the fighting arena. I struggled against them going in the other direction. Every step I took seemed to take me two steps back. Bending forward, my shoulders bumped other people's shoulders. A man stomped on my foot and knocked me down.

"Sorry." He grabbed my arm and yanked me to my feet, then left me standing on my own.

The crowd carried me closer.

I ducked lower, squirming through the bodies. Their sharp accessories stabbed me and scratched my skin. The scent of over-powering perfume and sweat filled my nostrils. The harder I pushed, the more I was pulled forward.

"Be careful." A woman wrapped her arm around my shoulders. "The men always hog the spots up front."

"I don't want to be up front."

She ignored my objection and tugged me closer. To her and the action.

The wires of the arena sizzled with energy. Spotlights glared into the center of the blue mat.

A troll stumbled out of the tunnel, his green slimy skin glistened. He wore a dirty and torn brown cloth draped over one shoulder and reaching to his knees. Tufts of dark hair stood out on his back and legs, similar to studs more than hair. His large mouth and pointy teeth could swallow me in one bite. Maybe he wasn't defenseless.

The troll stood in the center with a defiant expression, flared nostrils and flatlined mouth. Yet looking closely, his gloppy eyes shined with fear. How many majiks had been hurt or died in this terrible sport to entertain the regent, prince, and their cronies?

Maybe my fairy godmother was right, and the majiks should rule the kingdom.

A clinking came from the tunnel. Fire spurted from the opening and the heat traveled toward the spectators. The crowd *oohed* and *ahhed*.

How had they captured a dragon?

Most dragons hid in the mountains. They couldn't leave the kingdom because of the dome. I'd been told by my teachers the dragons lived peacefully and didn't bother humans. Did humans bother them?

A large orange snout stuck out of the tunnel. I quivered. And I thought the troll's teeth were big. The dragon's teeth were bigger than my hands. Her fire-red gaze flashed with anger and intelligence. Her enormous wings unfurled like a wind sail. She stomped out of the tunnel and her mouth opened wide. Flames flared.

Heat singed my eyebrows and the people leaned away. A rotten burnt smell filled the air. The flames couldn't pass through the electronic cage. The humans were safe. The troll had no protection and no powers to defend itself. The dragon had fire. And real, sharp teeth. She could even beat the troll with her powerful wings.

This wasn't a fair fight. This wasn't a fight at all. This was slaughter.

My fingers sparked. I couldn't let the troll be butchered. How could anyone be okay with this terrible sight? I remembered Olivia's clapping, the cute guy's description of the event, the women laughing about executing zaubers. Each image blazed a wildfire beneath my skin. The troll was a living, breathing, thinking creature. It didn't deserve to die this way.

The dragon screeched and beat its scaly wings. A special type of chain held her down. She kicked her clawed feet into the stage shredding the padded floor.

The troll took a step back. His tiny legs trembled. His arms were stiff at his side. He had nothing to shield himself.

The people behind pushed against me. My body pressed against the stage bringing me closer, letting me see and experience the troll's fright firsthand. I gasped, dragging in air to breathe.

The dragon fired again.

The troll ran. He tripped on the dragon's chain and went sliding across the mat landing in front of me. His slime splattered, and a drop hit my cheek.

Gross.

The dragon's talons clawed, stalking toward the troll. I could make out each scale glinting in the light. Flames shot out of her mouth again. Her wings thumped creating a wind. A wind fanning the fire and making the space hotter and hotter.

Sweat poured down my back.

If the troll had a club, he could use it to fend off the dragon's teeth, claws, and wings. I couldn't do anything about the fire. Electricity rolled through my body igniting every nerve ending. My fingers sparked and waved and jolted.

The troll jumped upright holding a club with metal spikes.

My chest clutched. A club like I'd imagined. That wasn't troll magic. It was *my* magic.

Did I just expose myself as a majik?

Chapter 9

Every muscle in my body went on high alert and I stood on my toes ready to fight. I hadn't even started my real mission, and I'd exposed myself as a majik. My chin trembled, and my gaze darted around wary of a call to apprehend me.

None came.

I released some of my tension and uncurled my fists. Everyone stared at the troll with wide eyes and open mouths. No one realized the magic had been done by me. They must believe the troll had conjured his own club. Humans really didn't understand the different majiks and their different powers. Not smart if war between us erupted.

The troll's eyes still shone with fear, but a light of hope gleamed between the puffy green lids. Maybe he believed he had a chance because he held a weapon.

Maybe I had a chance to uphold my secret.

The dragon was released from the chains and screeched, sending a chill down my spine. Her large orange wings flapped creating a draft that carried an acrid scent.

The crowd leaned back. I pinched my nose.

The dragon lifted her enormous body into the air and hit

the wires on top of the arena. Sparks shot out and rained down on the crowd. I hunched my shoulders, protecting myself from the ashes.

"Come on, troll," I whispered. "Fight."

Or at least defend himself. I'd wanted to give him a fighting chance.

Instead of charging the dragon, the troll ran in the opposite direction. He moved fast for a fat, slippery majik. Lifting the club high, he gave a blood-curdling yell. "Yaya! Yaya!"

The scream attacked my ears and I covered them with my hands.

Everyone else did, too. The ball attendees hunched, and yet managed to continue to watch the arena.

The troll slammed the club down on the electrified wires surrounding the edges of the arena. Strong flickers of fire darted from the cage. He used the club to hit the wires again and again and again. The sparks hit the ceiling and exploded. Small tiles from the fresco hit people and fell onto the marble floor. The rat-a-tat-tat sounded similar to rapid gunfire.

It wasn't.

Chaos hit the dance floor. People screamed and scrambled away. Wires collapsed and broke, the torn ends wriggled with the disconnected power resembling an attacking snake.

The troll climbed out of the arena brandishing the club. He bared his jagged teeth. "Yaya! Yaya!"

The screech was a sonic attack howling in my head. I'd thought the troll was defenseless, I'd been wrong. I had just as much to learn about my fellow majiks. Why had I felt sorry for the troll's plight? He could take care of himself.

The fallen wires had pinned the dragon down, trapping her inside the arena. She tried to flap her wings. The wires held her in place. Sparks hit her scaly skin and extinguished. Flames lobbed from the dragon's mouth sending a scorching heat through the ballroom scaring the terrified people even more.

They continued to scream and run, shoving others to the ground. They covered their heads to protect from falling tiles and flame.

I ducked and worked my way toward the back of the crowd.

The royal guards pointed weapons from where they stood on the balcony that ringed the ballroom. None of them discharged the guns. If they did, they might hit a guest. They weren't equipped to deal with a wild majik inside the palace because they believed they'd kept them all out.

I couldn't stop a small smirk. Little did they know.

The troll plodded toward the back of the ballroom near the kitchens. He disappeared behind the potted grove of palms.

Great idea. I darted into a run knowing I wouldn't look suspicious because everyone was running. I dodged and bolted my way through the crowd heading toward the double doors the cute guy had told me about. Pushing the door open, I stepped inside and halted.

The kitchen was the complete opposite of the ballroom. Everything here was calm and organized. Dozens of cyborg waiters picked up trays and headed out the door toward the ballroom not even recognizing the chaos existing out there.

I'd never seen so many cyborgs in one place. We didn't own any. The closest thing we had was the broken robo-vac. School employed a few in the cafeteria, which were scratched up and dented with metal generic faces.

These cyborgs glistened with the latest technology. They had real expressions and plastic blinking eyes. They hovered slightly above the ground without making a noise. Their arms moved smoothly with no jerky motions.

Other cyborgs operated the kitchen equipment punching

buttons on the food preparation machines. Conveyor belts carried plates from one station to another. First a beam of light to cook the food, then a garnishment plopped from a tube, and the process continued.

No humans or guards were present. *Phew.*

I caught the attention of the closest cyborg. "How do I get to the dungeon where they hold the majiks?"

Her pupils flickered from blue to yellow to blue again. "All garbage goes in the chute."

I studied the robot. Did she not know or not understand? "The majiks." Maybe they didn't use that word at the palace. "Where do they lock up the," I cringed, "zaubers?"

"All garbage goes in the chute." The cyborg pointed to a white door with a handle. "All garbage goes in the chute."

Was the cyborg saying majiks were garbage or that's how they fed the prisoners? Garbage thrown into a chute? *Gross.* Poor Arbor! She didn't eat much, but she enjoyed the best.

I pulled the handle and peered down. Molding vegetables, sour dairy, and rotten meat scents assaulted my nose. Scrunching my face, I considered my options. "Are you sure the majiks are down here?"

The robot nodded. "All garbage goes in the chute."

My jaw tightened. She *was* calling majiks garbage. Meaning me, and Arbor, and all the others. I fisted my hand wanting to rearrange the cyborg's perfectly arranged features.

The kitchen door opened, and a cyborg rolled inside with a metal arm dangling at its side. Guards, with weapons drawn, positioned behind the cyborg.

I rocked back and forth on my heels. They'd want to know what I was doing in the kitchen. They'd search me and my bag. They'd know, even dressed nice, I didn't belong.

I peered down the chute and the stink grew stronger.

No, I couldn't.

"Check the entire kitchen," a guard ordered.

The six guards split up each going in a different direction. One headed toward me.

Adrenaline spiked and sweat broke out on my upper lip. I paused to the side of a commercial flash-frozen freezer. I couldn't get caught.

The chute yawned open—a disgusting tunnel of gross. Nothing I'd ever cleaned smelled this bad or appeared so vile. I regarded the guard working his way in my direction. He checked under the equipment and opened every cabinet. If I didn't go now, he'd see me.

Question me.

Arrest me.

Holding my breath, I dove into the chute. One of my glass heels got caught on the door and fell off. I couldn't grab it before I slid *down, down, down.* The oil and grease caused the shoot to be slippery fast. Debris clung to my skin. The tunnel went dark. I pinched my lips together to keep from screaming.

Bang. My head hit the side of the chute.

"Awwww!" I pulled my hands up in protection.

Bonk. My hip hit the other side making me gasp.

My dress rose up my legs—good thing I wore shorts underneath. I used my knees to dig into the floor of the chute. Sharp edges cut into my skin making them burn. Nothing slowed my progress. The dress tugged lower on my front. The skirt flew behind me like a cape. And the bag strangled around my neck.

The chute went on forever. Deeper and deeper. Darker and darker. Dirtier and dirtier.

And I became desperate and more desperate.

My mouth went dry and my pulse raced. Why had this seemed a good idea? The slope of the chute curved, and my body slowed. Food waste clung to the side of the slide and to my arms and dress. So much for looking beautiful.

I plopped out of the chute and onto a high pile of garbage. The stink in the air burned my eyes. The lightless area resembled a cave. How far down had I traveled? The palace was built on a mountain, and only the visible part above ground was made of crystal, metalloid and glass.

Beneath the palace? Who knew.

Standing, I shook off the waste clinging to me. My feet sunk into the garbage. "Eww."

I took off the remaining shoe and shoved it in the bag. Would there be majik sensors under the palace?

Patting my hair, I confirmed the dagger was still twisted in the strands and found a wilted lettuce leaf. I threw the leaf on the ground. I shoved my hand in the bag and thought of a flashlight. Immediately, my fingers grasped a cylinder-shaped object. Taking it out, I clicked on the flashlight. Thank you, Gardenia. Now I could see the mess I was standing in. I sniffed. Maybe that wasn't a good thing.

A large metal scoop swirled toward the pile of garbage. The mechanism pushed into the pile and shoveled a bunch. The pile I stood on shifted and I lost my balance. I tumbled back and rolled down hitting the ground hard.

"Ouch." Rubbing my hip, I watched the scoop carry the waste to holes along the wall and shove it in.

No way was I climbing in there.

Standing, I scanned the area trying to decide my next step. Going up the chute wasn't possible, and I wouldn't fit in the small holes the garbage was being shoved into. The only way out was forward through a narrow tunnel. My only choice.

The dirt ground felt cold on my bare feet. When I took a step something gross squelched between my toes. The stench was worse here. The tunnel narrowed. Tall enough to stand and wide enough for maybe two or three people to walk side by side. Solid rock surrounded. The darkness was my only companion. I trudged on.

My nose twitched. Another smell wove toward me, much worse than the garbage. Sharp, tangy, bloody. My foot stepped in something wet and sticky. I stopped and flashed the beam of light at the ground. A mixture of green and dark red.

Blood, but not human blood.

Uh oh.

I followed the trail of bloody ooze and came upon a green mound. The mound shifted and moaned. A troll. An injured troll.

"Are you okay?" Keeping my distance, I thought about tiptoeing past, except I wasn't a monster. If I could help I would.

"Hey, there. Are you okay?" I tapped on his shoulder and my finger came away coated in slime.

Which was more gross than the garbage I'd waded through.

The troll moaned again and rolled onto its back showing a large, bloody gash across his chest. His labored breathing proved his agony. His eyes flickered open and pain swam in their depths. With his mouth closed, he didn't appear so scary. Beside him lay a spike-studded club.

I sucked stinking, stale air into my lungs. "Are you the troll from the fighting arena?"

He struggled to sit up straighter. His clawed hand wrapped around the club. He must've taken the garbage chute down, too. The reason why the cyborg said the majik had gown down the chute. Maybe she hadn't been calling majiks garbage.

"It's okay. Don't be afraid." Taking a step back, I reached into my bag and thought about first aid for a large cut. "I can help."

A tube of ointment shoved from the bag into my hand. I held the tube up for the troll to inspect.

"Why would you help me?" His gruff voice held disbelief. His hand held the club.

"Because you're hurt." I had the ointment and there was always more in my Necessary Bag. I'd already helped by giving him the club. Though, I wouldn't share that tidbit.

He placed his other hand over the wound and blood spread onto his clawed fingers. "Really? I didn't realize I was injured."

His sarcasm lifted my spirits reminding me of myself. "You *are* the troll from the arena."

"And you're a human. Why do you want to help a troll?" He must not be that injured if his comebacks were so quick.

"Why would you call me human?" An offended tone spewed out of my mouth. I wanted to be known as human, didn't I?

"Look at you with your fancy dress and your perfect human body." His disgust ripped through me. "What're you doing in the waste tunnels?"

Not so fancy anymore. Every inch was stained or torn.

"I'm searching for someone." A tremble slid from my head to my feet. What if I was too late? "What're you doing here?"

"No humans, and especially guards, come here." He growled, baring his sharp teeth. "Who are you searching for?"

"Do you want my help or not?" I refused to overshare or tell him about my mission. Bending closer, I held up the tube.

"The ointment will help?"

"It should." I squeezed ointment onto my hand and used my fingers to rub it on his chest. His skin felt squishy and damp, similar to a lizard, and I controlled the impulse to jerk away. Starting at the narrowest part of the gash, I worked my way up. The wound oozed whenever I put on pressure with my hands and his greenish-red blood squirted on my skin. My stomach roiled.

He flinched. We both needed a distraction and I needed more than ointment to stop his wounds. Focusing on my fingers spreading the ointment, I pictured the wound healing. My fingers tingled.

The ends of the gash pulled tight, an invisible thread sewing the wound closed. The tingles spread through my bloodstream creating a euphoric sensation. My magic was working the way I wanted.

"What's your name?" I couldn't continue to think of him as the troll and I needed to distract him from my magic.

He grumbled before asking, "What's your name?"

"Elle." Focused on healing, I answered automatically. I was healing the troll. Maybe having magic was a big deal if I could use it to help others. Is that what Gardenia was trying to tell me? How had my mother given up this power?

"Elle." Another male voice repeated.

My concentration broke, and the wound stopped healing. I gaped at the newcomer and my pulse skipped.

The gorgeous guy who'd asked me to dance stood there. Why was he here? How had he gotten here? Had he noticed my magic?

"I never even got a name from her." His highbrow scoff told me that didn't happen very often.

His fine clothes weren't a mess like mine. His hair wasn't disheveled and didn't have bits of garbage stuck between the strands, although he'd lost the hat and coat. His dreamy face was clean.

My face flushed knowing I must resemble a disaster. He probably wouldn't want to dance now that he'd seen me touching a troll. "I didn't give you anything."

"That's my point." Gorgeous crossed his arms and the material of his vest pulled tight across the expanse of his shoulders. "Not a name. Not a dance."

"Not a chance." I couldn't afford to tell him anything.

He grabbed my un-bloody hand and tugged me to standing. "Elle."

He pronounced my name with a lilt as if he enjoyed saying the single syllable. It struck a song in my heart.

Tugging my hand to his chest, he said, "You wound me."

Heat swamped through my center and I wanted to melt at his feet. Or was that his ego talking? Is that why he followed me? We stared at each other and time warped.

"I'm the one wounded here." The troll grumbled his complaint. "Thought you were helping me, not romancing him."

I tugged my hand free already missing the connection. Kneeling beside the troll, I squirted more ointment onto the wound hoping it would be enough. I couldn't use magic in front of Gorgeous.

"How'd you get down here?" I glanced at him before returning to the troll's wound.

"This passage leads back inside the palace." Gorgeous pointed past the pile of garbage I'd landed on. If I had turned in the other direction, I would've ended up right where I started.

"Good to know," the troll grumbled.

"There. That should help." Setting the tube down, I used a mostly clean piece of skirt to wipe the ointment and blood from my hand.

"Is this part of your school project?" Gorgeous bent down and picked up the tube and screwed the lid back on. He studied the container as if he'd never seen anything like it before. He probably hadn't if it had come from Gardenia's private stock.

"My what?" I wanted to snatch the tube from his hands but that would make me appear more suspicious.

"Your school project? The reason you couldn't dance with me at the ball?"

Right.

Just because I could lie, didn't mean I was any good at it. "Oh, my school project. Yes. Yes, it is."

He scanned the area around us. "Are you supposed to be down here?" His nose scrunched.

At least he couldn't smell me with the other foul odors.

"Why not?" Defiance jammed through my bones. Taking hold of the troll's thick arm, I helped him to his feet. "Unless the regent has something to hide."

The troll harrumphed.

Gorgeous appeared confused. "I thought you didn't…"

"Didn't what?"

Shoving the tube in his pocket, he took the troll's other arm. "Never mind."

I couldn't become distracted again. "Can you walk on your own?"

The troll needed to escape the palace before anyone else tumbled down the chute. Both the guy and I let go.

"Why because I don't have dainty feet like humans? Don't wear shoes?" The troll took a step and almost fell.

We both grabbed the troll's arms again. Gorgeous peered at my bare feet. Was he comparing me to a troll? I lifted my chin.

Using my free hand, I waved to focus attention on anything aside from my feet. "What're you doing here?" I put force behind my words. He could be a spy or a guard. I had to stay on my toes and be suspicious of everyone.

Pink stained his cheeks. "Well, I…followed you."

Energy sizzled up my spine hitting the back of my neck and morphing into a tickle-y shiver. "How? Why?"

He kicked his not-as-shiny shoes into the dirt ground. "I was worried about where you went when the troll," he regarded the troll in front of him, "got free. I knew you were headed to the kitchen, so I asked a couple of the servants. One said you came down here."

Had the cyborg told a guard? Of course, a guard wouldn't have known to ask about me.

"The area beneath the palace can be dangerous." His concern touched.

"It's a hellhole." The troll grumbled between them. He seemed familiar with the layout below the palace. He must know the location of the dungeon.

My pulse leapt. "Do you know how to get to the dungeon where they keep the majiks?"

The troll growled, and his entire body rumbled. "Held me there until they put me in the arena with the dragon."

Gorgeous stiffened beside me.

I ignored him. "Can you take me there?"

"Why would you want to go?" He jerked on the troll's arm.

"Watch it!" The troll bared his teeth.

Served him right. Humans shouldn't mess with an injured and angry troll.

Gorgeous waited for my answer. His eyebrows rose causing the scar on his forehead to widen.

"For my school project?" Biting my lip, I hated how unsure I sounded. I needed to be forceful with my lies.

"What about the palace guards?" Gorgeous glanced behind displaying slight nervousness. It was the second nervous tell I'd noticed. The first had been at the ball when my sister had come close.

"Those wimps never come down here." The troll pulled back his shoulders in a proud stance announcing he wasn't afraid of the guards. "I'm surprised you did."

Gorgeous' pupils contemplated the ceiling possibly thinking of an imaginative response.

Turning to the troll, I didn't ask. "You'll take me there."

"Because you helped me, I'll show you to an access point, then I'm leaving." The troll grumbled something incoherent. "I'm not getting stuck in that torture chamber."

Gulping at his descriptive words, I swallowed the lump in my throat.

Gorgeous' silver eyes widened, and his expression flashed with something. What was he thinking?

"Great." I patted the troll's arm several times knowing this would not be great. I needed to get rid of Gorgeous. The joke was on me because I'd never attracted the attention of a guy before and always wanted to. "Thanks for your help. I can take it from here."

He dropped the troll's arm and fisted his hands. "Are you dismissing *me*?" His voice filled with disbelief as if he'd never been rejected.

Which I knew wasn't true because I'd already rejected him twice at the ball.

"You don't have a school project now, do you?" I challenged him. Why did he want to tag along?

"I want to be educated on all matters with regards to the kingdom." His arrogance caused me to raise my eyebrows.

It was the first time he'd ever used the tone and I didn't appreciate it.

"Besides, you need help with the troll so I'm going." He grabbed the thick arm again needing to prove his worth. "Which way, troll?"

"Don't call him troll." Humans treated majiks like they

were animals. If I couldn't stop him from helping, I could put him in his place. "He's got a name."

"What is it?"

"Well, I don't know." Squirming, I peered at the troll and at Gorgeous. I couldn't keep using that label either. The word gorgeous might slip out. "I don't know your name."

Still holding onto the troll's arm, he made a courtly bow similar to the one at the ball when he'd asked me to dance. "I'm Rye."

He was named after a wheat plant? It suited him in our current environment. Poor soils and low temperatures.

Shaking away the thoughts, I looked at the troll. "What is your name?"

The troll scrunched up his snout. "Never tell people your real name. It gives majiks power over you." The troll believed we were both idiots. "Don't they teach humans anything?"

Really, what could a majik do with my name?

"If you won't tell us your name, what should we call you?" Rye's request sounded reasonable.

"Jayunja." He took a step forward and Rye and I moved with him, supporting the troll as he gained his strength. Trolls were known for healing fast, and the ointment and my magic definitely helped.

I nodded my head. "Nice to meet you, Jayunja."

"What? It's not nice to meet me?" Rye's teasing revealed he wasn't offended and lightened the weight I carried.

The problem was, meeting him was too nice. Too confusing. And too troublesome.

Chapter 10

Jayunja set a slow pace even though we headed downhill. We headed deeper into the mountain that supported the palace. The awkward silence between the three of us made the distance longer. I didn't really know how to talk to a cute guy and my mind was on my mission to save Arbor. The troll snorted and grumbled not really saying a word. And Rye studied every inch of the dark tunnel we traveled.

"Why are you helping?" I feared trusting this handsome stranger because I wanted to trust too much.

"Why are you helping? I thought you didn't like majiks." Rye's retort dug under my already bruised and scraped skin.

Jerking, I glanced at Jayunja to see if he cared what we talked about. The troll kept his head down. "Why would you say that?"

"What you said in the ballroom about your ridiculous project." Rye's hand shot out emphasizing my insinuation that majiks were of a lower class.

"I was only saying it to fit in." The honest statement landed solidly in my gut. My entire life I'd been trying to fit in, lying and concealing my true thoughts and identity. I was tired of not being myself.

The troll's brown eyes narrowed. I wanted to shout out I didn't hate majiks. That I was one. And remind Jayunja I'd healed him. I kept my mouth shut.

"Because of how the regent feels about majiks?" Rye's astute questions and observations had me answering honestly.

"And the prince."

His stare slid to me, studying and assessing. "How do you know what the prince feels?"

I blew out an exasperated breath. "He's the prince. He'll be the ruler soon. I'm sure he's in the regent's trust, knows the evil things the man is planning."

Rye huffed. "You have too much confidence in the prince."

"Confidence he'll be as big of a rat as the regent." Just thinking about the changes the regent had made in the last few years caused my blood pressure to soar. It had never been fair. It just hadn't been relevant to me until now.

Jayunja snorted in agreement.

"Why do you say that, Elle?" Rye's quiet tone didn't dim the authority in his question. Was he surprised or hurt by my opinions?

My opinions.

Finally, I voiced what I truly believed. Is that because I was comfortable with his company? Or, after seeing the arena fights was I too disgusted to care?

My lungs filled with hot, righteous air. "The prince is the rightful ruler. At this point, he should be thinking for himself, forming his own opinions, and stopping some of the Regent's more restrictive majik laws."

The hot air seeped out on a whine. I was the same age. I hadn't done any of those things either. I hadn't stuck up for my family home or my heritage against my stepmother. I hadn't defended Arbor. I still hid behind my half-human self.

The silence deafened.

Had I said too much? Did Rye support the prince and the regent? But then, why would he help a troll?

"Maybe the prince is only just learning about the atrocities." He whipped his free hand in a loose salute. "Maybe he's been kept ignorant about what was going on in the kingdom. He's been gone for a year." He saluted a second time. "Maybe, once he's educated, he'll surprise you." His hand dropped to his side and he fisted his fingers.

"I hope so." If the prince changed the laws, I wouldn't need to hide any longer. The thought buoyed my step.

The tunnel narrowed and grew darker and the slope became steeper. Jayunja had to duck his head. Spiderwebs hung from the roof and dangled in my face and hair. I swatted them away more in annoyance than fear. These simple things didn't scare me anymore.

"Elle, you're not really here for a school project, are you?" Rye's soft question rang with seriousness.

I wanted to tell him everything and have him on my side, help me with my mission. The journey would be less lonely. And yet, why would I trust him? Because he was attractive and nice? Because maybe he was interested in me? My shoulders slumped. Why would a gorgeous guy be interested in me?

Maybe it was a ploy to learn the truth. A trick. He was smart. He'd already figured out part of the truth.

"No. Not a school project." My mind swirled in varying directions. *Tell him. Don't tell him.* I teetered on the edge about how much to confess. "I'm here to save a friend."

And assassinate the prince.

No use telling him I'd been tasked to commit treason. Besides, I planned to avoid the offense by leaving the palace as soon as possible. In my head an alarm went off. Time wasn't ticking, it was charging full speed ahead. My transport would change back into an ugly chair. My stepmother would leave the ball and go home. My friend would be tried and found guilty and kicked out of the kingdom.

"Save your friend from what?"

"She was arrested by the SCUM."

"The what?"

My jaw dropped. How could he not know the acronym for the most hated security unit in the kingdom? All the citizens feared them, majik or human. "S-C-U-M. The Security Collectors of Unique Magic."

His chuckle echoed in the tunnel. "I hadn't heard that one. It fits."

I smiled at his recognition of the truth.

"My friend is a smoke sprite and she wasn't performing magic." *I was.* "She didn't deserve to be taken into custody."

"She'll have a fair trial and prove her innocence." He sounded innocent. Or naïve.

"A trial?" Jayunja snorted and snot flew out of his nose. "I didn't get a trial."

"Not possible. Alandaska gives everyone a fair trial." Rye's indignation seemed personal as if a slight against the kingdom was a slight against him.

"Did you read that in a textbook?" The troll's laugh sounded more like a gurgle.

I *had* read it in a textbook.

"What were you arrested for?" His serious tone showed he was gathering facts.

For what I didn't know.

"Stealing food for my starving children." The troll smirked, his puffy lips twisting into a half-smile. "And, insulting the SCUM."

Rye quirked a dark eyebrow obviously realizing he was the only one who hadn't heard the nickname.

"Your children?" My heart squeezed. The troll children must've been starving even before Jayunja had been imprisoned. My blood boiled. The kingdom had become a jail for half of its citizens. "There are majiks starving because they're not allowed to work or to move someplace where they could get a job. They're afraid of their shadows in this kingdom."

"I've never seen a lack of food." Shaking his head, Rye's befuddlement came in raised dark brows and a slight frown.

"Where do you live? The palace?" The troll elbowed him in a sly way.

Rye coughed and tried to clear his throat. The troll must've hit him harder than I thought.

"Careful of your wound." I squinted at Jayunja's torso. Between the ointment and my lifesaving magic, the wound had healed. He appeared steadier on his feet. I let go of his arm. "Can you walk on your own now?"

"Sure."

Rye let go of the troll's other arm. "Wow. Your wound healed fast."

"Trolls heal fast." I spoke quickly. He couldn't figure out the truth. "You're still going to show us the way."

Jayunja nodded. "Majiks don't get fair trials. They don't get trials." He stomped his foot harder and winced. The wound had stopped bleeding. Still, he wasn't completely healed on the inside.

"I've never seen a majik who's taken into custody let go." Dryness crept up my throat. "And the rumors about this prison." A chill slid down my spine. I waved in the direction we headed.

"Zauber Tomb." The troll's response rang a death knell.

"Once a majik goes in, they never come out." My voice rose repeating the rumors.

"Because if they're found guilty, they're sent out of the kingdom." Rye's hard tone hinted at knowledge. "We don't have the capacity to hold all the majik prisoners."

"We?"

His lips puckered. "The kingdom. *Our* kingdom."

I'd heard so many stories at school. Gardenia had repeated the gossip as fact. I hadn't believed most of it. But now? After seeing the arena fights and hearing the people chitchat at the ball? I didn't know what to think. Jayunja didn't get a trial. "You're living in a fairytale if you believe that."

Narrowing my gaze, I studied Rye. Who was this guy? He'd attended royal balls before. He wore nice clothes. He knew his way around the palace. How close was he to the regent and the prince? They couldn't be related. Not with Rye's tanned skin and long, dark hair. He was the exact opposite of the fair-skinned prince. Besides, I wanted to kiss him, not kill him.

Jayunja huffed. "I wasn't shipped out of the kingdom. I was forced to fight a dragon."

I remembered his fear as he'd stood in the center of the arena waiting to face a much stronger foe. "An unfair fight."

Rye's scar turned redder with his furrowed brow. "You made a club magically appear. You escaped."

"Trolls don't have that kind of magic." *I did.*

"I was told he could use his magic to defend himself." How could he be so unaware of the majiks and their abilities?

"Shows how much you know." The boiling in my stomach bubbled again, roiling with his ignorance. With all humans' ignorance. No wonder they didn't appreciate majiks.

"Trolls can blend with the environment." Jayunja's entire body went gray and it was hard to see him. "We can see in the dark and hear from long distances away." He pointed to his chest. "We heal quickly."

I stretched my neck and shoulders. There was another explanation for his wound healing so quickly. It hadn't been only my magic, and so there would be nothing for me to explain.

Rye's brow furrowed deeper as he put everything together. "You were defenseless in the arena?"

"Yes."

"How did you get the club?" His intelligence added to his attractiveness, and to my worry about him figuring things out. About me. About my mission.

"I don't know. A majik nearby must've helped." Jayunja glanced at me and back to his friendly interrogator.

My abs clenched. Did the troll know who had helped him? Is that why he'd been willing to accept my medical aid? Most trolls were independent loners. They lived their lives with minimal contact with other majiks according to my textbooks. And yet tonight, I'd learned so many things I'd been taught were wrong.

He shrugged his large, furry shoulders. "This is the farthest I go."

My hands flailed. "You said you'd show me the way."

He pointed around a bend in the tunnel. "The Zauber Tomb has an access point through there. It's not the dungeon, but it will take you there. I'm not getting any closer. And I'm not going back. Ever."

Rye's gaze widened turning the silver orbs into gray slates. "Was it that bad?"

"Do you know where trolls live?"

"Under a bridge?" He really had no clue.

"Where have you been? Under a rock or stuck in a palace tower?" I couldn't believe his ignorance. One second, he seemed to be the smartest guy I'd ever met, and the next it was if he didn't know what was going on in the kingdom.

His brow smoothed, and he sucked in his cheeks. "I've been away for a while."

"We live in caves in the mountains." Jayunja tilted his scruffy chin. "Dirty, dank caves with no light. No real possessions because the SCUM would regularly search the mountains. No privacy. And that is better than Zauber Tomb." Pivoting, he headed back in the direction he came.

"Goodbye." My voice cracked.

"Good luck." The troll grumbled. "You're going to need it."

His parting shot echoed through the cave and vibrated into my soul. I was alone with Rye at last. A guy who had risked danger to follow me, and I didn't understand why. A guy who was smart, except about things having to do with the kingdom. A guy I didn't understand and wanted to, yet couldn't trust.

An awkward silence descended.

"Shall we continue?" He pointed with a flat palm.

"Why?" I had to understand his reasons.

"Why what?" He flashed an animated smile, showing bright white teeth. A smile that made me forget my common sense.

"Why are you coming with me? It's dangerous, according to the troll. What are you getting out of it?"

"Can't a guy be gallant?" He sauntered forward skirting around the bend, leading the way.

I should be the one leading. Thundering to catch up to him, I repeated, "Gallant?"

He didn't glance back, just kept walking as if this was a stroll in a garden. His shoes squelched in the mud on the ground. His once-crisp pants had splatters of dirt near the bottom. He'd removed the vest and his shirt tugged across his broad shoulders.

"You're trying to rescue your friend. You're going

somewhere dangerous. Having a partner is a good idea." His longish hair curled slightly in the dampness, highlighting the lighter tips.

"Partner?" I'd gone from leading my mission to becoming a parrot.

"Partner." He kept moving forward and suddenly came to a quick stop.

I slammed into his strong back. "What the—"

"The zauber betrayed us."

Flinching at the slur, I took a step away.

"Jayunja sent us on a false path." Rye had called the troll a zauber, not a majik. Not a friend.

Is that what he thought of us? Of majiks?

Us? Swallowing at the realization I'd included myself in the grouping, I tried to control my fast-beating heart. Was I finally starting to accept my majik side? Although not out loud. Admitting it now would be stupid. With Rye I needed to continue to pretend to be human.

"It's a dead end." He pounded his fist into a wall of rock.

The gray wall had lines etched into it by water over thousands of years. It looked as if someone had taken a large knife and scraped in the horizontal design. Moss had gathered in the cracks creating a miniature forest.

Defeat pressed down like the tunnel. I'd failed in my quest. We were stuck underneath the palace and I didn't know how to get out or how to move forward. It had to be past midnight by now, and I had no clue how to find Arbor. Giving up wasn't in my human nature. I'd suffered through years of abuse from my stepmother so I could be accepted and in control of my own destiny. Getting in trouble for sneaking out was the least of my worries.

Taking a deep, calming breath, I ran my palm across the stone. My skin caught on the tiny outcroppings. What appeared to be a smooth surface actually had hundreds of tiny indents. I'd seen a similar rock in the small park by my house. Arbor had called it crystalline limestone and said it could become a passageway.

I glanced at my companion. Could I trust him? He'd used the word *zauber*. So had I. The slur was casually thrown around by everyone and he must not realize the negative connotations. He was ignorant about a lot of majik things. And I wouldn't be using my fairy powers.

He'd been pretty obstinate about staying by my side and I didn't have the time to walk back with him, find a way out, dump him, and then make my way to this spot. Trust him or not, he was about to witness powers from Mother Earth. Anyone could call on nature for help. It was one of the things I'd allowed Arbor to teach me.

I rubbed my palm against the rock, thinking the thoughts Arbor had taught me.

Earth, open for your loyal servant. Show me the way.

The rock beneath my hand trembled. Rumbling and creaking filled the small, dead-end cavern. The ground shook. It was working.

"The tunnel's caving in." Rye rushed forward and pressed his body against mine. He hunched over my small frame, protecting me.

My body liquefied. He cared enough to protect me. He was gallant, and brave. And each quality made him more appealing. My pulse raced, and his heat scorched my skin. I twisted around to face him wanting to see his expression.

The muscles in his cheeks and chin relaxed. His silver orbs changed to a silkier gray. He tilted toward me inch by inch.

Licking my lips, I tried to control my galloping pulse. My eyes got wider as he got closer. I was already in his arms. Was he going to kiss me? A squeal ran the length of my midsection, from my quivering stomach to my zooming heart. Now?

His mouth brushed mine sending tingles across my lips and lighting a fire inside my skin. I burned from his slight contact imitating a match igniting a forest fire. His lips caressed mine again in a light, testing touch.

My lips grazed his. There were no open mouths or tongues. Only sweetness and light and hope. In this kiss, I wasn't alone, that he'd be beside me always.

His fingers palmed my cheek and chin. "Elle?"

I didn't know what he was asking or how I should respond. Biting my lip, I tried to control my awkwardness. "The tunnel is not caving in."

The ground stopped trembling and the rock stopped vibrating because I'd stopped concentrating on earth to concentrate on Rye. I placed my flat palm back on the rock trying to settle my emotions. My first kiss. From a gorgeous guy. And totally at the most inappropriate moment.

"You're right. The shaking has stopped." He didn't move away from me and I was hyperaware of our bodies so close. An inch or less. Too close, or not close enough.

Just because the kiss was special did not mean we started a make-out session in the middle of a quest. I needed to stay focused. And while I enjoyed the intimacy, I couldn't concentrate with him so close. "Can you step back? I'm trying to concentrate."

"On what?" He took a step back.

It was enough room to let my pulse return to normal. Almost.

"Watch." I couldn't stop my small grin and I wasn't sure if it was because of the kiss or what I was about to show him.

Placing my hand back on the rock, I concentrated once more. The rock vibrated, the ground shook, and rumbling filled the cavern.

Rye's gaze widened, and his mouth opened. His body stiffened. He didn't move though. Maybe he did trust me. How could he not after the kiss?

The crystalline shifted and became translucent resembling a shiny quartz stone. The shaking stopped. A strong vibration came off my palm and the passageway opened.

"How did you do that?" He spoke slowly.

A thrill zoomed down my spine and electrified my nerve endings. I'd called on earth and it had answered. "Mother Earth has mysteries still to explore."

"Magic?"

I paused and surveyed him. "Not magic. Mother Earth. Anyone who connects with nature can do it. Even humans."

"Where did you learn how to do that?"

"It's a long explanation. I'll tell you later. Let's go." I stepped through the opening first not wanting to explain to him all the things Arbor had wanted to teach me about magic and fairies. Learning about Mother Earth's powers had been a compromise between me and her.

Entering, a sucking tugged at my skin. My ears popped. I glanced behind to make sure Rye was coming.

He was right behind me. His slightly lost expression made him look adorable. His eyes appeared more silver filling with wonderment, and his lips quirked in an enchanted smile. Lost in his smile, I released an appreciative sigh. I wanted to kiss him again.

"Put your hands up, humans."

About a dozen majiks stood sentry at our entrance on the other side of the rock. In a semi-circle so we couldn't get away, each either fisted their hands or carried a homemade weapon of some sort.

And the weapons pointed at us.

Chapter 11

The demand bulleted through me and sent a thrashing through my ears. I jerked up my hands, but not in surrender. In self-defense, and a we-come-in-peace gesture.

A female elf, a fairy, a couple of ogres, and a troll stood in attack position. They surrounded us, blocking us in. If this was the way to the dungeon, what were majiks doing running about on their own? With weapons! The palace guards must be slacking off.

"Hands up!" the female elf repeated. She jabbed a sharp stick, coming within inches of my chest.

Rye stepped in front of me, taking a protective position. My heartbeat quickened, and I wanted to trace my fingers across his broad shoulders. Totally inappropriate thought at this moment. He held his hands in a flattened karate-chop position, instead of fists. Did he know the ancient defensive arts? With no weapon—against a dozen majiks with powers—he'd lose quickly.

I recognized more majiks in the background. Some laid or sat on the ground. Others leaned up against the walls, interested but not participating.

Rye glanced back and whispered, "Just as my uncle said, zaubers are all bad. They want to kill us."

My head swam. I'd thought he was different, even though the same thing had been drilled into me at school.

The female elf growled and raised her pointy stick. Elves had excellent hearing and she must've heard Rye.

Hmm. Why are the majiks using fists and rocks and sharpened sticks? They could use magic.

"We're not here to harm you." I held my empty hands higher to prove my point. They'd called me human, so they believed without a weapon I was defenseless. Since I didn't know how to use my powers, in a way I was. Guess, I should've started training before I needed my powers in an emergency.

"You're human." The elf jabbed with her stick and the movement caused her deep red bangs to slosh across her forehead. "Of course you want to harm us."

There was that word again. Human. All my life, I wanted to be recognized as one. After the way Arbor, and my fairy godmother, and now the majiks I'd met on this journey, had pronounced the word, I wanted to shout I was a fairy. My gut jittered. I wasn't confident Rye wouldn't turn away in disgust or abandon me on my quest. He was right about one thing. I did enjoy having a companion, especially one who gave romantic kisses.

"Why do you think humans want to harm you?" His fierce expression said he believed the exact opposite.

The elf, who appeared to be around my age, moved as fast as lightning and stuck the stick against Rye's throat. The point pressed against his jugular. He'd had no time to react. "Because humans stuck us in this hellhole."

She had a point. *Literally.*

"Not us. We don't want to hurt you." I stepped beside him

and pushed away the stick. "I'm Elle, and this is Rye. We're not guards, and we don't work in the palace."

The elf pursed her lips in a fierce scowl and repositioned her stick near my face. A jeweled necklace tied together with twigs hung low on her neck. She wore brown breeches and a cape with a tight top underneath.

Rye tensed behind me. He must be worried we'd die right here. The majiks were only defending themselves.

"If anything, we want to help you." The minute I spoke the words, I knew the truth of it. The certainty settled in my soul and centered me. Yes, I wanted to find Arbor. But I couldn't ignore the plight of the majiks. I'd already helped Jayunja.

"Why would a couple of humans want to help us?" The female elf acted as leader of this ragtag group.

Tilting closer, Rye whispered, "We should slip through the rock and get out of here. I don't trust them."

I bristled and caught the attention of the elf, who'd probably heard his comments. Her gaze narrowed. "I'm trying to find a friend of mine. A smoke sprite."

"Anyone willing to enter Zauber Tomb of free will is either brave or crazy." The elf gave the signal to the other majiks and they relaxed their positions, although none of them let their guard down completely. "I'm Keltie."

I'd been called a lot of things, although never crazy even though this quest had insane written all over it. "You're right, Keltie. I probably am crazy."

I might not find my friend, but I wasn't giving up. And in the process, I was discovering truths about myself and what I really wanted. For example, I didn't want to only be known as human. At least to some.

Rye relaxed his hands and let his arms drop to his sides. "Brave."

My lungs expanded, and I pulled my shoulders straighter. For the first time since my dad's death, I felt brave.

The cavern we entered appeared more disgusting than the trash chute and half the size of my tiny attic room. Stench permeated the hole. Dark and dirty with piles of garbage laying around. Cramped with a dozen majiks. The only light came through the crystalline rock. The ragtag group with weapons stayed near.

"What is this place?" Rye didn't hide his disgust.

"A hidden tunnel from Zauber Tomb." Keltie used her stick to jab at the ground. "We thought we'd found an escape, except we can't get out."

The fairies in the room didn't know how to ask Mother Earth? I figured I'd show them once they answered a few questions. I scanned the vicinity and caught on something I originally thought was a small pile of garbage.

It wasn't.

A small brownie lay against a wall several feet away, her head coated in blood. She wore a long, green skirt with a matching vest. She clutched a pointy hat in her hands.

"What happened?" Reaching in my bag, I searched for my magic ointment.

Keltie and the other majiks raised the makeshift weapons again. Tension escalated between us. A large ogre wearing only baggy shorts dove in front of the brownie.

An ogre defending a brownie. Now, I'd seen everything. Their legendary battles were written about in history books.

I stopped a few feet away. Slowly, I took my hand out of the bag to show I didn't have a weapon. "I have something in my bag to help heal wounds."

"She does." Rye charged beside me, again protecting me. My own personal defender. "She used an ointment to heal a huge gash on a troll."

I raised my chin to a proud angle. First because I had helped, and second because he bragged on me.

A chorus of *oohs* and *ahs* echoed around the small cavern. The majiks' reaction was a mix of surprise, disdain, and disbelief.

"You're a healer." Keltie sized me up and nodded in a superior way. "Let the human take a look."

The weapons were put down and I kneeled at the brownie's side. "My name is Elle."

Rye snorted.

"I'm Tos." Her over-round eyes darted, and her tiny body shrank into the ground. A large scratch ran across the brownie's bald head. Her ear had been ripped.

"That cut is deep." Majiks fighting majiks was common. "How did this happen?"

"We were waiting in the holding cell near the auraguillotine." Her high, squeaky voice filled with emotion. "The collection time was drawing near."

One of the SCUM had used the same term— auraguillotine—at my house.

She held up her hand. "One of the guards took pity on me because of my size."

"The guard thought you were a child not a teenager," Keltie scoffed.

Tos stuck out her tongue at the elf, showing no fear of reprisal. "The guard opened a small grate in the collection room and let me go through. Some of the other majiks noticed, and a stampede started."

"A stampede to move toward the auraguillotine?" Rye didn't believe any of the brownie's story.

"No. To escape." Tos jumped to her pointy toes to demonstrate. "The other majiks saw their chance and pushed and shoved through the grate. They trampled me."

"Sorry." A fairy nearby flapped his wings.

"Me, too," another ogre grunted.

I held my breath, waiting to hear what happened next. They'd all survived. They were here, together. They'd escaped.

"Ugoki protected me while the others trampled." The brownie hugged the ogre's slimy bare leg. "Keltie grabbed me off the ground and carried me away." Tos let go of Ugoki's leg and hugged the elf.

The good will between these three normally arguing types of majiks lifted my spirits. Brownies and elves were known to fight over the forests. Their wars were sources of legends and taught even in human school. And ogres were just grumpy.

"What happened to the guard?" Rye scowled, his expression sour.

Why would he care what happened to a mean guard? Although since the guard let Tos free, maybe he wasn't so cruel.

"He was fine. Slammed the grate closed after me." Ugoki's chuckle imitated a rasp. "Probably got in trouble from his superiors."

"We worked our way through the small tunnel, met Hokima," Keltie waved her hands at a troll standing nearby. "and ended up here. Now, we're stuck."

All the majiks in the room had worked together to escape. They'd formed a team to defend themselves against me and Rye when we'd entered. They'd worked together.

I shoved my hand in my bag. *Hmm.* The only items inside were a lipstick, comb, and mirror. None of those things would help cure wounds. Focusing on the ointment, I stuck my hand inside the bag again. My hand came up empty. Could I be too far underground for the magic in the bag to work? I shoved my hand back in the bag and imagined any kind of first aid. Gardenia had said I needed to think of what I wanted, and it would magically appear.

Nothing happened. It wasn't working.

"Are you looking for this?" Rye held the ointment in his hand.

Good thing he'd picked up the tube when I finished working on the troll. If I'd put it back in the bag, it might have disappeared.

I squeezed the ointment onto my finger and smoothed it along the brownie's cut, hoping that even though my magic bag wasn't working, the ointment would. Once I helped the majiks through the crystalline rock, Rye could direct them out the way he'd gotten below the palace.

Tos pointed at my decorative bag. "Do you have any food?"

"Are you hungry?" I tore off a strip of material from my skirt and wrapped it around the brownie's head as a makeshift bandage.

She nodded and so did everyone else.

"How long has it been since you ate?" Rye must care about majiks, even though he did call them zaubers. He was a good guy.

"Days." Tos sounded weak and afraid.

"I'm sorry, I don't have any food." If the bag was working, I could've given them a feast. Brushing off my hands, I stood. Time to get back to business. "Has anyone seen a smoke sprite named Arbor?" I held up my hands a few inches apart. "She's about this big and has multi-colored hair?"

Keltie shook her head. Her red braid whipped back and forth.

Rye angled toward the elf with a curious expression. "What did you do to become imprisoned?"

"Nothing." Her pointy ears went red.

"You must've done something, or you wouldn't be here." He acted like a judge, leaning forward aggressively.

I scowled. Why didn't he believe her? Arbor had been arrested for doing nothing. She and Keltie were similar to birds with their wings clipped unfairly. Imprisoned through no fault of their own.

The elf's green gaze narrowed. "My mother was dragged out of our home because she met with an unsanctioned group of elves."

"What do you mean unsanctioned?" I'd never heard of an unsanctioned or a sanctioned group.

"It's a new law being discussed." Rye dismissed the elf's claim. "The law hasn't been put into effect yet."

"Tell that to the SCUM who attacked our house with my younger brothers and sisters inside." Keltie's voice went frigid.

A shiver passed through me. "That's criminal."

"But how did *you* get arrested?" He accepted the reason for her mother's arrest, as if it was okay to be arrested for something so innocent.

My face tightened, and I crossed my arms.

Red, as dark as her hair, stained Keltie's cheeks. Her stance stayed defiant. "I tried to stop the SCUM from taking my mother."

"By attacking the authorities?" His wide eyes and dropped jaw showed his disbelief. He didn't understand most citizens didn't like the SCUM.

"They were hurting my mother." She stomped her stick on the ground. "In front of her children."

Where were her brothers and sisters now?

"What happened at your trial? Did they understand the extenuating circumstances?" Rye whipped out question after question.

His official tone sent a chill down my back. Whose side was he on? One minute being kind and considerate, helping Jayunja and me, the next going on a verbal attack.

Hokima tugged on a bedraggled blue sash around his neck. "Majiks don't get a trial. We end up in the dungeon until they feed us to the auraguillotine. Never to return to our parents."

"They take our families, too. I'll never see my baby brothers and sisters again." Keltie sounded small and sad, the exact opposite of the fierce leader she'd proved herself to be.

I gulped. "What is this auraguillotine?"

I couldn't imagine what it did and why it scared them so much.

Keltie's bottom lip quivered. Tos' eyes went so wide she resembled a kewpie doll more than a brownie. Hokima grimaced. All three shook their heads. Did they not want to talk about it or tell me? They must not trust me enough with the information.

Rye ran a hand through his thick, dark hair. "What about you? Why are you in prison?"

Ugoki glared. "I picked plants from a human's garden. Only weeds, something a human would pluck and throw away from the precious wheat growing. The SCUM arrested me."

"You were guilty." Rye nodded, satisfied with the answer.

"Of trying to feed my family," the ogre growled. "My parents are too old to work, and I'm not allowed to travel to the part of the city where I had a job. I had no way of earning creds. No way to provide for them."

The ogre's chuckle and smirk disappeared. I could hear his pain and patted his shoulder.

"What about you?" Rye challenged a gangly teenage fairy with a handsome face, cherubic cheeks, and narrow lips. "Why were you sent to prison?"

"Murder."

A sudden coldness hit my core. The fairy with an angelic face and thin as a pole body committed murder? His loose shirt and pants hung on his frame. No muscles or malice that I could detect. "What? Who?"

He shrugged his thin shoulders. "The SCUM threatened to kill my parents unless I confessed to a crime. I figured if I was going to confess, I should confess to a big one."

Shaking my head, I stared at the fairy. The same thing could've happened to me. I was a fairy. I'd heard rumors about forced confessions. Here was proof.

"The Security Unit—" Rye glanced around at the majiks. "I mean the SCUM who forced your confession must've been punished by their superiors."

He had noble beliefs. People who had money and were shielded must not hear what was really happening on the streets. My spine crumpled. I'd thought the same before Arbor started pointing out the injustices.

"I haven't heard. Then again, I'm not cozy with the SCUM." The fairy insinuated maybe Rye was.

"What happened to you?" Rye reeled toward Hokima. The gorgeous guy sounded desperate to find one guilty majik.

"I came through the crystalline rock to find my girlfriend." Hokima's globby eyes secreted more liquid. "And now I can't get out."

"We found him wandering in the tunnels." Keltie pointed to a large boulder in the cavern. "He led us to this spot."

"You weren't arrested?" Rye kept hammering at the same point.

"No." The troll heaved a big sigh and his large stomach rumbled. "I wanted to save Xefroz. She's everything to me."

My heart softened. I hadn't realized the extent a troll could love, which made me as bad as the humans. Thinking of other majiks, not fairies, as being less.

Not anymore. I'd helped the troll in the arena, and I'd administered first aid to a brownie. Keltie, an elf, had saved the brownie and now was the leader of this little group. Ugoki had protected Tos, too. The majiks were working together for their survival.

Unlike their bloody past.

For example, the time the ogres decimated the brownies in the Crystal War. Or when the elves put a curse on the sprites. Or the Bloody Battle between the giants and the fairies.

"This is an intolerable situation." Rye waved his arm in an arc resembling a salute and turned it into a wave.

I admired how he might care about the majiks, even while using the slur. "What can we do?"

"I'll tell the Regent what's happening. Make him see how the majiks are being treated."

The ogre started with his horrible chuckle. Keltie, Hokima, and the fairy joined in. Tos added her high-pitched giggle. Maybe they laughed because they couldn't cry. Not after the injustices they'd faced.

Their off-key laughs thrust like a dagger in my midsection, pinching my anger to a sharp point. Rye made it sound so easy. As if a citizen could waltz up to the regent and have a conversation about injustice. I massaged my temples, sensing the beginning of a headache.

"The royal family doesn't care about the majiks." I thought about my daily fears. "The rules are getting more and more restrictive. They can't work for a living. They can't do magic. They can't take care of their families. And now they can't even meet as a group."

The troll swiped the snot from his large nose. "The only thing the royal family cares about is the majiks' power."

"That's not true. I don't think that." Rye's brows gathered

in ferocious determination. "The prince doesn't think that."

Misgiving trickled slowly through my bloodstream. How closely aligned was he to the palace? "How do you know?"

Keltie raised her stick toward him. "Yeah. How do you know?"

I wanted to trust Rye, except I'd just met him. He was familiar with the palace and knew the laws being discussed, or ones being implemented before being passed. If he was so close to royalty, what was he doing beneath the palace with me? Helping me? Wanting to help majiks?

Or did he?

Fear flashed in his expression. "I know the prince. I'll talk to him."

Keltie lowered her weapon, deeming him not a threat. "It's the regent who holds the real power."

His jaw clenched. "He did hold the power. The…prince is now of age and will be taking control of the kingdom."

Huffing, I couldn't help wondering how that would be possible. "But will the regent give up the power?"

I totally related to the situation. After Continuum, I was supposed to inherit my ancestral home and take my rightful place in society as Lady Milford. Would Sybil hand the house over? Worry had gnawed at me for the last several months as I'd gotten closer, and I thought constantly about how she might slip a rug out from under me at the last second. I'd been naïve believing she'd let me go to the ball.

"Laws of the land." His eyes grew hard as slate. "Order of succession."

"Laws change." Keltie swirled her stick in the dirt, creating a drawing. "When the kingdom was formed, majiks helped the royal family rule. Their magic is what put the family in power and gave them the ability to hide from the rest of the world. As technology developed, magic was no longer necessary and became a threat to the ruling class." She swiped the image on the ground, making it disappear. "Regent Theobald has slowly eroded our rights. One teenage prince isn't going to give them back."

Rye's cheeks grew red and he waved his hand about. "Uh…he will. We need to inform him of the situation and let the Regent know our wishes."

"If it was easy, we wouldn't be in this hellhole." Hokima paced away.

Keltie stabbed her stick into the ground. "The majik council tried to reason with the regent. The council was forcefully disbanded."

"We'll go right now." Rye wrapped his strong fingers around my arm. His smooth palms caressed my skin, causing goosebumps to blossom. He made me believe this was more than a partnership, especially since our kiss. I trusted him to help. "We'll talk to the regent after the ball and make sure the imprisoned majiks get a fair trial as soon as possible."

"We're all innocent." The fairy waved his hand, encompassing everyone. "The only thing we're guilty of is being majik."

"We'll see." He didn't believe in them one hundred percent, but he was willing to investigate, to give them a chance. "It might take time to sort out who belongs in here and who doesn't."

I pulled back, finding our partnership uncomfortable. "None of them belong here. Look at this place."

The cramped quarters closed in on me. The heat and the terrible smell had been infiltrating my nose, making me woozy. The piles of garbage on the dirt ground seemed bigger than they had moments ago. The majiks stared as if he had come from outside the dome.

His nose crinkled. "This place is awful. I'll do something about the terrible conditions." He tugged me toward the crystalline rock. "The sooner we talk to the regent, and the prince, the sooner we can make things right."

Stiffening, I resisted. If we met the prince, I'd have to kill him. I wouldn't have a choice. And then, I'd be executed immediately. If Rye had so much confidence in the prince, why would Gardenia want the royal killed?

And I hadn't found Arbor yet.

He kept tugging me forward. "Do your thing."

With a shaking hand, I placed my palm on the rock. I'd open the entrance for him and the other majiks and then I'd return this way to continue my quest to save Arbor. I'd prove to her how much I'd changed.

Earth, open for your loyal servant. Show me the way.

The rock beneath my hand trembled. Rumbling, creaking, and clattering filled the small, dead-end cavern. The ground shook.

"Do you think I didn't try that, human?" Keltie sneered at what she believed was my pathetic attempt.

Connecting with Mother Earth was a natural and ancient art passed from one generation to the next, both human and majik. Humans believed technology was superior to nature and most of them had lost the art.

Hokima watched with beady eyes. "It's how I got in, but I couldn't get back out."

"Let me concentrate." I pressed my palm harder against the rock.

Earth, open for your loyal servant. Show me the way.

The vibration became more rhythmic. The rock became translucent.

"You did it." Rye powered through the passageway, holding my hand.

Why could I do it if Keltie couldn't? She probably had sufficient training while Arbor had only taught me a few basics before I'd received my powers and a few fairy magic tricks once I'd turned sixteen. To make a joke or ease a cleaning task or while telling a story. Subtle teaching methods my mind had soaked up.

Rye tugged me harder and my fist slammed into the rock. My hand wouldn't pass through. It was like hitting a brick wall.

The pain shattered up my veins from my fingers to my head. I took a shallow breath, finding it hard to take in oxygen. The troll had said he couldn't go out through the passageway. And neither could any of the other majik creatures.

Apparently, neither could I.

Chapter 12

I yanked my arm out of Rye's to stop him from banging my hand into, what was for me, solid rock. My half-fairy blood must be keeping me on this side of the passageway. That's why Keltie and the other majiks couldn't get out. The earlier image of the clipped bird's wings applied to me. My back throbbed at the spot where I should've sprouted fairy wings.

Rye stuck his head back through the wall. His lips quirked in that adorable way. "Elle?"

The torment spread from my back to my ribcage and had me hunching my shoulders. He'd want to know why I couldn't pass through and discover everything. I couldn't tell him the truth. Not now. Not like this. I knew he thought some majiks were okay. But would he want to hang out with one? Date one? Kiss one again? My cheeks heated.

"What's wrong?" An impatient demand stamped in his question.

"Um, I think…I think I should stay here." My mind scrambled. "The majiks need my medical assistance. I'll wait with them until they're freed."

"It might take a while. There will be steps to go through and things to prove and…" He ran frustrated fingers through his hair. "Come with me."

"Is that an order?" My jaw tightened. I was tired of people telling me what to do. First my stepmother and stepsisters, then my fairy godmother, and now this guy. Even though this adventure had been scary, I'd enjoyed making my own decisions. Going back to servitude would be difficult.

"It's a reasonable request." His pupils darted around to glance at the other majiks. "For your safety."

Aha! He didn't believe in the complete equality of majiks. He was worried about leaving me behind with them. Which was sweet, and also degrading.

I crossed my arms outwardly displaying determination, while my nerves shimmied. "I'm staying here. With them."

Obviously, I couldn't waltz out of the cavern as Rye had. I needed time to strategize. Maybe if I put my elfin shoes on, I mean shoe, I could use the passageway. I couldn't attempt that with him here.

"Besides, I haven't found my friend yet." My sole reason for coming to the ball tonight and letting Gardenia put an enchantment on me to kill the prince. Another good reason not to go with Rye.

He frowned. "I don't relish the idea of leaving you."

"You didn't even know me before tonight." I needed to push him away even if it made him mad. Since I'd probably never see him again, why worry about what this one guy thought?

Because I felt something toward him. The inner reflection jarred. He was the first guy to pay attention to me, listen to me, and kiss me. And I hadn't been pretending. I'd shown my true personality. Shown him everything except what I was.

Exactly. I hadn't told him I was half fairy and didn't want

to now. But Arbor was more important than a possible future date. And I didn't need him to get caught up in my mess. If we both got caught, we'd both suffer. I needed to force him to go by himself. "I'd planned to come here on my own. I wasn't expecting a traveling circus or a knight in shining armor."

His skin went pale and his glare could've shot poisoned arrows. "So be it."

His venom already spread beneath my skin.

"I'll be back with help." Wheeling around, he disappeared behind the translucent rock.

Collapsing against the wall, I took a couple of heavy breaths. I couldn't leave the way I'd come. And what would happen when Rye came back with help? How would I explain myself? I was stuck in this cavern with a roomful of majiks that had been arrested. Even if the crimes had been made up.

"What's the real reason you didn't leave?" Keltie leaned forward in a threatening way. She didn't trust me either, yet she'd kept quiet while I'd dealt with Rye. She must trust him less.

The cavern became smaller, hotter. Tugging at the top of my dress, I wanted to stop the strangling sensation. I needed to trust her and the others if they were going to trust me. I wanted their help finding Arbor. Maybe together we could get out without Rye's assistance, without the prince and the regent ever knowing we'd escaped.

If they were going to trust me, I needed to tell them the truth. Take a leap of faith and put my future in their hands.

Blowing out a large breath, I stood. "I believe majiks can't pass through from this direction."

"Why do you think that?" Keltie scowled.

Swallowing, I pointed at Hokima. "He could come in but couldn't go back out."

Keltie and the troll nodded.

"Well…" I stuck out my chin. "I couldn't leave either because…" My chin wobbled. "Because I'm a majik, too."

"What?"

"No way."

"I couldn't tell."

Their responses ranged from shock to disbelief. All things I would've been proud of in the past. The fact I could pass as human.

I stuck out my chest, pumping with a new pride, a different kind of pride. The unveiling of my true self felt good and freeing. Maybe I should've accepted my identity a long time ago. "I'm half-fairy."

Tos shuttled to my side and put her arms around my legs. "I knew you couldn't be a horrible human."

Cringing, I noted the opposite type of prejudice. The races uniting seemed impossible. Too much bad blood between the groups. Majiks didn't trust humans and for good reason. Would they trust me as half?

"You don't look like a fairy." Keltie sized me up and her gaze slid to the other fairy comparing.

"I'm shorter than most humans. I have this silver in my hair." I tugged out a strand to reveal the ends. "And I have a little magic I'm not very good at using."

"Half-fairy?" The other fairy's snooty nose lifted high. "Half breed."

His words cut through me. Being half meant not being accepted on either side. Good thing my bargain with Gardenia wasn't to go to the fairy academy. I'd never be accepted. More years of being bullied. And the other students could use magic, no less. No thank you.

"If you're half-fairy why were you stupid enough to come through the passageway?" Keltie's tone also wounded. "The humans have used technology to subvert our magic and keep us locked inside the underground dungeon and caverns. Under the palace, our magic doesn't work."

"I didn't know I couldn't go both ways." My whine pained my own ears.

Jayunja had led me to the crystalline rock. He'd never said anything about technological locks. Had he known? Either way, I was determined to find Arbor. I would've gone through no matter what.

Hokima shook his head. "You're stuck with the rest of us."

"Maybe." I reached in my bag and pulled out the elfin shoe. Slipping it on my foot, I placed my palm against the rock and said the magical phrases.

"What's the shoe for?"

"What're you doing?"

"Might as well give up."

The chorus of naysayers didn't stop me. I continued my internal chant.

The rock vibrated and the ground trembled. I'd opened the passageway for Rye, that wasn't the problem.

The rock shifted to its translucent state. I shoved my foot with the shoe forward. It wouldn't go through. On the other side of the rock, I vaguely saw shadows, and yet I couldn't cross the line. Pinching my lips, I knocked my forehead against the rock.

"Why did you and Rye come down here?" Keltie crossed her arms, her long braids covering her shoulders. I appreciated how she protected those she felt responsible for.

"I told you, I'm searching for my friend." And being completely unsuccessful. I snapped off the shoe a little too hard and shoved it back in my bag. "And Rye, I'm not sure why he decided to come with me."

He'd said he followed me. He'd tried to protect me. He'd

kissed me. My pulse thudded. He wanted me to return with him. Was the kiss only taking advantage of the opportunity or did he care? The thought spiraled into warmth in the center of my chest. A good-looking guy being attracted to me was a new sensation.

"I overheard the SCUM talking about a smoke sprite who was arrested for shooting fireworks. They were really interested in her abilities." Hokima understood the urge to search for someone you cared about.

He was a hero. A troll hero who believed in love.

"Where did you hear?" I pounced on him.

"I've never heard of a smoke sprite who could do that kind of magic," the fairy murmured.

Keltie's gaze grew wide with alarm. "How is that possible? How are majiks changing their powers?"

"Where did you hear about the smoke sprite?" Yelling, I needed to know so I could find Arbor.

Hokima glanced uncertainly between me and Keltie.

My earlier frustration blasted my blood pressure. I threw my hands up. "It was me who shot off the fireworks. Not my friend Arbor. A smoke sprite doesn't have that kind of power. A fairy does."

"You let your friend take the fall for you?" Disgust threaded through the elf's voice.

"No!" My heart shrieked remembering the anguish during my friend's arrest. "I tried to tell the SCUM it was me. They didn't believe me because of how I look."

Peering at the spots and stains on my dress, at the ragged hem, at the scratches and bruises on my arms and legs, no one would believe I was a human who'd attended the prince's ball.

The majiks closest to me wore skeptical expressions. Both Keltie's brows rose, and her head did a little noodle-nod. Hokima's fatty, lower lip stuck out. The male fairy's eyes slitted, studying me like a bug. Only Tos appeared satisfied and my spirits lifted. I had one ally.

I didn't want my quest to end here and I needed their help with directions on how they'd gotten to this place underground. I'd convince them by telling them the entire truth.

"I'm a half-fairy who passed for human. My plan was to go through Continuum, attend technical college, and be known as officially human. I had my life planned out. A safe life." My throat clogged. I'd been through a lot in the last several hours. Thinking about what Arbor must've gone through, my eyes teared. "Until, my best friend was arrested by the SCUM because of something I did."

The image of her being taken away in the small cage flashed in my brain. Her departing words seared into my consciousness. *Have a nice human life.*

"I'm not one hundred percent human. I don't want to pretend anymore. I want to claim my fairy heritage. And I need to save my friend."

Everyone went silent and the tension stretched.

Bowing my head, I sniffed. "My friend didn't do magic. I did those things. And at her trial if they try to test her—"

"Torture her." Hokima's hard truth punched.

I held back tears. "I have to find her. I have to set her free."

"What about us?" Tos stomped her tiny foot.

Keltie raised her red brows. The fairy glared in agreement.

"If we work together, we can figure out how to save Arbor and others. We can escape." My gaze alighted on each of their special faces. Expressions filled with doubt and fear, and maybe a little bit of hope. "If we do nothing, we've already lost."

Keltie's expression lit with fire. "Let's do it." Her stamp of approval meant a lot.

Tos jumped up and down on her toes. "Yeah, let's do it." She was enthusiastic about everything.

"I'm in." Hokima had tried to break in already. Why not a second time?

"What can we possibly do?" The fairy crossed his arms and leaned back against the wall. "We're stuck in this evil place."

They stared with rapt attention as if I was their new leader. My lungs wheezed. I had no idea where to start. We were stuck in the cave and we couldn't wait around for Rye to show up. But I had to take the momentum and do something now.

"We'll start where we began." Hokima pushed aside a rock exposing an opening.

I didn't have answers, but he did.

"That takes us back to the holding cell for the auraguillotine." Tos shivered.

The shiver must be contagious because I trembled even though I hadn't shared their experience.

"It's the only way we can get out of this cavern." Keltie proceeded to the hole. "There was more than one tunnel. We might find a way out of the prison and the palace."

"Yeah, right." The fairy's doubt deflated the charged atmosphere.

"What's your name?" I tried to not make it a challenge.

The fairy pursed his lips and narrowed his gaze. He was on the tall side for a fairy, and equally thin. "Bim."

"Nice to meet you, Bim." I kept my tone pleasant and scanned the dozen majiks in the cavern. All of them had watched the exchange. I'd never been a leader before, even so I stepped up to the line. "Everyone can't go. It would be too difficult to be stealthy."

"And if the human boy comes back, someone has to stay behind." Keltie understood where I was headed.

"If he comes back," a doubter from the back murmured.

"Rye will do what he says." I injected positivity. Even if he accomplished meeting with the prince and regent it didn't mean he had influence. Still, he'd find a way to help. I had to believe in him. I didn't have any other choice.

"The mission will be dangerous." Keltie had gotten them this far and protected them. The warning was fair.

"Sitting here is dangerous." Hokima huffed.

I agreed. I didn't want to die without trying. "I'll take volunteers only. Who is willing to take a risk? To go deeper into the tunnels not knowing where we'll come out?"

Keltie, Tos, and Hokima's hands shot up.

I didn't want to sugarcoat. "This isn't going to be easy. It's risky and we don't know what we'll find on the other side."

Bim raised his hand.

"Okay, then." Pushing away my misgivings, I nodded. "Hokima will lead since he went this way once before."

The troll got on his knees to crawl through the opening. Tos and Bim followed behind.

My lungs expanded, and I took a few satisfying breaths. I was taking a new step on my adventure with new companions I didn't know well. They risked their lives to help me, and I needed to live up to my end of the bargain.

Some way, I'd get them out of this dungeon prison.

Keltie's gaze swept over the remaining majiks. "Good luck to you. With good fortune, the human will rescue you."

"We hope you all survive." Another elf held her hand up and fisted it in a gesture of respect.

Swiping at my eyes, I firmed my resolve. "I don't want to survive. I want to triumph."

This wasn't only about saving Arbor. I needed to rescue these majiks too, and any others we came upon. Gardenia might be starting a revolution, but I was starting a mass escape.

Chapter 13

Crawling through the tunnel, my little speech rang through my head. The ringing became more silent as our little group progressed. The tunnel became darker and colder.

I tripped on the skirt of my dress and my elbow banged the rough rock wall. "Ow." I might need to use another strip of the skirt for myself.

"You okay?" Keltie crawled in front of me, sure and brave.

I wished I could be more like her.

The tunnel got taller. We went from crawling, to stooping, to walking fully erect reminding me of Darwin's Law which I'd been taught in class. I huffed. Returning to school held less and less appeal. I'd learned more tonight about the world and myself, than I'd learned for years with human teachers.

To go back and be restricted on what I could say. To go on pretending I believed what was being taught. To carry on as if none of tonight had ever happened. The thoughts attacked putting chinks in my plans. After a couple of hours, there was a lot of doubt. And too much silence.

Getting to know my companions might inspire trust and pass the time. "Where in the kingdom did you live, Keltie?"

"I lived in Elvenstad in the Metsa Forest." As she walked, the tails of her top swayed with the movement of her hips.

I'd noticed the flowy-cape top covered a tighter material that stretched across her clear, pale skin. Long, bright red hair was tied in a braid going halfway down her back.

My ancestors came from the same forest. "Is that anywhere near where the fairies live?"

Fairies, elves, sprites and brownies shared the forests. Fairies and sprites lived and worked together. The elves and brownies fought over territory with each other and the fairies.

"At one time, there was plenty of forest for the different majiks. For an elf to meet a fairy was rare." She shrugged her elegant shoulders. "Now, with the repatriation of majiks, space is limited, and natural borders are being crossed."

And yet, we worked together. An elf, a brownie, a troll, a fairy, and me. "Repatriation because the majiks are leaving the city and returning home?"

The law basically said the only place a majik could move was back to their natural habitat.

"Forced to leave the city." Bim's chilliness struck like ice. "If a majik loses their city job, which is happening more and more frequently, they are not allowed to get a new job. They're forced to return to their homeland."

"Which makes the habitats more and more crowded." I could picture this happening.

The regent was causing problems he didn't even realize. The ignorant man didn't understand he was creating bigger issues for the future. If the majiks fought for territory, the battles would affect humans.

"Less places to make a home. More people to feed." Keltie twisted around to scrutinize me. Her flawless, white skin glowed in the dark. "More majiks, at least the elves, are getting restless."

"The trolls are agitated and overwrought." Hokima swiveled around to make his point. "There's talk of war."

He sounded like Gardenia. How a war was brewing, and I needed to pick a side. The battles would be magic against the elite's technology. Who had the greatest power? And who would be hurt the most?

I wanted to understand what drove the different majik races. "Are many trolls going home to the mountains?"

The mountains had stood as a sentry behind the castle. Shadowed and foreboding.

"They're trying. They are fearful for their kids." Hokima started trudging forward again. "Trolls believe if they can return the children to the homeland, they will be safe from the humans."

I didn't fully understand the kids' thing. Humans liked kids. Many thought troll children were cute, resembling dolls, while disgusted by the full-size version. Glancing around, I noticed all of us were young. And most of the other majiks in the cavern appeared to be in their teens as well.

Coincidence?

Hokima raised his hand imitating a bird. "The dragons don't like our returning in such large numbers."

Leaning back, I quivered remembering the dragon in the fighting arena. It must've been captured and brought down from the mountains. I understood why the trolls would fear one.

Keltie's braid swished. "Have you ever seen a dragon?"

"When I was a little kid." Hokima sounded far away remembering happier times. "They flew peacefully in our skies. Soaring and majestic. They never injured or killed a troll. Stayed mostly to themselves."

"I want to ride a dragon." Tos jumped up and down. "Do you think I ever could?"

"No!" Keltie and Hokima both shouted.

I was thinking the same thing. Why would anyone want to get close to a dragon? Let alone ride one?

"A dragon isn't an animal to ride." Bim disapproved of everything. "They're majiks like us."

Not with fire-breathing capabilities they weren't like us. The one at the ball could've roasted everyone if it had escaped. "I saw a dragon inside the palace ballroom tonight."

"What was it doing inside a ballroom? Let alone inside a building?" Keltie's shocked tone rang out.

I told them about the arena and the fighting. And about Jayunja.

Hokima stomped a foot before continuing on. "That's why the dragons have been patrolling more heavily. They're being captured by the horrible humans."

The adjective should've gotten a reaction from me. I'd always identified as human. Except I wasn't fully human, and I'd declared myself on my new friends' side.

"Tell me, Elle." Bim shuffled behind Keltie. "Where do you hail from? I haven't heard of many half-fairies."

The insult cut harder than it should, harder than the horrible humans the troll had used. At least Bim didn't call me half breed again.

"I was born in the city of Lindenhamn where my parents lived. My mother was fairy and my father a human."

"Even though you look human, how did you pass for human if you're registered as a majik?" Keltie asked.

"My parents never registered me." My dad must've suspected registering would be the start of more restrictions.

"Where are your parents now?" Tos sniffed. Was she missing her parents?

My legs slowed, and the air weighed heavier. "They both died. My stepmother is my guardian for a few more months."

"Does she know you're in danger?" Keltie was always thinking of others. Especially her team.

My spirits lifted. A team experience that came with new friends and compatriots. Even though we were surrounded by darkness, I was inspired by the light of friendship.

"My stepmother wouldn't care." Although she wouldn't want to lose her slave. I kicked at the ground.

"What was your mother's name?" Bim's shortness didn't upset me. Maybe he could help me learn more about my ancestry.

"Lily Kunglig."

"What is her heritage?" His tone whined higher with either excitement or suspicion. He hurried his pace to catch up to me in the front of the group.

"She's a fairy." *Duh.* I'd explained already.

"No." His irritation and intensity came through in the speed of his reply. "Who are your mother's parents? And her parents before?"

I didn't realize I'd be taking a genealogy quiz. "I don't know. My mom died when I was a toddler and my dad never spoke of her past life."

"Ignorant humans." Bim shook his head and lifted his nose. "When did you come into your magic?"

My cheeks warmed. "A couple of months ago when I turned sixteen."

"Do you prefer wands or enchantments?"

A genealogy quiz and an inquisition.

"Um, I don't know." The warmth burned to scorching. "I haven't been trained."

"What?"

I might as well confess everything. "And my magic doesn't work very well."

His nose went higher. "So not from one of the higher placed families."

Shrugging, I really hadn't cared until this moment. "I don't know."

"Why weren't you trained?" Bim tossed out another question.

I was getting tired of the interrogation. "Because I lived with a human family and was trying to pass as human." The scorching went through my veins shifting into frustration. "I didn't know fairies' powers didn't materialize until they turned sixteen. I didn't think I had any magic."

Another reason I'd wanted to pass as human. What good was being a fairy if you didn't have powers?

"And then my fairy godmother Gardenia showed up on my sixteenth birthday and wanted me to join her."

Bim's gaze widened. He recognized the known fugitive's name.

"Do you know her?" My turn to question.

"We haven't met." He twisted his lips together and looked away. "I've heard of her."

"She's been harassing me ever since." I didn't dare tell them about the Binding Promise I'd made in my stupidity. The team would never follow me anywhere. "Let's keep moving."

I scrambled to the lead because I didn't want any more questions. There were so many things I didn't know about being a fairy. I didn't enjoy feeling ignorant.

"Eep. Eep."

The strange chirping caught my ear. I signaled the others to be quiet.

"Eep. Eep."

The noise came from inside a pit at the bottom of the rock wall in the tunnel.

Slipping out the dagger from my headdress, I braced myself for attack. I peered inside the pit, and my eyes adjusted to the even darker space. Bright red eyes stared back.

"Eep. Eep."

An orange snout bumped against my arm.

"It's a small animal." I stretched my hand out.

Keltie knocked my arm away. "Small animals bite."

"It's so cute." I squealed. "And it's shivering."

Tiny, scaly wings flapped. "Eep."

Ignoring the elf's glare, I picked up the creature. Its rough scales chafed against my skin with its trembling.

Hokima leaned toward me. "It's a baby dragon."

"A dragon!" Tos clapped her hands.

A tiny spurt of flame came out of the dragon's mouth. Tos must've scared it.

"It can breathe fire." Keltie pulled back.

"Only a flicker because it's so young." Hokima demonstrated his affection in his tone. "It's a Wyvern. I'm surprised it's alone. There's usually multiple eggs and the mother is never far from her babies."

The Wyvern dragon wrapped its wings around its body and ducked its head beneath a wing. The entire creature quivered.

"It's freezing." I cradled it closer experiencing an instant, almost-motherly bond.

"Eep." It sounded thankful.

"It's sooooo cute."

"What if the mother is nearby?" The fear in Bim's voice had us glancing around.

"I don't think a grown dragon could fit in this tunnel." I'd seen a fully-grown wyvern dragon at the ball. The animal was as tall as a tree. Was this little guy and the monster related?

Removing my ripped skirt, I used the material to wrap up the dragon trying to get it warmer. The poor guy, or girl, had lost its mother and was now alone in the tunnel.

"Eeeep." The dragon drew the mewl out settling into the material.

Keltie inspected the shorts beneath the skirt. "Nice, and useful."

Too bad the thin fabric wasn't thick enough to warm the dragon. I opened the bag hanging from my shoulder and gently set the dragon inside. "There you go, cutie."

Now our group had a mascot.

"Why was the dragon in the tunnel by itself?" Bim asked.

No one answered.

The baby dragon wasn't mean like the one in the arena. It was cold and afraid. Lonely. Things I could relate to. "Let's call it Drago, short for dragon."

With a few mutterings, we continued on.

The tunnel became wider forming into a subterranean grotto. Stalactites and stalagmites grew from the floor and ceiling. The rounded room had several tunnels leading from it. Which one should we take?

We stopped in the center. Keltie scanned each of the tunnels.

"Do you think the mother dragon could fit in any of the other tunnels?" Bim's voice trembled.

"Let's hope not." Clutching the purse to my side, I peered in each of the tunnels. All of them were as small as the one we'd traveled. All were dark. All appeared to round off around a corner. "Hokima, any ideas?"

The troll shook his head. "Everything looks the same."

"Eep." Drago lifted his head out of the bag. "Eep. Eep."

"Let's just pick one." Keltie clipped her words.

Debating, I pivoted on my feet about to use the childhood game of *Eenie Meanie Miney Troll.* Which would be politically incorrect in this situation.

A harsh war cry pierced the silence.

My heart rushed up my throat.

A human war cry.

At least it wasn't the mother dragon.

Chapter 11

Time slowed as I processed the sound. Or should I say sounds?

A second war cry. Boots stomping on the ground with threatening force. The crackling of radio communication pinching my ears. Deep voices echoing off the cavern walls. The noise wasn't coming from more escaping majiks.

My muscles tightened. "Thoughts?"

"We can't go back. It might lead them to the others." Keltie spoke fast holding the stick in front of her, ready to attack.

"If we run, we'll make too much commotion." Hokima growled and raised his fists. He probably wasn't much of a runner, either.

Tos wound between our legs. "We don't know how many are coming."

"Maybe they'll go a different way." Bim flicked his fingers as if he could do magic.

I wish.

There were no nooks and crannies to hide in. No way to be certain which way they were coming from. No way to save ourselves except to stand our ground and fight. Yanking the dagger from my hairpiece again, I tried to fortify my shaking knees.

The five of us scurried into the center of the room, backs to each other in a defensive position. Depending on how many people, maybe, just maybe, we could take them. It was our only hope.

The stomping and crackling and voices came from every tunnel. Advancing.

My heart rushed like my feet wanted to. I stayed planted in position.

Shapes emerged from each of the tunnels in a coordinated fashion like a sweep. Wearing SCUM uniforms with their large bills and neon stripes, ten guards surrounded us.

My rushing heart dropped into my stomach weighing me down. Terrible odds.

The guards held guns with long, thin shafts. Instead of a cartridge for bullets, a bulb held liquid that sloshed with their movements. New weapons I'd never seen on the streets.

I gasped and blew out a breath, as if by breathing I proved I was alive. At least for the moment.

Keltie raised her stick preparing to strike. Hokima stood his ground. Had I led my new friends into a slaughter? I ground my teeth together. What was I thinking believing I could lead?

"Zaubers." An older guard with gray hair and beard charged toward us. He wasn't afraid of our powers which must mean he knew we couldn't use magic. The humans must've done something to strangle our powers beneath the palace.

"Aiea!" Keltie's distinctive battle cry echoed in the chamber. She blocked the guard and pushed him back. The old man fell to the ground and his face reddened. She wasn't giving up.

Neither was I.

"Get them!" The old man yelled from his spot on the ground.

Another guard took on Hokima and Bim. Hokima threw a punch. The guard evaded. Bim broke off a stalagmite and poked him in the eye. With no magic, they fought with whatever they could.

"My eye!" the guard screamed.

Another moved in to take his place.

I swung my dagger toward the guy moving closer to me. He resembled a rock.

"Oof." I swung and missed.

The Rock jumped away from my slice on quick feet. He had one stripe on his uniform which meant he wasn't high up the ladder. He didn't appear to be much older than me.

"Careful. They're teens." He stared at me sending a frisson of warning across my skin.

Was the warning tone for me or the other guards?

Battle noises clanged. Other guards tramped in to fight my friends. They surrounded us with their advanced techno weapons. We had nothing but our muscles and our wits.

Tos ran up and kicked my pursuer.

I stand corrected. We had our determination and grit.

The Rock wasn't fazed by the brownie's kick. He was tall, and big, and buff for a guy only a couple years older than me. He probably overdosed on banned steroids.

Two guards held Hokima down. Keltie held her hands up in surrender. Her stick was broken in two and lying at her feet. Bim lay on the ground. Tos and I were pressed against a wall by Rock.

We were surrounded. Ten guards against the five of us, blocking the exits. Our battle hadn't lasted long.

"Don't move." Rock's deep voice held authority. The muscles on his arms bunched.

Click, click, click. The guards prepped their weapons. Pointed.

My heart clacked at the sound.

"This won't hurt." Rock's assurance didn't assure.

I froze in place. My friends did the same. There was nowhere to go. I was too young to die. We all were. And poor Arbor. She'd never know I'd tried to save her, that I cared about her.

The weapons fired. Streams of electric light shot from the nozzle. The streams curved and waved in varying colors of blue and purple and red. The colors wove toward us.

Bracing for death, my last thought wasn't of my family or Arbor or my new friends. It was of Rye. I'd never get to dance with him. Never get to see his smile again. Never get a second kiss.

As the red color hurled toward me, I swung my bag away from the light trying to protect the dragon. Maybe it could live by sneaking out of my bag when my body fell to the ground. The light hit my torso and I felt...

Nothing?

I slapped my hand against my chest and stomach. I was alive. What about everyone else? "Keltie?"

"Yes?" Her confusion made me worry.

"You're okay?" I wanted to make sure. "Tos? Hokima? Bim?"

"You're all fine." The old man got back on his feet and spit. "Stupid Zaubers."

"The tasers take away your will to fight. Much better than the serum." Rock's even-tempered tone made him seem nice, except he was SCUM and I couldn't let my guard down.

"Don't get ahead of yourself." The old man's reprimand of Rock caused him to narrow his glance.

He wanted to respond. Instead, he faced me and my

friends. "Hand us your weapons." He said the word weapons with his lips twitching. Was he making fun of us? "Now."

Keltie slapped the broken stick in his large hand.

I tossed my dagger to the ground. "What do you want with us?"

Rock picked up my weapon and studied me. If he wasn't a human and a jerk, he'd be attractive. "What're you doing in the tunnels beneath the palace?"

My skin tingled. It wasn't a foreboding-bad tingle, more of a wary sensation. Was it the effect of the taser gun?

"They're a group of dirty, teen zaubers." The old man grabbed Tos, avoiding Keltie's wrath. "More power for the regent's auraguillotine."

The repetition of the machine name sent a crisp shiver down my spine even though I didn't understand what the machine did. Just the fact that it was real was terrifying.

"What does the auraguillotine do?" If I was going to die, I wanted to know how.

My friends cringed. They knew or had heard stories. The guards' cruel chortle echoed through the chamber and sent goosebumps racing across my skin.

Even Rock choked. "You'll find out soon enough. Take them."

One of the guards' hands clasped around my shoulder. His fingers dug into my skin and signaled my demise. "This one is human."

I bit my lip and my thoughts ground against each other. If the guards believed I was one of them they'd let me go. Then, I could find a way to help my new friends and save Arbor.

"Magic." The old man scoffed and veered away, not really looking at me.

Okay, maybe they wouldn't believe I was human. Probably best to stay with my new friends. I opened my mouth and slammed it shut. Although, if I was set free, I could help. Somehow.

"Magic doesn't work down here." Rock ogled me again, making my entire body prickle.

I squirmed from the uncomfortable attention.

Now, we understood why none of our powers worked. Some type of magic containment system resembling the sprayers the SCUM had used at my house. And if magic didn't work down here it meant I couldn't be using a glamor which meant…

"He's right. I'm not a majik. I'm human!"

Keltie sucked in making a low whistle. Hokima snorted. Bim's eyes popped in surprise. And Tos dropped her jaw open.

"What?" The hurt in the brownie's voice dug the deepest.

I'd pulled the human card and they felt betrayed. A dark cloud enveloped me. I never would've claimed being human if the guard hadn't made the suggestion. I saw a way out and fallen back on the lie I'd lived my entire life. Smashing my lips together, I wished I could take back the claim. And yet, maybe if they let me go, I could help my friends.

The old guard leered. "What're you doing underneath the palace where the prison is located, girly."

"I was searching for a friend."

My new friends' expressions grew hostile.

"Right." He smirked. I was sure he'd heard plenty of lies before.

"I can prove I'm human." I spoke fast out of desperation and remorse. It was too late to take back my words. I needed to push forward even if my friends didn't understand. Everyone who saw me believed I was human. I'd passed for sixteen years. "I was at the ball. I'm wearing a ball gown."

I peered at my dirty top and where the skirt should've been. Only the shorts existed with most of my legs showing.

Rock leered at my bare legs and shrugged. "Doesn't matter. You were helping the zaubers escape." His tone went hard and unforgiving.

Similar to my friends' glances when I peered at them. Their gazes changed to glares and I became a target on both sides. Was I being selfish or smart? I scrubbed a hand across my face regretting my plan and yet pushing forward.

"We were heading deeper into the prison." I forced myself to speak slow so the guards would understand. "If we were trying to escape, we'd be going the other way."

"Not my problem zaubers are so stupid they don't know which way is out." The old man's bias tore at my insides.

They didn't believe I was human. My friends were mad because I'd claimed the status. My betrayal hadn't helped and had made things worse.

Twisting away, I broke the guard's hold and took a swing. My fist connected with his stomach and pain billowed through my fingers. The guard doubled over. I took a step ready to run when the same guard grabbed my arm and jerked me back. Stumbling, I fell to the ground and scraped my knee.

"I've got her." Rock's hands gripped my arms and he lifted me to my feet, and away from the now-angry guard.

"Why wasn't her will to fight taken away?" the angry guard asked.

"I must not have connected to her body correctly with my aim." Rock spoke through gritted teeth. He must hate admitting doing something wrong.

Had he done it on purpose? First, the weird warning and now missing me on purpose? By his actions, I'd guess he was normally a perfect shot.

"What do you mean by will to fight?" Because my will to fight was strong. I tried to jerk away, jostling my bag.

"Eep."

"Fine. I'll go peacefully." I didn't want the dragon to face the same fate. He was only a baby. "This bag is strangling me. Can I take it off and leave it?"

A thick blond brow curved in question. Rock's gaze went from me to my small bag. He nodded.

I slipped the bag from around my neck and shoulder knowing I was throwing away any future magic. Saving Drago was more important.

"Eep. Eep."

"What's making that yelp?" The old man quirked his head to listen.

"Nothing." I set the bag down on the ground.

The old man handed Tos to another guard and stomped over to me. "Pick it up."

Was the old man afraid it was a trick? A magical explosion or something that would help us escape.

"Pick it up!" He yelled.

I glanced at Rock and he jerked his head down in an almost imperceptible nod. Bending down, I picked the bag back up wishing the dragon would be quiet.

The old guard ripped it out of my hand and opened the bag. "A dragon?"

"She's got a dragon in her bag?" Rock's other eyebrow rose.

"It's a baby." I ached for the tiny creature. "Drago won't harm anyone."

"Drago?" Rock's smirk showed his amusement. He thought I was ridiculous for naming the dragon.

"This is the escaped baby dragon we were looking for." The old man held the bag out as if it was toxic. "It was born earlier than expected and snuck away."

"Smart Drago." Maybe he'd find another way to escape. I certainly wasn't any help.

Rock took the bag from his superior. "The *only* reason we were in the tunnels." His tone sent a message.

To me?

Why did I sense he was trying to send me secret messages? He was my enemy.

"Now, we can kill two birds with one stone. Or at least at one time." The old man's triumph rang in his voice. He took a position in front of the group. "Let's get them back to where they belong."

We trudged forward. Worry zipped through my midsection and zinged across my skin. I didn't want the dragon hurt and didn't want the purse to become magical again. My friends hated me, and we were going to die. I'd never see Arbor again. And Rye would return to the cavern and wonder what had happened.

At least, I hoped he wondered.

Dragging my feet, I slowed our progress and the two of us fell behind the group. I tried to tug out of Rock's grip. He held me tight.

"Play it cool." His whisper was so light I wasn't sure I'd heard.

"Excuse me?"

"The Compliance Taser doesn't work as well on half majiks."

I sucked in a breath. He knew.

"You can't get away so stop trying." His voice went loud, and his fingers dug in tight.

His scent of evergreen wove around me, making me more relaxed. Which was ridiculous. I needed to be afraid of him. He was one of the most handsome humans I'd seen with his chiseled chin and strong cheekbones. His thick blond hair looped in front of his face. Even though I liked Rye, I could appreciate this guy's looks. The two of them were opposites in appearances and prejudices.

Rock was SCUM and holding me prisoner. Rye had influence in the palace and wanted to help. He'd been sweet and nice and protective. Rock had shot me with the Compliance Taser. His messy blond hair and hard green eyes reeked of authority and superiority. Rye's long, dark hair had burnished highlights at the end as if he'd been kissed from the sun above.

Jerking my arm again, I needed to stop thinking of Rock like a vid star. He was the enemy. And yet, something about him was different. The veins around his thick neck were greener than the usual purple of bodybuilders. And how could he have a scent if he'd been hunting for the dragon underground?

"What's your name?" I needed to get my mind off his handsomeness and dig for information. Maybe finding out a human's name was an advantage, too.

"Stone."

A laugh gurgled out of my lungs. My nickname hadn't been too far off.

He flashed an annoyed glance. "What's so funny?"

Bim watched us. Keltie did too, giving an aggressive scowl. They must still be angry at me for saying I was human.

"Your name."

Stone tilted his chin up. "Nothing's wrong with my name."

"It's so descriptive of you."

His lips lifted in an egotistical grin. "Thank you."

Way to boost the enemy's ego. I berated myself. "In an ugly, stone-stupid kind of way."

"Ouch. That hurt." He didn't look hurt. He looked as if nothing could hurt him.

The rest of the journey I stayed silent, stewing in my thoughts. The more I thought the more my gut churned with emotions. Fear because I didn't know what would happen to us. Sadness for Arbor and my new friends for suffering the same fate. Humiliation because of our easy defeat.

The tunnel grew wider and taller with a metaloid door. The old man opened the door and led us inside.

"Welcome to the holding cell for the auraguillotine." Stone released me and pushed forward.

I blinked at the brightness of the room.

Steel walls and a shiny floor glared from the brilliant lights built into the ceiling. The sterile room reminded me of a hospital or a laboratory. The antiseptic smell burned my nostrils. The metaloid door on the opposite side had a small window. My friends and I filled up the space.

Not a caring place. Or even a comfortable one. I wrapped my arms around myself.

"Don't get too cozy. You won't be here long." The old man took out a set of remote keys. "Welcome to the end of your lives."

Chapter 15

After the guards left, the memory of the old man's cackling laughter echoed in the sterile environment giving me a headache. The entire night had gone from one bad scenario to another. And now everything was worse. I was a captive in the palace's infamous holding cell waiting to be tortured by an auraguillotine, the stuff of legends.

I pounded my fist into the wall, unsure if it was frustration or the will to get out. At least I still had my will. The others had just marched alongside the guards as if on a stroll.

"Way to flirt with the enemy." Keltie's haughty tone caught me off guard. Her angry red cheeks matched her hair. She scampered to the other side of the small, sterile-smelling cell.

"Flirt?" I didn't even know how to flirt.

"I saw you giggling with him."

I expected them to be angry for trying to pass myself off as human, not for flirting. I wasn't about to explain the reason for my laughter. "I was digging for information."

"What did you find out?" Bim's wings flapped, clearly distressed.

My shoulders slumped knowing I'd achieved nothing. "Only his name. Stone."

Bim stopped his flapping. "Stone?"

Hokima slumped onto the ground with a dire expression. "Just like a human trying to save their own skin."

"I'm not human." The room was cold, but the other majiks were colder. I understood why. I'd denied my majik heritage after claiming I was one of them. After asking them to trust me because I was a fairy.

"That's not what you told the guards." Tos, who'd believed in me from our first meeting, now doubted.

"I know and I'm sorry." Heat plowed through me making my knees weak. "The one guard believed I was human, and I thought…" My head dropped. "I thought if they let me go, I'd be able to save my friend and—"

"Your old friend is more important than your new friends." Keltie crossed her thin arms and faced the metal wall. "We understand."

Hokima joined the elf by the wall, turning his back to me. So did Bim and Tos. My new friends hated me. My eyes burned. I didn't know how to make it up to them. I hadn't meant anything negative about them by my claim.

"I said it to help all of us." I stepped closer and hung my head. "And I've been pretending to be human for so long it was a natural reaction. It won't happen again."

"Because we're not going to live much longer." Hokima with his death-and-gloom outlook didn't seem so wrong.

"Forgive me." Blinking, I forced the wetness in my eyes away. "I didn't mean to hurt any of you. If we're going to die, then please, please forgive me before we do."

No response.

Shivering, I hugged myself and paced away. I couldn't promise to help them in the future because there'd be no future. I couldn't convince them I was one of them. I paced toward them again. Each of their profiles were so different. The tiny brownie. The skinny fairy. The stout troll. And the brave and muscular elf.

So different and yet we'd worked together.

The thought gave me hope. Even though my friends and I might die, maybe the majiks in the kingdom would learn to work together. If our small group could do it, so could others.

Pivoting, I paced the other way. Arbor had left her habitat because her home had been destroyed by trolls. Legally, she wasn't supposed to come to the city. She'd found me, and I'd helped her. Not as much as she'd helped me.

Becoming my best friend, my one ally, my tutor in the ways of the majiks.

I hadn't been a willing student. I'd resisted learning about fairies. She'd managed to slip in a lesson here and there. She'd talked about the powers of Mother Earth. She'd been there when my powers activated. She'd defended me. Most important, she'd made me laugh.

My lungs squeezed, and I stumbled. I'd never find her. I'd failed my best friend. Was I going to fail my new friends too?

Pressing my hand against the wall, I closed my eyes trying to get a grip. I couldn't give up. Rye was going to talk to the prince and regent. He planned to better the conditions of the prisoners if he couldn't secure their release. I only hoped he made things better before my time was up.

Bim swished to where I slumped against the opposite wall. He surveyed me as though he was seeing me for the first time.

I wiggled, trying to get him to un-focus. "Why are you willing to be seen near me? Won't they get angry? Believe you're a traitor?" I couldn't help sounding harsh. I'd apologized, I'd begged, and they were still mad.

They thought my claiming human status was a betrayal to them. Just as I'd betrayed Arbor by not finding a way to prove my guilt. My throat thickened and my mouth went dry.

Keltie leaned against the wall with her eyes closed. Tos and Hokima sat on the ground whispering between them.

"Us fairies have to stick together." Bim tugged on my crossed arms.

"You're not mad at me for claiming to be human?"

"I'm trying to figure you out." His curious gaze continued to study me, imitating a teacher or a scientist, puzzling out things by observation.

I shifted on my feet trying to get comfortable with being dissected by inspection and questions. "Not much to figure out. I'd planned to pass as human for the rest of my life until my best friend was arrested for doing something I did."

"The fireworks?"

"And music."

He ticked a thin finger on his chin. "You didn't come into your powers until you were sixteen. That makes you a Fire Fairy."

I jerked back. "I didn't know there were different types of fairies."

"Of course. The types are based on the elements you get your power from." He counted on his fingers. "Water Fairies, Air Fairies, Earth Fairies, and Fire Fairies, just as there are different types of trolls and sprites and elves."

Mind blown. Most humans had a hard enough time distinguishing a troll from an ogre or a sprite from a wisp. To actually categorize different types of the majiks would boggle their minds. It boggled mine. Arbor had taught me sprites and fairies were related.

"If you're a Fire Fairy, your mother must hail from Fae Forest."

I remembered hearing my dad talk about Fae Forest. We'd visited a park once near the entrance. Arbor had said something about the area, too. I couldn't remember what. My interest peaked. Too bad it was too late to learn about my mom and her heritage.

Shrugging, I pretended nonchalance because I was unsure if Bim had actually forgiven me. "What type of fairy are you?"

"I'm an Earth Fairy. We get our powers at birth." A slight nod had his hair moving up and down. "That's why you could fit into the human world so easily. As a child with powers lots of mistakes happen."

I thought about the magical mishaps I'd had since receiving my powers. "What about as a Fire fairy? Do mistakes happen when they get their magic even though they're older?"

Was I normal? Or a really bad fairy? Or did mishaps happen because I was only half fairy?

He tapped his finger again. "There's usually a few, but with training…"

I remembered Gardenia's nagging and rolled my eyes.

"With training mistakes can be controlled." Bim must've noticed the eye roll because his voice went harsher. "Training is important to every type of fairy. We need strong fairies to rule and guard our empire."

"Rule?" I choked. I'd never even considered the order of succession for fairies or any other majiks assuming they were ruled by Regent Theobald. "Who rules the fairy empire now?"

"Our queen is aging." Bim's frown communicated more than sadness. "The Fairy Commander is mostly in charge because the queen's three daughters died unexpectedly."

Empathizing with the queen, I understood loss. I'd lost a mother and a father. To lose three daughters must be terrible. "What about the king? Or their sons?"

"Succession is through the female line. It's a matriarchal society."

Go girl power!

His gaze clouded. "Although because of the deaths of the queen's daughters there's been discussion of letting a male grandchild assume the role when the queen passes."

"What do the fairies think of that?" Was trouble brewing in the fairy empire? Better to learn as much as possible if I decided to join their ranks. If I lived.

"Most aren't happy. I mean, consider the human world with their male succession. Regent Theobald has been a disaster. And the new prince has been mostly brought up by the man." Bim shivered. "Things will only get worse for the majiks."

"Rye thought the prince would be different." I hoped he was right.

Bim's disbelieving snort scraped across my skin. "Your boyfriend is clueless."

Keltie pivoted. Her one eyebrow raised in a question. She understood we had nothing to laugh about.

"Rye is not my boyfriend. We just met." Saying his name tugged at my heart. He was special, and we'd kissed. I didn't know if he'd care that I was half-fairy. He'd wanted to help the majiks. And yet, if I survived and announced my fairy-side, would he want to be with me? And wouldn't having a human boyfriend make me more different from the other majiks?

Why was I even thinking about him as a boyfriend? For the little I knew, he could kiss girls all the time.

"There is hope." Bim avoided my gaze. "There are rumors of a granddaughter."

A sliding noise had me stiffening. The locked door opened, and dread rose like bile in my throat. Was it time?

The other fairy's eyes flipped wide open and his lips slammed shut. Someone backed into the cell.

Turning, Stone faced us. Sweat formed on his forehead and his hair was in disarray. He scanned the room stopping at me.

I swallowed. My thoughts ran around in panicked circles. It was time to die and I was going to be first.

"Here comes your *other* boyfriend." Keltie's smirk contradicted the fear on her face. She was worried this was the end for us. She must've been listening to Bim and my entire conversation. With her elf ears that shouldn't have surprised me.

Scowling, I glared back. I did not want them thinking I'd betrayed them or flirted with the enemy. "He's not my boyfriend."

For a second, Stone's brow furrowed. Wiping the expression off his face, he stormed toward me. Even with his bulk, he moved like a commando. His muscles rippled beneath the guard uniform and his broad chest demonstrated strength. Why would Keltie think for one second this masculine specimen would be interested in me? He must be two to three years older.

He clicked the weapon in his hand and grabbed my arm. "Let's go. Quietly."

My pulse stuttered to a stop and then raced ahead of my mind. Not a chance. I refused to be taken to my death without speaking. Unfortunately, I couldn't think of anything eloquent to say as my final words. Instead, I opened my mouth to scream.

Before I could utter a single sound, his large hand clamped over my lips. "Quiet. Don't want the guards to hear and wake up."

I closed my mouth too shocked to speak. "You're a guard."

Okay, not that shocked.

Keltie raised both eyebrows. Bim scrambled away because he probably didn't want to be taken with me. Tos and Hokima leaned forward interested in the exchange.

"The guards watching your cell are asleep." Stone spoke through gritted teeth. He removed his hand from my mouth. "Let's go."

"Go where?" I refused to lead my new friends into a slaughter. As their infamous leader, I'd already gotten them captured. I needed details.

"Escape." His single word response sent a jolt through my body.

"You're helping?"

"You're certainly not helping yourself." His smug expression was emphasized by the upward tilt of strong, male lips.

I wanted to slap him for teasing at a life or death moment.

Quirking my head, I studied those lips and those eyes. "How do I know I can trust you?"

"You don't have much choice."

Another person taking away my choices. He seemed an okay guy. He'd told me why the weapon hadn't affected me like the others. But, honest? He was SCUM, and huge and threatening, and too good-looking. And he wore a palace guard uniform.

He tapped the weapon against his shoulder. "Why don't you take your time with your decision? The guards will wake up in a few minutes and we'll both be stuck."

Right. We needed to go with him. And if he was lying, we'd find a way to escape from him later. The five of us could fight one guy. Couldn't we?

I glanced at my friends. Hokima's gloppy eyes appeared wary. Bim's chin raised with confidence. He'd trust my decision. Tos stood on her toes ready to run either with me or against me. Keltie's crossed arms and angled chin exhibited she was waiting for my answer too.

Nodding at our would-be rescuer, I uncrossed my arms and pointed at the elf. "I told you I wasn't flirting with the enemy. Stone is helping us escape."

"Only you." His always hard expression went harder. His gaze narrowed to slits. "Time's ticking."

My stomach rolled. Why would he want only me? With more majiks fighting at his side we'd have a better chance of escape.

Keltie's eyebrows went even harder, challenging me. Tos quivered and leaned into Hokima's fat legs. Bim's gaze veered back and forth between me and Stone.

I couldn't leave them behind. I'd already betrayed them once by claiming my humanity. They'd agreed to follow me on this journey without knowing me, putting themselves in additional danger. "I'm not going without my friends."

"They don't look like your friends to me." Stone must've analyzed the situation in the cell when he'd barged in. He'd seen how far from me they stood and their hostile glares. He'd sensed the tension and heard Keltie's cruel banter.

Determination to not only prove to my friends I cared, but I was with them, hardened in my fairy blood. I was committed to being a majik and helping the majik cause. I might've hurt them, I wouldn't abandon them. We would live or die together.

"We're a team." I took a deep, calming breath. "My friends come, or I don't."

Chapter 16

The silence stretched. The quiet, crowded cell held its collective breath.

Stone's large brow furrowed, and his lips pinched. His carved cheekbones didn't flinch. His body appeared petrified. He thought I was crazy.

Maybe I was. I'd been called crazy before. Had that been only earlier tonight?

My bones hardened and I tilted my chin to a righteous angle. This was right. These majiks, my new friends, were worth saving.

"Don't be stupid, Elle." Keltie crossed the distance. "This guy is offering you freedom."

My other friends nodded.

"I wouldn't feel free if I left you guys behind." I stood my ground. Arbor was important and so were my new friends. And right now, looking at the odds, I had a much better chance of saving them than Arbor.

"Why are you siding with us now?" Hokima grumped.

"I've always been on your side." I needed them to understand my dedication to them and the majik cause. "I hadn't fully realized it until very recently."

"She's helping." Tos tugged on the hem of my shorts. "We can argue about logistics and loyalties later."

"Tos is right." Keltie glared at Stone. Her stares had power. Not magical power, the power of persuasion. "Well?"

Bim, Tos, and Hokima glared at Stone, too. Their gazes weren't as challenging, but they were effective.

Stone held their looks. He knew I was half-majik, so prejudice wasn't the reason for only wanting to rescue me. Who would blink first? It wasn't about winning. It was about convincing.

"My friends matter." My voice revved up with purpose and passion. "*All* majiks matter."

He stiffened, and an expression of shock crossed his face. Somehow, I'd touched a nerve. His shoulders dipped giving in and agreeing in one smooth move. "Fine. Help me drag the guards into the cell."

My chin dropped. He'd conceded easier than expected.

Keltie nodded, a thin smile on her lips. Hokima actually grinned. Tos and Bim cheered, clapping their hands together.

"Shh!" Stone put a finger to his lips. He tossed a death glower my way, telling me if we got caught, it would be my fault.

He wore a guard's uniform. If we got caught, he could say he was recapturing us. Why was he helping? Although, now was not the time to ask or dissuade. We were taking a chance by trusting him. We had no other options.

As I followed behind him through the cell door, tension seeped into my bones. My stomach tied into tight knots and fancy bows. If we got caught, would we be killed on the spot? Probably better than this auraguillotine.

The area outside the cell reminded me of a hospital nurse's station. Except instead of the large hospital doors, there were strong, metaloid, locked doors with a small window similar to ours. Several guards lay on the ground or dozed in chairs near the console at the center of the room.

Tos reached for a bowl of grapes sitting in front of one of the sleeping guards.

"Don't." Stone slapped her hand away. "Sleeping potion."

Interesting the human used majik potions in his scheme.

He shrugged at my inspection. "Grapes are a rare treat under the palace." He picked up a guard and lay him over his shoulder. "Hurry, before shift change."

Hokima used his strength and picked up a second guard. Keltie dragged a third guard, pulling him from underneath his arms.

I wrapped my hands beneath another guard's shoulders and dragged him toward the open cell door. Tos helped by lifting a leg.

"This would've taken forever if I had been the only one helping you." Already my friends proved their value.

"I would've left the guards where they slept. When they woke, they wouldn't have noticed one majik missing from a cell. They'll notice all of you gone." Stone's sharp nose turned up making me feel the size of a full-fledged fairy.

Short and inconsequential.

"We should take the guards' weapons." Keltie was already taking a gun from its holster.

"Yes." His agreement had everyone stealing the sleeping guards' weapons.

After Hokima and Stone got the last two guards in the cell, he slammed the door shut. "Exit is this way."

I stood on my tiptoes trying to peer inside the window of another door. "What's in these other cells?"

"Majik prisoners." He shoved a weapon in my hand and trekked toward the hallway on the far side of the room.

I didn't move because my speech of *all majiks mattered* reverberated in my head. "We should let them out."

My friends stopped and stared, their mouths open. Did they think I was crazy or brave? The question of the day. Maybe I was a little of both.

Stone halted and turned in a slow pivot controlling his response. "No."

"Why not? You've got the keys." I pointed at them jangling from his waist. "We could free the majiks in this area."

He stomped to me and grabbed my arm. His fingers dug into my skin setting off a heated reaction. Because his grip hurt. "I wasn't planning on rescuing an additional four majiks. You're my priority."

I jerked trying to get away from him. "Why?"

Dropping my arm, he scowled. He ran a hand through long blond hair. I could tell he wasn't used to having his orders challenged.

"If I manage to get five of you out alive, I promise I'll come back and release the others." His green eyes held integrity, not their usual laughing-at-me humor. His broad lips flatlined and his chin jutted out with determination. "Just no more questions."

My friends' gazes swung back and forth between the two of us.

"Okay." I had to believe he'd keep his word. "Why am I a priority?"

"I said no more questions."

Maybe this gorgeous hunk was attracted to me. I'd dazzled him with my wit when we'd been captured, and he wanted to help me. Yeah, right. That would be a first. Besides, Rye was the guy of my dreams.

Stomping interrupted my egotistical thoughts.

"Guard change. Hurry. They're going to discover you're missing earlier than expected and raise the alarm." He grabbed my arm again and tugged me toward the front of the pack. "Follow me and keep quiet."

The grip on my arm didn't feel like an interested male's hands. Not that with my very-limited experience I'd know. He didn't look back with longing as we traipsed down the hallway. He made rapid strides, dragging me along for the ride.

As if I was a package.

The hallway resembled the cells. Sterile, shiny, and cold.

The stomping feet echoed through the corridor, getting closer.

My hands became clammy gripping the gun. Why were we walking toward the noise made by the guards' feet? We should be running in the other direction. Did Stone not understand the danger? He'd promised to get me out, yet he could be leading me to my death. I'd trusted Rye too, and I had no idea where he was or if he was truly helping the majiks stuck under the palace and in its prison. I had no experience with guys, no instincts.

I considered my friends standing behind me. Their expressions didn't display doubt. They were confident in me and my trust in Stone. I gave a hesitant nod.

He plastered his back to the wall and pulled me against him. "*Hvitspyd.*"

A swear word. Had to be by the intensity and the tension radiating off his hard body.

My stomach tangled, pulling tight. "What's happening?"

"Guards are ahead of schedule and we're behind ours." His eyes narrowed, and he glared at my friends.

My chin quivered. I'd caused us to be behind whatever schedule he'd had. In my defense, I didn't know we had a schedule.

He turned to my friends, concern written between the high cheekbones and strong chin. "Can you guys fight without magic because magic would send off a warning?"

Keltie huffed and cocked her gun. It had been her brilliant idea to take the weapons. "Of course."

Hokima took a fighting stance and held up his stolen weapon.

Bim nodded, his wings fluttering.

Tos shook her head. *No.*

"It's easy. Shoot anyone you see." Stone slipped the large automatic rifle over his head and demonstrated how to use it. "We'll need to surprise them. I have a special job for Bim."

Bim scooted ahead and the two of them whispered frantically for a few seconds. The fairy's face visibly paled when he snuck a glance at me.

My gaze narrowed. How was I involved in this discussion?

The fairy nodded, his bony head moving up and down several times. He took a position in front of the group.

Stone signaled to continue walking. "Can you fight, Ellery?"

"Did you not see me against the guards in the tunnel?" I took an offended tone. I'd fought valiantly against him.

"I did. That's why I asked." The egotistical grin on his face made me want to kick him.

"This isn't a game. And this isn't a time for joking."

"Killing someone isn't easy." His knowing voice spoke volumes. He'd killed before and it had affected him. "I might be only eighteen, but I've witnessed more death than you can imagine."

I put a hand on his arm. I might not have killed anyone before, but I understood death.

"I don't need your sympathy." He pushed my hand off. "Just stay behind me, princess."

My jaw locked. I wanted to shoot him with the weapon.

He thought I was a spoiled princess when I'd been slaving every day of my life. I'd show him I was tough.

Gripping the weapon tighter, I prowled forward staying a little behind him. He led the way because if the other guards saw him in uniform, they wouldn't immediately realize this was an ambush. Hokima and Keltie hugged the wall on the far side. Tos was slightly hidden by the group. Her gun pointed straight ahead ready for action.

A dozen guards marched this way in their menacing caps and stomping boots. They talked and joked even though they must know the majiks in custody were headed toward their demise. The one in the front waved to Stone.

No. Blood throbbed through my veins. He wouldn't betray us now. He wouldn't arm us with weapons if he was going to turn us in.

Moving ahead, he lifted his arm in what appeared to be a wave. His arm swung out and he clobbered the head guy. He made it appear effortless.

The guard collapsed to the ground.

The other guards froze. Questions and confusion stamped on their expressions. They glanced at one another as if they didn't know how to respond. Stone must've taken out their leader. Those few seconds gave us an advantage.

Stone pushed me back and signaled for the others to take a position and start shooting.

Zap. Zap. Zap.

A couple of guards went down. The ones standing took cover, ducking and lowering their bodies to the ground in defensive positions. They grabbed their weapons and answered our attack.

Tos let off round after round hitting the guards solidly in the chest. She had great aim. Hokima and Keltie worked together on the opposite side of the hall. Bim fiddled with something in his hand—it wasn't a gun. Their will to fight must've returned. Good to know the Compliance Taser didn't do permanent damage.

"Now, Bim!" Stone shouted. "I'll cover."

The fairy scrambled forward dodging bullets and strays of light. A bullet whizzed past Bim's head and hit his wing. He stumbled to the floor. Time sharpened to a point, slowing to a crawl.

What the heck was he doing? He wasn't firing back, just running forward.

I let off a volley of shouts and started to move toward him. "Bim!"

Stone yanked me back and I fell. Dazed, I sat for a second. I'd been trying to help the other fairy in his foolish charge. He'd been kind to me when the others were mad. We had a special fairy bond.

Chaos reigned through the lens of the floaty sensation in my head. Action seemed to slow. Stone, Keltie, Hokima, and Tos continued the battle, firing shot after shot after shot. The guards returned fire. The bullets and lasers zoomed in both directions of the hallway, more spectacular than the fireworks I'd conjured.

A large hand reached out. The close-up view of dark skin with greenish veins and thick fingers with trim nails snapped me out of my stupor. The hand was real. The bullets were real. The fighting was real.

I grabbed the hand and let Stone pull me back on my feet. Time sped up faster. Getting my head back in the non-game, I focused on the battle. I needed to do a better job protecting myself and my friends.

Bim crawled forward. Stone volleyed around the fairy with his weapon, trying to protect. The other majiks held off the guards. I joined in the fray, shooting recklessly.

It was like watching an inch worm as Bim dragged himself toward the main group of guards holding a defensive position. A loud shot rang out. The fairy collapsed, and blood spurted from his wound.

He'd been shot.

Horror bulleted inside me as if I'd been shot. The emotional pain blasted, and I wavered. A sudden coldness hit my core.

With jerky movements, Bim reached for the wound on his chest. But instead of pressing against the gaping hole trying to stop the flow of blood, his hand slipped into his pocket. He pulled out a round, shiny disc and tossed it into the middle of the guards' formation.

An explosion rocked the hallway.

A high-pitched wailing screamed through my ears. Torment coursed through my veins and raced toward my heart, revving the beat. I pushed my feet into the floor trying to stay standing.

The remaining guards fell. Shouts of agony rent the hallway. I couldn't tell who was screaming. The deafening blast had decimated the guards. Not one of them moved. They were all dead.

Stone tugged me against him. The evergreen scent of him calmed, made me feel safe. Through his clothes I felt his galloping heart. It beat as fast as mine. What kind of weapon had Bim set off?

Bim.

My pulse came to a screeching halt, and then picked up its pace. I struggled against Stone's grip to free myself and stumbled toward the fairy. Dropping to my knees, I placed a hand on Bim's wound. "Are you okay?"

His pale skin appeared paler than possible. His breathing labored. The acidic scent of fairy blood filled the air. "It was an honor…"

I glanced at Stone and the others who stood around in a vigil. Hokima's normally globby eyes watered. Keltie's face was stoic. Tos showed her emotion openly, tears dripping down her cheeks. And Stone, his eyes closed, sending up a message or a prayer.

"Pppp...." Bim stuttered.

"Don't talk." I pressed my hand against the wound. "You're going to be okay."

Even as I said the words, I sensed they weren't true. There was too much blood. His skin was sickly. His eyes half-mast. If I could get the blood to stop, we could find help and save him.

"You're going to be a great leader."

He must be delirious.

With the way I fought, I wouldn't be leading anyone anywhere. Stone had saved me more than once in this tiny skirmish. I was a terrible fighter.

Bim shuddered and took his last breath.

My own breath shattered, watching him die.

Chapter 17

A breath shivered through me, making my limbs go frigid. Pain squeezed my lungs tight. Bim was gone. Part of my team. A friend. A warrior. A fellow fairy. The shivers morphed into ice. He'd volunteered to come with me, to help me in my search.

Tos used her tiny fingers to close the fairy's eyes. Hokima knelt out of respect. Keltie hung her head. We were weary from battle and the loss we'd sustained. What had Bim been thinking running into the thick of the shooting guards? Where had he gotten the strange device that killed the guards?

And why hadn't it killed any of us?

My gaze swung to Stone. The sadness on his face told me the death had taken a toll and a tiny bit of sympathy squirmed through my veins. Except, he was the one who'd whispered to Bim and then the fairy had gotten himself killed.

"What did you say to him?" Jumping to my feet, I attacked him with my questions. "Why would Bim dive into the middle of the action? Where did he get the strange bomb?"

"I gave it to him." Stone's expression didn't change. His grass-colored eyes wavered—the only display of emotion.

I fisted my hands, pressing the nails so hard the skin on

my palm ripped. Anguish twisted through my body, tangling and knotting my common sense, scattering the shreds of civility. I lashed with my tongue. "It's your fault. Your fault Bim died."

Stone reached out, gathering me close in a comforting and containing hug. I stiffened. "I'm sorry. So sorry," he whispered in my ear. "I needed someone who could get close. We never would've gotten past the guards."

"You should've let me do it." I sniffed against his chest. I was small and fast, and this had been my mission.

"You're half human. I couldn't take the risk." His tone hardened, and his heart boomed beneath my fingers.

"What does that have to do with anything?" I pushed against his chest.

He talked in riddles and kept secrets.

He dropped his arms from around me. "We need to get going before we're discovered. I'd hate for Bim's sacrifice to be in vain."

My emotions wrung dry as if someone was twisting my insides in a tight bunch. "We can't leave him."

"We don't have a choice." Keltie's normally strong voice quivered. "With the commotion we made they'll come to investigate."

"We need to change the route." Stone scanned the long hallway. Corners and intersections were lit up ahead. Signs gave directions to places. Nothing resembling the confusion we'd encountered underground. "The way to the safe room will be crawling with guards."

Safe room? I shook my head trying to piece him together. Why would a guard need a safe room? "Do you have another route?"

"No. We'll figure it out as we go." His response didn't soothe.

"Are you familiar with the palace?" Keltie raised her questioning brow. The one that spoke volumes.

"Enough." He jerked his head in a move along motion.

"How long have you been a guard here?" Doubt seeped under my skin, stirring my already roiling nerves. We followed this secretive guy blindly. "Why do you have a safe room?"

He glared but I wouldn't budge without answers. "I'm undercover. Pretending to be a guard in the palace while working for someone else."

"But—"

"Nothing more right now. We need to go."

Tos snagged another weapon from one of the dead guards, loading her tiny body with weaponry. We each took one or two guns and continued. Stone leading a more somber group than before.

I couldn't get the image of Bim taking his last breath out of my head, of him talking to me as if I was important. I wasn't important. I'd gotten him into this mess. A sob clogged my chest, but I refused to let it out. I needed to pretend to be strong. For some reason, he believed in me and I wasn't going to let him down.

Not like I'd let Arbor down.

"Do you know where they keep the recently arrested majiks? The ones awaiting trial?" I didn't have a hope she'd get a trial. From all I'd learned tonight, majiks were treated the same as animals.

"Yes." He cringed. "Let us get out of one situation before we try and land ourselves in another."

Us?

The word reminded me of Rye. He'd indicated we were an us, and then he'd gone in one direction and I in the other. Not that I'd had a choice. Stone used the same word linking us together. How could we be when he was working for some secret organization? Thinking I was cute wasn't a good enough reason to break me and my friends out of the holding cell or to murder other guards.

"What was the device Bim used?" It had killed the guards, and yet not me or my friends. Although when it detonated the pain was so intense, I thought I might die.

"Natural Acoustic Discord. Or NAD for short." Stone marched on. His response short, clipped, and unhelpful.

My blood pressure spiked. "How did the NAD do what it did?" Keeping pace, I watched his expression instead of his backside. As nice as it was.

"The sound is the opposite of natural white noise exemplified to the highest possible pitch."

"The sound is intense enough to kill?"

"Humans, yes."

I gulped down a breath and choked. The noise had been intense. My body had reacted strongly, however the NAD hadn't killed me because I was half-human. I opened my mouth to ask another question.

He put a finger to his lips. "There might be guards close by."

Not the most promising statement. Blowing out, I tried to calm myself. Forget the death of Bim, forget my tiredness and hunger, forget the fact we were lost in enemy territory.

Yeah, right.

"This is the plan." At least Stone was informing us of his idea. "Try to hide your weapons beneath your clothes or behind your backs. Those you can't hide, we'll leave here." He indicated the side of the narrow hallway. "I'm going to pretend you're my prisoners and march you right through this maintenance area. Hokima, you'll go first followed by Tos who can hide behind your bulk. Keltie will be next. And then Elle."

No Bim.

The absence of his name struck a harsh chord. *Don't think of it. Don't think of it. Don't think of it.*

"Do you know what we're walking into?" I stared at the hinged door as if it held the answers to my questions.

"Cyborg maintenance operations." Stone pointed to the sign above the door which I'd missed.

I hung my head. How would I ever be a leader if I didn't observe? "Where do we go after we make it through the maintenance facility?"

Stone nodded, and his lips turned up slightly. "Yes, you guys should know where to go in case I need to stay behind to fight."

My pulse palpitated. I couldn't lose Stone. Another couldn't die on my watch. "Don't say that."

He ignored me. "If someone questions us, all of you keep going toward the single door on the opposite side of the room. There's one other exit. I'll distract them. And if I need to, unplug a few."

As if it was that easy to stop a cyborg.

"The safe room is through maintenance, past the podship garage, and through the supply closet."

We moved into position and left a few of our weapons. I mourned the loss although I didn't relish carrying guns.

Hokima pushed a button and the podship garage door slid open. His gun slung around his shoulder with the weapon pressed against his back. Tos had slipped a small gun under her tunic leaving the larger weapons behind. Keltie had strapped a weapon under her shirt and hid another at her side. Because of my outfit, strapless top and barely-there skirt, I had nowhere to hide a weapon. And even though I'd only been carrying a weapon for less than a day, starting with the dagger, I felt naked without one.

The loud buzzing in the room captured my attention. Large machinery working non-stop. Conveyor belts similar to the kitchen transferred the unfinished cyborgs from one stop to another. Metal torsos on one. Heads with wires sticking out on another. A stash of arms and legs lay on a counter. Docking stations where the completed cyborgs charged lined the walls. Fumes of grease and short-circuiting wires filled the air.

Cyborgs rolled around the room operating the equipment. They diagnosed and fixed their own problems. Humans weren't even needed in the process. Which for us was a good thing. No guards in the warehouse.

The commotion stopped.

All the cyborgs twisted to watch us. Even the ones without bodies, swiveled from their necks to glare. The red lights of their eyes flashed scanning, trying to determine our presence. I held my breath thinking if they didn't see me breathe, they couldn't detect us.

"Majik life forms detected," a robot with bright orange strings of lighted hair said.

Stone cocked his weapon. "I'm a guard taking these prisoners to new cells."

Another robot came forward on silent wheels. "Majiks are not allowed."

I huffed, remembering the kitchen cyborg who'd told me *majiks belong in the garbage.* "How can a cyborg with no real brain be prejudiced?"

"Programming." Stone's quick response told me he'd pondered the same question. "Ignore them. Keep heading toward the exit on the left."

We moved in unison, keeping a steady pace, not wanting to risk an attack or the cyborgs sending out a warning to the guards.

The robot with the orange hair swiveled its head around

in a complete circle. "Security for the Collection of Unique Magic headed this way."

Air squeezed out of my lungs. How did the cyborgs know this? Built in radar? Or had they squealed?

"Thanks for the warning." Stone's irony was lost on the robot. He picked up his pace. "Go."

We jogged the way he directed. A cyborg jumped in front of Hokima and he almost crashed into the metal man. Veering left, another cyborg got in our way. I went in the other direction. Another cyborg. And another.

Surrounded.

My pulse raced, and my muscles tightened with tension. I wasn't ready for another fight.

"Weapons out." Stone raised his gun and pointed.

The others revealed their hidden weapons. I wished I'd kept one. Stealth had been more important at the time.

"Security Collectors of Unique Magic," the cyborg even used the long proper name instead of the more appropriate acronym, "will come through the door in fifteen seconds." His orange head spun around. "Completed and deliverable cyborg servants go this way."

The cyborgs surrounded us like choreographed dancers. A space opened, and their metallic arms pointed in a different direction. Toward the conveyor belt where a small door opened and emptied into blackness. Completed cyborgs lay flat on the belt, their midsections straight and arms to the side.

"Only repaired and deliverable cyborgs. No guards," the orange-haired robot said in his monotone voice.

I looked at Stone. He regarded me and then the rest of our group.

"We should do what the cyborgs say." I edged toward the conveyor belt. They'd helped me in the kitchen and promised no guards would be this way.

The orange-haired cyborg beeped. "Security Collectors of Unique Magic will arrive in ten seconds."

"I don't know where we'll end up." Stone actually sounded unsure. I'd never heard uncertainty from him.

That made my decision easier. This was my mission, so it was my decision.

"Nine seconds." The monotone voice sent a chill down my spine.

"They're helping us." I pushed a cyborg off the belt and its metal parts clattered to the ground.

Keltie pushed up next to me. "How do you know?"

"Eight seconds."

My lungs smothered with my own lack of conviction. What choice did we have? Walk out the door and into the arms, or guns, of the guards or take a different option. A different chance. "I trust them."

"You trust a robot made by our enemy, *programmed* by our enemy." Hokima reminded me of the conversation seconds earlier.

"Seven seconds."

I'd trusted Stone to get us this far. I'd trusted Rye.

"If the SCUM are coming, where do you think they're coming from?" I pointed to the door we'd come through and the one we headed toward. It was logical to me.

"Six seconds."

"If we go through the exit, I know the fastest way to get us to a safe room." Stone's expression flashed with panic. "I don't know what happens by way of conveyor belt."

"Five seconds."

Tos jiggled her shoulders. "The conveyor belt might cut us up and throw us into a scrap garbage pile."

"Been there. Done that." Glancing between the two doors,

I had to persuade them. It wouldn't make sense for the SCUM to be coming from the way we came. They had to be marching towards the door in front of us and we had no other way to escape and not much time. I cleared away another cyborg. "I'm getting on the conveyor belt. Follow me or not."

It had to be each of their own choices.

"Four seconds."

I jumped onto the cleared space of the black rubber belt and laid down, so I'd fit through the door.

"Ellery!" Stone's panic bulleted through his shout. He tried to grab my arm.

I yanked it away.

Hokima struggled to sit on the belt. He pushed a cyborg off. "I'm with Elle."

"Three seconds."

"I hear them." Keltie's sharp ears must've picked up their approach. She pushed a metal man off and jumped on the belt. "They're coming through the far door."

Just as the cyborgs had warned.

Stone grumbled something about me being right and he picked up Tos and put her on the belt between two cyborgs. He cleared a space for himself and climbed on with his gun drawn pointing toward the door.

If the guards saw us, they'd switch off the conveyor belt and capture us. I hoped I made the right decision.

"Two seconds."

I slid through the small entrance door and into a darkness. I heard no shots or calls of distress, so my little group must've made it inside the conveyor belt's black hole before the guards entering the room noticed.

The belt continued traveling, and I relaxed for the first time in what seemed days even though it had been less than twelve hours. My muscles melted into the warming hum of the black belt and my eyelids fluttered. Fighting off sleepiness, I started counting.

Bum. Bum.

A loud clatter startled me. The noise grew louder and closer. The belt shook with each stomp.

My eyes flew open in time to see a metal rod with a flat plate at the end stamping the belt. It barely missed my feet. My heart jumped into my throat. I was going to be made into mashed fairy. Jerking, I rolled to the side narrowly avoiding the plate.

"Watch out!" I called up the line.

Literally, because we were on a production line. None of us just happened to be what was being made.

I sat up. No harrowing screams or smushing innards. "Everyone okay?"

Each of them answered affirmative.

"Is there anything else able to kill us ahead?" Stone's sarcastic-heavy voice filtered to me.

"Hard to tell. It's pitch-black." I tried to sound nonchalant, when I was pissing in my pants. "And you're welcome. You know, because I got us out of there alive."

He murmured something I couldn't make out.

"He said, *barely.*" Keltie chuckled.

Stone growled. He must've forgotten how well elves could hear.

"We should jump off." Tos' voice quivered at the end of each word.

"I can't see any type of ground." I swung my legs over the edge. "Can't even tell if there is a ground."

"I don't hear anything." Keltie chuckled again. She was enjoying her game of historical telephone.

"I can't see much of anything either. Just varying shades

of black." Hokima had excellent sight in the dark. "We're going up."

"How can you tell?" Stone asked before I could.

"Because I feel sick." Hokima emphasized his point with a loud burp. "Trolls can easily get motion sickness because we never leave the ground, even though we live in the mountains. Nice, sturdy mountains." Homesickness swelled in his tone.

"Good thing you're not flying on a dragon." Tos sounded excited at the prospect.

Paying attention, I perceived the movement too. The way the conveyor belt tugged slightly upward, how with each minute my body rose.

"Are we still beneath the palace?" Keltie asked.

"The cyborg maintenance center is on the ground floor, not beneath." At least Stone was acquainted with the palace layout.

I'd noticed how the hallways and corridors slanted. Underground in the dungeon had been cold and damp, but in the cell and running through the corridors the space had gotten warmer. Guess, I noticed more than I'd originally thought.

"We're moving up in the world." My joke fell flat.

My dream had been to move up in the world through Continuum and finally graduation. I'd inherit my house and officially become Lady Milford. The entire dream had changed overnight. Now, I dreamed of survival. Of saving my new friends. Of finding Arbor. And then…

I needed to consider Gardenia's offer.

"These cyborg servants are complete and being delivered." Something clanged and I realized it must be Stone examining a robot. "The question is where?"

The conveyor belt continued to climb in the blackness. If the maintenance facility was on the ground floor, we were higher now. The grand ballroom had been on the second floor and had been lined with balconies leading to other rooms.

"I can see the ground." Hokima's voice rose with excitement.

Now, maybe we could get off this never-ending carnival ride.

Our surroundings lightened, more gray than black. Small grates vented the room circulating fresh air. The floor was a glassy surface which made sense since the upper part of the castle was crystal and glass.

"I'll go first." Stone was always ordering us around, especially me. Sure, he rescued me and my friends, but that didn't mean I owed him my life.

Well, maybe it did.

He thundered to the ground. "Six-foot drop."

I inched toward the edge. Before I could jump, he dashed and grabbed me. His large hands spanned my waist. His fingers held me tight as if I was a precious fruit easily bruised. His powerful masculinity made me feel safe and protected, and yet he'd followed me onto the conveyor belt. He trusted me to make decisions.

He helped me jump down and held me for a second. His gaze captured mine trying to communicate something. An electrical tension sizzled to my toes. How could I be crushing on him while liking Rye.

I'd probably never see Rye again. My shoulders rounded inward, and my energy flowed out. I stepped away and out of Stone's grasp. "I could've jumped a few feet."

"Of course you can." His complete confidence brought a small smile to my lips. The only other person who'd had confidence I'd get something done was Gardenia.

Of course, she'd expected me to assassinate the prince, and my plan from the beginning was to avoid the royal teen.

The rest of the gang had jumped off and watched. Good thing it was dark because I knew I was blushing. What did they think was going on between me and Stone? They'd already accused me of flirting.

"Keep your voices down," Stone whispered. "I'm not sure exactly where we are in the palace and what those grates lead to."

The grates let in a little light and my sight adjusted. Since most of the servants were cyborgs it made sense we were near the servants' quarters.

Stone tiptoed to the closest grate. I held my giggle at the giant male on his toes like a ballerina. Wanting to see too, I snuck in front of him. The warmth of his body heated imitating a blanket. One I'd pull out on cold and lonely nights.

Voices came from the room below. I pressed closer to the opening trying to ignore my unwanted attraction to Stone.

One wall in the room had shelves filled with classic textbooks made from real paper. The other wall had multiple vid screens and enlarged text capability. An old-fashioned desk sat in the center of the room with a large velvet chair. Two smaller chairs were situated in front of the desk. A tray of sandwiches and fresh fruit sat on the desk.

My stomach growled, and I sucked it in trying to control the noise.

Regent Theobald strolled into view. He wore purple robes and black pants with a crisp pleat. His gut stuck out and a crown glistened on his head. I'd seen vids of him and didn't realize how short he was, or how bald. From this angle, the bright white patch of skin, which would be covered by the crown, was circled by thin patches of blond hair.

"The majik prisoners don't need livable conditions because they're not going to live long." The regent picked up a sandwich, took a bite, and tossed the rest in the trash. "I mean, they're not going to live long in prison. They're going to be transferred."

"Transferred where?" The male voice rang with authority as if he had every right to question Regent Theobald.

I gasped recognizing the tone.

Rye.

I warmed. He was asking about better conditions for the majik prisoners. He was doing what he'd promised to do. Squishing my eye closer to the grate, I wanted to see him.

Stone's body stiffened.

I ignored him focusing on Rye's words. I imagined how his mouth would shift when speaking, and for a second I lost myself remembering those lips on mine.

"Does it matter?" The regent moved out of the way, unblocking the view of half the room.

A second guy came into view. He appeared to be around my age and wore a nice suit. His blond hair was clipped short and his gaze darted between the regent and I'm assuming Rye.

This other guy must be the prince.

I fisted my hands together willing myself not to propel forward to kill him. Surprisingly, I felt nothing. No urge to assassinate as my mission dictated. Then again, I didn't have the enchanted dagger anymore. Stone had taken it when he'd taken my magical bag.

Rye paced into view. He gripped an odd-shaped piece of glass with white fingers, holding it too tight. The negotiations with the prince and regent must not be going well.

I believed in him, though. He was bringing our concerns to their attention and he was going to blast the royals about their unfairness. He was going to tell them what needed to be done. He was my hero.

I leaned forward even more, not wanting to miss a single word.

Rye twisted the glass piece and I caught a better glimpse. I sucked in a breath. The glass piece was a shoe. *My shoe.* He must've found the one I'd lost. My heart softened, and my bones melted like goo. I wanted to call out to him, to tell him I was okay, and that he needed to be strong.

Besides his white fingers, I couldn't tell if he was angry or upset. His expression didn't redden with anger. He didn't tilt forward to press his point. His expression stayed neutral. Blank.

What he said next almost made me gasp.

"No. Of course it doesn't matter. Majiks don't matter."

Chapter 18

Rye's cold response struck in the center of my chest and wallowed in trembling waves. He'd seemed so genuine, as if he'd wanted to help the plight of the imprisoned majiks. He had the opportunity. He was in the presence of the regent and the prince, and yet he hadn't even tried to persuade them.

My heart seemed to shrink, and my body slackened. I leaned against Stone using him as a crutch.

"You okay?" Stone whispered keeping his voice low.

"I guess." I didn't want to confess what a fool I'd been. I hadn't believed Rye would be successful, but I'd believed he'd try harder.

Stone tucked me closer. "You know the majik prisoners aren't being transferred anywhere or being sent out of the kingdom."

I gulped. Knowing and fully comprehending were two different things.

"Were you one of those foolish girls who crushed on the handsome prince?" His tone rose in a tease trying to lighten the atmosphere.

"No." It wasn't the prince I'd been attracted to. Rye wasn't the guy I thought he was. To cave so easily. To not care what happened to the majiks being transferred. To not demand something be done. "We should get out of here. Get to your safe room. Make a plan."

A new plan. One that didn't include Rye and his obvious lack of principle. One that saved Arbor and the other majiks. *All of them.*

Slowly, Stone slipped his arms from around me, almost reluctantly. "Yes, we should."

Gathering the group, he led us away. Once he'd figured out where we were, he knew what direction to go. We followed the conveyor belt's path for a while, then through numerous hidden corridors used by the cyborg servants. The few robots we came upon either didn't notice or didn't care.

Walking in a daze, I dealt with a second loss. We'd lost Bim to death, and I'd lost Rye to the regent. His convictions weren't strong. Similar to how I used to be. Knowing atrocities happened in Alandaska, and yet content to live my life trying to achieve my goal of being accepted as one hundred percent human.

Not anymore.

This one night had changed me. I'd been hoping to save Arbor and return to my regularly scheduled life. Even if I couldn't save my friend, I'd planned to go home and pretend nothing had happened, pretend I hadn't gone rogue. Sure, Sybil would punish me for not completing my chores. I could handle that. What I couldn't handle was pretending to be blind when I could see.

See the unfairness in our world.

See the suffering of the majiks.

See the torment and the dying.

I understood to the depth of my being. I couldn't sit back and watch.

"This is it." Stone had led us through the back of the podship station and into a supply closet filled with cleaning supplies and spare parts. He pushed the wire shelving unit away from the wall and tapped on an outlet from historical times. Something no one would need with today's electronics. A hidden panel popped open. He typed a code and a small doorway slid on silent hinges.

Shuffling through, I examined the door. When it had been shut you couldn't even see the seams. The craftsmanship was amazing.

"It's a place to rest until we head out again." He waited until we all entered and sealed the door.

"Who built this place?" Keltie's thoughts must've gone to the same place.

"Combination of humans and majiks. When they worked together instead of against each other." He waved in the direction of one wall. "There's food stored in the cabinets." He paced across the room. "And there's a small bathroom through the door. Sleeping pods over here."

My stomach growled again at the mention of food. I hadn't eaten anything since lunch the day before.

"Hungry?" Stone's chuckle sounded less stressed than any I'd heard earlier. He believed we'd get out of here alive.

Tension leaked away from my muscles and bones. The knots in my back untied. The daze I'd been in cleared similar to fog after the sun shone.

He pressed a button and a cabinet popped open. "Nothing fancy. Protein tubes to keep up your strength."

I snatched a tube and ripped open the cap. Sucking down the flavorful paste tasting of chicken and peas, I filled my belly.

He tossed Tos a protein tube and showed Keltie how to work the bathroom. He helped Hokima get comfortable on a sleeping pod and pulled a second one out for Tos. Both of them climbed in and went to sleep. Stone had been there for us since we'd met, getting us out of the cell, figuring out a new plan when the first had gone awry, bringing us here to recover. He was the hero.

Not the guy who shall remain nameless.

My lungs expanded. Stone resembled one of those gods from ancient Rome or one of the Alandaska fighters who'd left the kingdom to fight amongst the humans during one of their multiple world wars. Handsome and daring. Bold and courageous. Hunky.

"What're you staring at?" He must've noticed my intense inspection.

My cheeks baked at being caught studying him like a piece of cake. "Nothing. Nothing."

"Here." He trekked toward me on light feet. He held a small wet towelette. "You've got something on your cheek."

The red stains of embarrassment, no doubt.

Gently, he wiped my skin in a slow, circular motion. Mesmerizing, the way his thick, strong fingers proceeded with a delicate, subtle touch. He was taking care of me again, treating me special. His expression softened.

The white cloth came away with the color red. Not embarrassment, but blood.

Bim's blood.

A blow struck. Loss, strong and hard hit me. I gaped at the red stain knowing I'd never forget the dull, reddish-brown color. Knowing I'd never forget Bim.

Stone must've realized where my thoughts had gone because he pulled me into his arms. His muscled strength brought comfort and his big body oozed protection. I lifted my head to stare into emerald eyes changing with his emotions. His eyes swirled with longing and pulled me toward him. His full lips appeared hard. Would they contrast and be cushy like so much of the enigma of Stone?

Hard and soft. Caring and cold. Teasing and all-seriousness.

I ran a nervous tongue across my lower lip. He stared at my mouth. Did he plan to kiss me? I wasn't ready for a kiss from a different guy.

He cleared his throat and pulled away with a jerk.

This time heat flooded my entire body, not just my cheeks. He was providing comfort because he cared. He didn't want to kiss me. Romantic e-books spoke of how during times of high stress, emotions went haywire. That must be what had happened. I'd gotten caught up in the moment. My feelings simmered close to the surface with the fighting and the risk, the loss of Bim, the sellout by Rye.

Stone pulled out two sleeping pods close together. "Sleep."

Another order.

I was tired of people telling me what to do. I was also too tired to argue. And yet, my mind rushed with thoughts and my heart bled with loss.

Keltie chose a pod on the other side of the room, turned her back, and at least pretended to sleep. Tos was small in the human-sized pod. Hokima's rhythmic snores hypnotized.

I couldn't sleep, and neither could Stone. I could tell by his uneven breathing and restlessness.

Rotating on my side, I faced him. "Are all the majik prisoners kept in those same cells?"

The area we'd been in hadn't been large. Half a dozen cell doors centered around the middle guard station. Hi tech locks and magic blocking chemicals to keep the majiks inside.

He grimaced, expecting the question but not wanting to answer. "Teen prisoners."

"Why teenagers? Why the need to keep them separate from the rest of the majiks?"

He huffed, and his broad shoulders rolled. "Teen majiks' powers are the most potent because they've recently gone through puberty."

I cringed. The last thing I wanted to talk about with him was teenage puberty and how our bodies changed and how we became attracted to others. "The government is afraid teen majiks can more easily break out of the regular prison?"

"The government," he said, as if he wasn't part of them, "are harnessing the more potent powers of the teens."

"What do you mean by harnessing powers?"

"They are stealing the majiks' powers."

Reeling back, my own useless powers seemed to seep out of me. "How are they stealing their powers?"

"Auraguillotine."

I jerked. "I've heard of it. The majiks I met beneath the palace, the ones who are trying to escape, are terrified of the name."

"As they should be." Stone's solemn tone sounded so final.

My mind ran in circles trying to wrap my brain around what I'd learned. Teen majiks' powers were stronger. The regent and prince, and possibly Rye—a crack went through my heart—used an atrocious machine to pilfer powers for their own use. For what?

"What are they using the magic for?"

"What the rulers have always used magical powers for. To keep the kingdom a secret. To advance technology. To keep themselves in power. To fight against the majiks themselves."

Fairies against brownies. Brownies against elves. Elves against giants. Giants against trolls and ogres. The list went on and on. The humans playing one race against the other, always manipulating, always in control. And now, they had magic of their own. They'd used technology and turned it against us, creating their own magical power.

Stolen magical power.

Rolling into something hard and warm, I realized I must've fallen asleep. My eyes were crusty and my brain unaware of my surroundings. The wall of warmth felt good and I snuggled closer. During the ravishing dreams of weapons and blood, of Bim and Arbor, I'd twisted and turned.

The wall moved in and out. A living breathing thing.

Stone.

Relaxing, I cuddled into him. Close. Until I jerked to my senses. He'd almost kissed me, and I wasn't ready for another kiss from a different guy. Scooting away, I turned and studied his lips. How would he kiss? I'd only had the one kiss from Rye, and I'd believed it was the best kiss ever. But now, I realized Rye was weak and not worthy of my affection. Not with my new convictions. Not with my new plan.

A new plan that shouldn't include a romance.

"Good morning." Stone's rough voice created an uncomfortable response.

Fever flooded across my skin and drained like a riptide. I'd never slept near a guy before. I scooted further away. "What's good about it? And how do you even know it's morning?"

The ball had been in the evening. I'd traveled beneath the palace, gotten caught by Stone and the other guards, freed, fought a battle, and rode the conveyor belt of thrills and chills.

Rubbing his face, he stood abruptly. "We should get ready to go."

Without glancing back, he stomped to the bathroom and slammed the door.

Ouch.

The noise woke everyone else in the room.

Keltie sat up and stretched her long, elegant limbs. Her braid didn't have a hair out of place. "What's his problem?"

I shrugged, not willing to admit anything. "Grumpy in the morning, I guess."

Hokima and Tos stirred and after a few minutes of taking turns in the bathroom, grabbing more protein tubes, and organizing the few weapons we had, we were ready to head out.

The question was in which direction.

"We'll take a small tunnel which leads into the mountains behind the palace." Stone double checked the weapons hanging from his belt. He'd changed out of the guard uniform and into pants and a tight, black T-shirt. "I'll have you in complete safety in about an hour."

Was anywhere in the kingdom safe for a majik? With the regent's restrictive laws and the mass arrests of teen majiks? I wasn't running and hiding any longer. A battle was going to break out soon and I needed to choose my side. My dreams, or should I say nightmares, returned with force. I'd let Arbor down. Bim had died because of me. Hokima, Tos, and Keltie had been put in additional danger because of my quest. I'd failed in my unwanted mission to kill the prince.

I couldn't waltz out of here having accomplished nothing. I was done playing it safe.

"I'm not leaving without Arbor." And without at least attempting to destroy the auraguillotine.

"Don't be foolish." Stone's tone spoke volumes starting with asinine and ending with thick-headed.

I took in my friends. Not new friends or majik friends, just friends. I'd miss the ragtag lot. "You should go."

Tos didn't meet my gaze. Hokima's gloppy eyes widened with uncertainty. Keltie arched the ever-questioning brow.

Bracing myself, I whirled to face Stone's glare. "Tell me how to get to the auraguillotine."

He watched every movement of my pupils, every blink, every twitch of a muscle on my face. "Why would you want to go there?"

"I heard my friend Arbor was taken there." This wasn't about just my friend anymore. "And someone has to stop this terrible machine."

He ran a hand through his hair. "Majiks who go there don't come out alive."

His words landed inside of me like soft grenades. My tummy twisted, and guilt won over worry. Righteous topped fear. This had been building inside me all night. The conditions the prisoners lived under—and not for long, the unfair arrests and the separation of families, and the stealing of powers.

I stood taller and stronger, cement hardening in my bones. "I have to see if I can help. It's my fault Arbor was arrested and I'm going to do everything I can to save her and any others."

His pupils changed, deepening to a mossy color that might've been respect. "I'm going with you."

"No. I don't want anyone else endangering themselves." I was adamant about this point. Each of them had risked enough already. I wanted them out of the palace and safe.

"I'm a palace guard and you'll never make it without me." His lips formed a smug smirk. One saying he was right, and he knew it and I couldn't argue.

What he said made sense, yet I needed him to take my friends to safety.

"I want my friends," I pointed at Keltie, Tos, and Hokima, "to get out alive. You need to take them."

"I'll tell them how to get out." Stone's jaw set. He wasn't going to give in on this point. "Then, I'm coming with you."

His words nailed me to the spot. He was right. His assistance would be helpful. He was strong and knew his way around the palace. He was on my side and willing to fight.

He grabbed his electronic pad and drew a map with the stylo. Telling each of them the code word, he patted them on the back and said goodbye.

My lungs welled with a mix of emotions, pushing against my ribcage causing physical pain. This was goodbye, possibly forever. When would I run into an elf, a troll, and a brownie again? Right now, our kind were on separate sides, even so I was hoping the groups would find a way to work together against the human threat.

I hugged Hokima's fat, fluid body. The ickiness I would've expected to experience didn't come. "You tell the trolls how you worked with a fairy, an elf, a brownie, and a human." I wanted to be part of this coming together of races, even if I was the tiny flame starting the fire.

"Our escape will become legend." He bowed over my hand imitating a prince.

I pivoted to Tos. She was such a special majik. Proud, smart, funny. "You are the bravest brownie I've ever met."

"I'm the only brownie you've ever met."

Laughter sprung from my fear. "True." I hugged her close, lifting her off her tiny feet. "Stay safe. Look out for these two."

Setting the brownie back on the floor, I reeled toward Keltie. My throat tightened holding in tears. She'd taught me about being brave and a leader. "Thanks for your guidance."

"You think you're going to keep me away from the fun?" She wiggled her expressive brows. "I'm coming with you and Stone."

"It's not going to be fun." I didn't want her thinking this would be a good time. We were lucky to have survived so far. Our odds would lower significantly.

"I can help. I have skills you could use. I'm a warrior." She took a combative stance.

I knew she could fight. Knew her heart was in the right place. "It's going to be dangerous."

She stuck her hands on her hips in a superhero pose. "I live for danger."

No lightness entered me at her joking. We understood how serious the situation was. "Or because of it, you die."

Chapter 19

"Are you sure about this?" Stone straightened the lapels of the guard uniform I wore.

Extra uniforms were one of the staples stashed in the safe room. Keltie was dressing in a similar uniform in the bathroom. Tos and Hokima had headed out on their own with a promise to tell our story to everyone and drum up support.

"Never been more sure." My uncertainty had evaporated similar to Arbor's smoke. I knew I was doing the right thing. It was a step forward in proclaiming who I truly was and where I fit in this crazy world.

Still gripping my collar, Stone leaned toward me. His evergreen scent relaxed my bones at the same time the closeness created tension. A good-weird kind of tension. Was he a flirt? Did he want to kiss me? "You must follow my directions."

"Your orders you mean." Pressure to do what he wanted. Another form of coercion. "This is my mission. You're tagging along with me. Why?"

I'd asked before and he'd never answered. Why would this human risk his very thick neck? He was obviously part of some underground insurrection. Who did he work for? Humans would never work for the fairies or anyone else trying to rebel against royalty.

Humans were part of the royal system. Aristocracy based on race.

"Why not?" His lips twitched in an all-knowing and annoying quirk.

"You're a human guard and you took out other guards to help majiks escape. You have connections to some sort of underground network. Why risk your mission for me?"

"You're taking a risk by trying to save your friend." His tone stayed even, not giving away any secrets.

It was comparable to facing a solid rock. One I couldn't touch and say a chant to get through.

"She's my friend." My voice cracked and my chin quivered. Guilt was not a helpful emotion. "I'm nothing to you. Tos, Hokima, and Keltie are nothing to you."

Stone's eyes changed color again. The green morphed into something deeper and darker, something more intense. "Maybe you're something to me."

Before I could comprehend his meaning, his mouth descended onto mine. His lips besieged while mine dropped open in an *O* of surprise. My heart thudded, and my brain ran around in circles as if competing in a marathon. Confusion and chaos won the race.

His mouth was hard, punishing. My lips didn't respond to his aggression. He tasted dark and dangerous, and concerned about the future. Our future.

Not about our future together. We didn't have a future together, in a relationship. I wasn't sure if I felt hero worship or physical attraction. I'd really liked Rye, but had I even known him? Did I truly know Stone?

Not really. He kept too many secrets. Which wouldn't be

good for any future relationship. I couldn't decide whether to respond to the kiss or slap him. We were in a precarious situation and I didn't want tangled emotions getting in the way of my task.

"I don't think this uniform goes with my complexion." Keltie's statement snapped into my bungled synapses.

Stone jumped a step back and I ducked my head, trying to straighten my collar and my expression. The attraction spiraling between us severed like a tight thread leaving me gasping. My chest was tight, and I couldn't speak even though her question was directed at me.

He waited for me to respond and when I didn't, he said, "As long as your skin doesn't match a body bag you should be good."

Keltie chuckled.

Their gallows humor soured in my stomach. The kiss must not have meant much if he could go from kissing to sarcasm in seconds.

Leaning in, he straightened Keltie's collar, too.

I held my breath waiting for him to kiss her. As I suspected, I didn't mean anything to him. I was a distraction. He was a flirt.

"One last thing." He took a fancy clutch and a jewel-encrusted dagger out from a locker.

"My bag and knife!" I swiped them both from him. "Where'd you get these?"

"I told the commander I'd put them in a secure place." His flirtatious smile had my pulse quickening. With anger, not attraction.

Peering in the bag, I checked the contents. "Where's Drago?"

"I don't know. The commander might've put him with the other baby dragons."

At least Drago was with his siblings.

I tucked the dagger inside the front of my uniform for safekeeping. "I should leave the bag here."

"Its magical capability might come in handy."

"Magic doesn't work under the palace."

"We won't be under the palace where we're going." He snapped his weapon at his belt. "Everyone ready?"

Slipping the bag around my neck, I followed them out. The opening slid on its silent hinges and we entered the hallway of our enemy. No safe place to hide.

Not from the palace guards, not from Stone, not from my emotions.

The kiss had been too aggressive to show any depth of emotion. Not that I had much to compare it to. The two kisses I'd received were like night and day.

Rye's kiss had been sweet and light and filled with hope. While Stone's kiss had been hard and desperate, a clinging to what could happen. Both had been good. Just different.

And I had no idea what either of them meant. If anything at all.

Stone must've been taking advantage of the situation and the adrenaline. If I hadn't been standing there, he probably would've kissed Keltie, too.

Avoiding Stone, I kept pace with her. She had her head down knowing her elf heritage would be recognized at first glance. The hat she wore barely covered the tips of her ears. The first and second hallway had been empty, except for the occasional cyborg whirring past. The shiny metal walls fractured our images as we swept passed. The lights glared causing me to squint. The cold became colder with each corridor we tread.

"What did you do for fun before?" I whispered the question.

"After the human school I attended kicked me out and

my father lost his job in the city, we relocated to Elvenstad. My father tried to get work in the area. Manual labor." Her scoff came from a place of pain. "He's a lawyer, and a good one."

"Why did he lose his job?"

She shot me a furrowed forehead and narrowed gaze. "Because he's an elf. And since elves don't get trials anymore, his firm didn't need his services."

The unfairness gutted me, and I wanted to put a stop to it. Destroying the machine would be the first step.

Stone paused and checked around a corner. When he gave the clear sign, we moved forward.

Wanting to change the subject, I asked, "What did you do with your free time since returning to Elvenstad?"

I'd never had free time. Maybe that was a good thing because as soon as I spent time the way I wanted, I'd gotten in trouble. Gotten Arbor in trouble.

"I watched my brothers and sisters a lot." Keltie's wistfulness pulled at my sympathy. "My mom started elves' rights meetings."

Stone shifted to stare. His eyes had grown larger than normal. Had what she said meant something to him?

"The reason my mom got arrested. I'm sure of it." Her voice rose with bewilderment and anger. "Why would she put me and my brothers and sisters at risk?"

I didn't have any brothers and sisters and I'd always wanted them. Ingrid and Ilana didn't count. They didn't act like sisters. We weren't a real, loving family. "How many brothers and sisters do you have?"

"Had." The single word exploded. "When I fought the SCUM, they arrested me and took them, too." Keltie swiped at her nose. "I'll never see them again."

I didn't know what to say. I didn't care for my stepsisters

although I wouldn't want them dead. Just out of my house and my life.

"That's why I volunteered to come with you. If my siblings are alive, I don't want them put in the auraguillotine." Her tone hardened. "If you plan to destroy it, I want to be there to watch it crushed."

We arrived at a supply door and Stone used a code to get inside. He made quick work of piling up supplies in a way appearing haphazard on a quick scan, except the items acted as a ladder to the ventilation shaft. This was how he knew the direction from the ventilation area behind the regent's library to the area near the safe room. But why? Curiosity about him burned.

Keltie went first and easily climbed into the shaft. I went next. Stone went last and readjusted a couple of crates to make the ladder look even more random. The dark shaft was quiet, and my nose tickled from the dust. I held back a sneeze.

We crawled what seemed miles, however, was only yards. My knees ached, and my palms were raw. It must've been much harder on Stone because of his size. His shoulders barely fit. He didn't complain. He stopped where a darker spot stained the wall.

Facts about Stone started to pile up into an unclear picture. He was a guard helping the majiks and working for a secret organization. He knew his way around the palace. He had contacts because he couldn't have built and supplied the safe room by himself. Questions about him swirled and this time while we waited, I was going to get answers.

I settled in next to him. "I'm not going to shut up until you tell me who you are and who you're working with." And why you kissed me.

The strength to ask the last question disappeared. I'd

conquer that aspect of our relationship another time. I had to know who he was and what he stood for.

"Does it matter? Know I'm on your side." Using a hand tool, he pried off the back covering of a grate. Once the cover was removed it was similar to the other grate we'd peered through. "The less you know at this very dangerous point, the better."

Meaning if I was captured, I couldn't squeal. My hands fluttered. "You can kiss me, yet you don't trust me?"

"Look, Ellery—"

"My fairy godmother calls me Ellery." It hit me. He knew my real name and he knew about the magic purse because he'd asked me to bring it. I reeled back and the hairs on the back of my neck stiffened. "Gardenia. You work for her and her organization."

Chapter 20

My fairy godmother was high commander of the fairies. Her word was on par with the queen's. Gardenia must've formed a sub-army dedicated to destroying the monarchy. How many other groups were out there working against the crown? Against the regent and prince? Her spies had infiltrated the palace and Stone was one of them.

And he'd rescued me. Of all the captured majiks, he'd found me.

"That's how you knew who I was." My blood pressure spiked to a dangerous level. I'd been tricked by Stone and Gardenia. My chest squeezed, humiliation drowning my lungs. She hadn't trusted me and sent him to save me.

I hung my head. Gardenia hadn't sent an inexperienced fairy to assassinate the prince. She wanted something else from me. I'd been tricked into the quest for some other reason.

"I'm part of the queen's elite unit. I report to Gardenia." His carved cheek had a small tic.

My shoulders dipped, and my body deflated. Had I been led around on purpose? That must be why he'd kissed me— to get my cooperation. "My fairy godmother sent you to watch me."

"These are dangerous times for you." His bland explanation didn't soothe my quiet seething.

He knew everything about me and yet hadn't shared who he was. He'd thought I'd turn into a besotted fool after one kiss and do what he wanted. Anger pinged at each of his lies, bouncing off a rib and then an organ creating chaos inside. Everyone I became close to lied to me, kept secrets from me, tried to manage me.

With blackmail. With lies. With kisses.

"These are dangerous times for all majiks." I swiped at my mouth and the memory of his kiss. "Why didn't you tell me who you were?"

"And if I did, if I'd whispered the truth during your capture, would you have believed me?" The scoff telegraphed his doubt.

I opened my mouth to say of course, but he was right. I never would've believed him. I smashed my mouth shut.

His lips lifted in his trademark sexy, flirtatious, and too-smart smile. "Exactly."

I'd thought he was attracted to me. Now, I realized I was part of his mission. He was tasked by my fairy godmother to protect me. I was a job to him. And if teasing and kissing and flashing his killer smirk helped get me to do what he wanted, he'd use whatever was at his disposal.

"I don't need a babysitter." My eyes prickled. I refused to cry proving him and Gardenia right.

He didn't believe in me. She didn't trust me.

"Is destroying the auraguillotine part of your mission?" Holding my breath, I repeated to myself, *say no, say no, say no.*

"That was all your idea." There was a steel note in his voice. "And a good one.

At least he respected my mind.

"Why did you kiss me?" The urge to slap my hand over my mouth shot through me. I stilled the action.

He blinked several times. "It got you to listen, didn't it?"

I gritted my teeth trying to control the air rushing in and out of my lungs. Trying to control lashing out. "I'm listening to you because we have the same goals. To destroy the machine. Not because of some kiss that wasn't very good."

"Not good?" His expression flickered with what appeared to be hurt, before a bright gleam shined from his emerald orbs. His lips quirked. "I'll have to do better next time."

"There won't be a next time." My mouth tingled with the memory. "No more kissing. I'll follow your orders when they make sense."

"My orders always make sense." His chauvinistic confidence had returned.

I refused to argue. "Who else is part of the organization? Is Keltie part of the group, too?"

Her eyebrows arched. "What're you talking about, Elle?" She must've heard everything.

I pursed my lips in a tight grin. "Call me Ellery. My real name. You probably knew it all along."

"Ellery, stop." Stone grabbed my arm bringing my attention back to him. "I've never met Keltie before today. She doesn't know your fairy godmother, doesn't work for her."

He defended the elf. Why?

I sagged like a wilted flower. He'd insisted on coming with me to destroy the machine because of my fairy godmother. Because he was protecting me under her orders. And, Keltie I didn't know about yet.

Because I didn't know anything.

"We'll talk about this later. Right now, we have a task to complete."

True. My task. Not a quest Gardenia had sent me on. Not one of Stone's orders.

He shuffled forward on his knees to the next grate and pulled out an old-fashioned hand tool with no cord or battery. As he de-magnetized the grate cover, he whispered, "Those holding cells lead directly to here." He pointed with the tool. "The majiks wait in line."

I squinted to see the area he indicated pushing my emotions aside. I'd deal with his betrayal later.

A queue formed on the far side of the machine. A couple of fairies, an elf, and a giant stood docilely staring straight ahead. No fear on their expressions. No gazes darting around seeking escape.

"Why don't they run?"

"Or fight?" Keltie's preferred method of dealing with conflict.

"Remember the Compliance Taser that defeats your will to fight?"

The taser had made even Keltie docile.

"Before the majiks are taken out of the holding cell they are given a serum with their last meal." He sounded as if he was swallowing a disgusting morsel. "The serum makes them loopy and they follow the majik in front of them. They're sucked into the auraguillotine one by one, where they are processed."

From above, the shiny metal parts of the machine glinted. Red, orange, purple, and other colored lights flashed on and off resembling an out of whack podship light. Silver tanks aligned around the largest portion of the machine with wires and electrodes sticking out. A black flap sucked in and out where the majiks took the final plunge.

Too clean for a killing machine.

I'd always loved the hi-tech gadgets at home making my

life easier. The robo vac, the self-cleaning sink, the dish sanitizer. Arbor had been afraid of anything I'd cooked in the insta-oven, saying it couldn't be healthy. She believed one needed love and care and tradition to make a meal. According to her, magic was the most important ingredient. She didn't understand humans didn't have magic, so they'd developed tech.

But at what cost?

The main part of the auraguillotine was round and about the diameter of an adult dragon. It had small windows on the surface where guards could watch the process. Sick. Had technology made humans removed and non-attached to others?

"The majiks are conveyed to the extraction chamber where their powers are stolen. The power ascends those coiled tubes and is collected in the various tanks based on kind."

The tanks' colors related to the lights. Red for one kind of majik, say fairies. Orange for another. Purple for a third. And so on.

"What happens to the majiks after their powers are stolen?" Keltie asked.

"In order to steal the power, the majiks are tortured." His disgust strummed through his vocal cords in an angry clash. "The machine fractures a majiks' power and sucks their souls."

Agony tore through me as if my soul was being ripped. Imagining the torment and the helplessness my knees buckled and I wanted to sink to the ground and bury myself. For a half-second I thought about turning around. This wasn't my struggle. It would be risky, and I could fake being human for the rest of my life.

But I wasn't human, and I was done pretending. I'd made the decision during the past twelve hours.

"Torture?" I squeaked. Resolute didn't mean unafraid.

He put an arm around me. "They die, Elle. They're tortured to access their powers, and they die."

The arm might've brought comfort, and yet his words delivered nothing but fear. I shook his kind of comfort off.

Watching the majiks placidly plodding to their abhorrent deaths, I struggled to take a breath while trying to stay quiet. I had to help them. Had to stop this now. Even if I couldn't save Arbor, I could save others. A rod spiked through my spine keeping it straight. I'd never again doubt my intentions or even think about pretending to be human again. This was a fight I wanted to be part of, and if we could make a dent on their side by taking one risky step now before the war, I'd take it.

"How do we destroy it?" I turned to Stone for guidance.

Keltie leaned in closer. "Do you have another one of those explosive devices?"

"No."

I shivered at the memory of the painful effects the device had on me.

"What can you pull out of your bag?" Stone inspected the evening bag hanging around my neck.

"Are we far enough above ground?" The bag hadn't worked in the tunnels and caverns.

"The majiks need their magic in order for the machine to steal their powers."

Keltie snapped her fingers. "The reason why the majiks are drugged into compliance."

I swallowed. "Does the serum make it easier for the majiks during the torture?"

"No. Their minds are drugged." Stone's hard tone hit like a hammer. "They can feel everything."

A hammer that swung down and pounded me into an emotional fury. I wanted to dash into the room and scream at the majiks to run, and for the humans to stop. I knew the action wouldn't be successful. We had to have a plan.

I snapped open my bag and peered inside at the comb and lip cover. "What device will work best to destroy the machine without harming the surrounding majiks?"

He regarded the bag as if he expected it to grow wings. His contemplative gaze roamed from the bag to study the machine. "The key is destroying the machine. There isn't another one. It would take weeks to build a second. Then, my unit will have time to rescue the remaining trapped majiks. Can you pull a bomb out of the bag?"

"I can try." I reached my hand inside. "Explain to me how it looks and what you want it to do."

Closing my eyes, I listened as he told me what he needed. I pictured the shape of the device, the way the mechanisms clicked and connected, the way it would explode the machine in a terrifying boom.

My hand wrapped around a cylinder device made of metal and plastic. I pulled it out of the bag and held it up. "Got it."

"Neat trick." Keltie arched her brows expressing her doubt. "Will it work?"

"It will work."

Did Stone have confidence in me or Gardenia's Necessary Bag? Most likely the latter.

He detailed what had become his plan.

I was okay with that. He had more experience and knew how the machine worked. I understood there were going to be losses. Majiks would die by the auraguillotine while we got ourselves and the explosive device in position. Others would die when the explosion occurred. We could die, but it was worth it.

We each had a task based on our abilities and appearances. Poor Keltie had the most challenging part hiding her elfin features. She pulled the broad cap down low and tucked in her pointy ears. She was chosen for her task because of how she looked.

Stone slipped into the grate opening and dropped to the ground on almost-silent feet. Keltie went next, landing next to him like a cat. Shaking out my arms, I squirmed above the opening and stuck my feet through. My legs dangled and I swung my feet, hoping to keep my balance and not fall. I wiggled further down wanting to get as close as possible to the floor.

Strong arms wrapped around my thighs and lifted me down. "Thanks."

Nodding, he let go of my legs and stood. He studied my face and then turned to Keltie. "Ready?"

My knees trembled, and my stomach churned. My head felt slightly dizzy and my throat dry. I was terrified. Terrified of being caught. Terrified of dying. Mostly, terrified of not taking a chance at bringing this machine down.

"Keltie, keep your head down and move as if you're following orders." He examined me. "Elle follow behind me and when we get to the side of the machine where there are no guards posted. Start climbing."

I wished I'd paid attention in gym class when we'd done rock climbing. I wished I'd listened to Arbor when she'd wanted to go to the park and climb large boulders. I wished I could wish my way to the top.

Magic tingled in my fingers. Did I dare try and use my untested powers?

Stone marched us into the room with the machine. The excruciating screams hit a raw nerve and I froze. How could I proceed calmly when majiks were being tortured right in front of me? He angled his head. I gave him a confident nod. I could do this. I had to do this.

He slapped a guard on the shoulder. "Guard change."

The head guard signaled to two other guards and the three of them left leaving around a dozen who could figure out what we were up to. Stone marched around the far side of the machine with me and Keltie following him. I stopped on the side with no guards and crouched out of view.

Stone tapped another guard who stood near the front of the line of majiks. The guard took another position and Keltie took his place. She put a finger to her lips when an elf in line recognized her heritage.

Please stay quiet. I put my foot on the lowest rung of a built-in ladder that led to the top of the auraguillotine. The ladder gave access to mechanics fixing the machine. I was going to blow the machine to smithereens.

Keltie led the first elf toward the back door. This exit led back to the holding cells where all the teen majiks had been housed. It wasn't saving the majik's life, at least not yet, but it got the elf out of the assembly line of death.

The majiks didn't doubt her orders, just as they didn't doubt the humans' evil directions.

I placed my foot on the second rung. One step closer to victory.

Stone slipped into a spot by another guard and nodded. He had the best view to warn and protect both me and Keltie. I admired how he fit in so seamlessly.

A sharp scream soared over the suctioning tumult of the machine. The tanks had a unique jangle of their own, filling and emptying and filling some more.

Chills ran down my spine and I sprouted goosebumps across my entire body. I wanted to cover my ears. Unfortunately, I couldn't climb without my hands. With nerves stretched to breaking point, I hoisted my foot onto the next metal step and lifted my body. The sooner I accomplished my goal, the sooner we could save the teen majiks and get out of here. That's what I focused on.

Using my arms, I pulled myself higher. The machine hissed and hummed beneath me—a sinister song.

I got to the halfway point and spotted Stone. He stood tall with his broad shoulders and large arms. Big by human standards. He pretended to be looking straight ahead, except I saw his gaze dart to me and to Keltie. He was keeping watch.

My nerves soothed a bit.

Keltie took about every other majik in the long line and led them to the back door. I had no idea what the majiks thought. We weren't saving them all. Not yet.

Adrenaline gave me a boost. I continued my climb and nearly reached the top.

A large horn bellowed drowning out even the majiks' harrowing screams.

My hand fumbled and I lost my grip. Air whooshed from my lungs and I dangled by my other hand, my white-knuckled fingers curling around a metal handle. My body hit the side of the machine and my knee slammed into the metal. That was going to bruise.

The large bang caught the attention of the nearest guard.

I couldn't get caught now. I was so close to the top and the most vulnerable spot to place the explosive device.

Stone said something to the attentive guard. He'd been watching my actions, seen my stupid fall.

Flinging my free hand high, I gripped the ledge and pulled myself back into position. I scrambled higher and placed the explosive device near the top. I needed to set the timer and flick a switch and my task would be complete.

The horn rang a second time and the double doors we'd walked through earlier opened. The auraguillotine came to a halt. The hissing stopped, and the screams cut short.

I breathed a sigh.

"Regent Theobald and Prince Zacharye are here to assess the operation," a royal guard announced.

The machine guards came to attention and put their hands to their foreheads in a salute.

The regent strolled in wearing full regalia. The long red robe, the gold crown, the rubied scepter.

The guards bowed at his entrance.

A second person paraded in behind the regent. His shiny shoes glared. His pressed pants didn't have a piece of lint and his starched shirt appeared crisp. A bejeweled sash adorned his chest. He wore a familiarly endearing expression of concern.

Rye.

My heart lurched and tumbled. He seemed so different and superior than when we'd parted. He must be more than a friend of the prince. Maybe bringing the prince and regent here was part of his plan to help the majiks. To prove to the prince what was really going on in the palace. If he couldn't convince them with his words, he could show them the torture device. Maybe that's why his words had sounded so harsh earlier.

Or maybe it was the prince convincing Rye to believe in the evil plot.

I pulled myself higher to get a glimpse of the prince behind him.

The nearest guard bowed.

To Rye.

My lurching heart stopped beating for a second, and then pitter-pattered to the rhythm of a fast song. Not a love song. Not a song of friendship. Rye had lied. The prince was not coming in behind him because Rye was the prince.

Prince Zacharye.

Chapter 21

Squeezing my eyes tight, I willed away the vision. This couldn't be right. When I opened my eyes again, there Rye stood. Except he wasn't just Rye.

Rye was Prince Zacharye.

My brain buzzed with the fact. My friend was not my ally. He probably wasn't even my friend. He'd tricked me. My body sweltered and I wanted to bang my head against the auraguillotine. He'd made a fool of me.

But if he was the prince, why hadn't I killed him when we met? The Binding Promise should have forced me to assassinate the prince. I'd spent time with him at the ball and under the palace searching for Arbor. And yet, Prince Zacharye was still alive.

The buzzing in my head swarmed like gnats. Like magic, had the enchantment not worked under the palace? Yet I'd met him at the ball. Did the Binding Promise not recognize the prince as I hadn't? I didn't know enough about my fairy background or the rules or the magic to understand how the dagger or the promise worked. I pinched my lips together. Gardenia had said the weapon would seek justice.

Had the dagger recognized the goodness in Rye? Was that even possible for an inanimate object?

I frowned. There was no goodness in him. He'd lied about who he was. Lied to me.

He'd pretended to be an acquaintance of the prince, someone with influence, not overall control. He'd pretended to care about the plight of the majiks. What was his game?

"I want to understand how torturing teen majiks is saving the kingdom." Rye's strong tone carried toward me in my position high on the auraguillotine.

My breath fractured in cold crystals. He knew about the torture. He must believe in this terrible contraption. So much for goodness. So much for hope. How could I be fooled into thinking he'd wanted to help? How could I fall for him?

With each step he took closer, my pulse throbbed. I willed him to glance up at the same time I prayed he didn't. I wanted him to see me and my wrath. Although if he saw me, our mission to destroy the machine would end.

His dark hair had been cut short, chopping off the lighter highlights. His thick brows curved above his eyes in a stern expression. His patrician profile appeared to be carved by the gods covered by a flawless complexion. Perfection for a teenage guy. Amazing, how handsome can cover the ugly underneath.

Dressed in full regalia and with the shorter hair, I now saw the resemblance to the old vids of the prince. The brown hair color appeared more natural matching his eyebrows, than the blond hair he'd always sported. The old color had matched the regent's hair showing a resemblance. Now, they looked nothing alike. Too bad they thought alike.

Rye's silver orbs roved over the machine, up and down and up and up.

My body tensed, *waiting, waiting, waiting.*

His gaze connected with mine. Every breath I took synched with his. No one else existed in the room except him and me.

Us.

Then, his eyes widened in horror realizing who I was and what I was doing.

His gaze shot daggers that plunged into me and punctured my heart. My body froze, and I couldn't do anything to stop him or warn the others. I was paralyzed.

Would he command his guards to arrest me? Would he stay silent about my position? Would he come to my rescue?

Twisting around, I focused on Keltie and Stone trying to warn them with my I've-been-discovered expression. Keltie couldn't see the prince from where she worked behind the large machine. Stone didn't know I'd met the prince, so he didn't understand the ramifications.

Pressing my lips together, I forced myself to wait for Rye to say something. Good or bad. For me or against me. My hand numbed holding the position for so long. My nerves screamed and tightened. I lost my grip.

And, I fell.

My body jolted with the fall putting my emotions back in place. My muscles tensed and tremors spread in my arms and legs. The ground rushed up to meet me. This was going to hurt, and I was going to get caught. In this weird-slowing-down-sense-of-time, my gaze swung to Keltie who wore a shocked expression. Stone charged in slow motion toward me, fear and concern etched on his square face. He was too far away. I squeezed my eyelids shut not wanting to witness my own demise.

Because when I fell, I'd be captured and killed.

My body hit something hard and solid. And warm. Instead of hurting me, it embraced, breaking my fall. This wasn't the hard floor. My bones didn't break, and my body didn't bruise. The scent of sandalwood enveloped me making me feel alive.

At least for the moment.

I let myself relax for a second before opening my eyes.

Rye held me in his arms. His mouth was open, gaping. The silver sizzled, and electricity leapt inside me.

"Elle?" He spoke with a sense of wonder. His gaze slid from my face to my uniform. "What're you doing here?"

Destroying your machine. His machine. My rage reignited.

His chin tilted, and I remembered he'd asked a question.

What was I doing? My lungs seized when the reality of the situation returned. *What was I doing?* I tried to think of an excuse. *What. Was. I. Doing.*

"Fixing the machine." My answer came out fast and totally the opposite of my actions.

His silver eyes zapped through me as if trying to connect with my soul. My truth.

The truth.

Stone cleared his throat. We had an audience. An audience besides the prince. The regent, the other guards, Stone, and Keltie squinted at the two of us believing we were mentally deranged. An unknown guard having a normal conversation with the prince while in his arms.

My cheeks scorched, and I wanted to disappear.

"Fixing the machine?" Rye repeated my words with a flavor of disbelief.

Stone growled, and Keltie inched forward. They were both ready to defend me. I needed to defend them. Maybe I could use whatever connection Rye and I had so he'd use his influence to let us go.

I'd lie to him just as he'd lied to me.

"I can stand." I shoved against his chest and wiggled my legs.

Rye didn't let me down physically, even though he'd let me down in so many other ways. His grip tightened. He continued to study me. "I don't understand."

He didn't believe me. I could see it in his expression, how he glared and roved down my body once more. Why was he mad? Did he not want to believe I'd switched to the other side? The guards' side. *His* side.

My mind whirred. How could he be upset with me when I'd been so wrong about him? I'd thought we'd had a connection, that he liked me, believed he was trying to help. My shoulders dropped with the weight of my own deception. I'd been pretending to be human for my entire life. Were our lies similar?

No. I refused to compare myself to him. My lies hadn't scarred anyone except myself. His lies were far worse.

"Let me down." I put authority in my voice as I'd heard him use. Now I understood why.

Stone bowed. "I'm sorry this guard is bothering you." He tried to sound humble, but I heard the roar of anger beneath the quiet words. "You can put her down now, your majesty."

I cringed.

The prince swung my legs down and set my feet on the ground as if I was cherished, which I found hard to believe after his earlier expression of horror. "Are you sure you're okay?"

He peered at me and Stone and back to me again. The prince's body stiffened, and his gaze narrowed at my new protector. Did Rye care?

I wanted to bang my fist against my head. The connection I'd thought we had still seemed to live inside both of us. Yet how could I judge a guy's feelings when I'd only known him for hours? When he'd lied about who he was? When he was the prince!

He'd saved me from a brutal fall. He'd run so fast he'd been a blur. How could he be evil when he'd saved my life?

"Did you finish *fixing* the machine?" Stone grabbed my arm and pinched bringing me back to our current situation.

My face muscles slackened. It really didn't matter how Rye felt because we were on opposing forces. "Almost."

My answer hit me, sharp and strong. I'd failed to set the timer on the explosive device.

"What is going on?" Regent Theobald's question demanded.

Stone bowed to the prince again. "I'm sorry this guard caused a problem. I'll take care of her for you, your majesty."

He started pulling me toward the back when Keltie caught my attention. She was climbing up the side of the machine and was going to finish the job I'd ungracefully abandoned. The air leaked out of me.

The prince and the regent and the guards continued to leer. If I created a distraction, Keltie could finish the job. I yanked my arm out of Stone's and faced the prince. The two of us talking distracted everyone in the room, including the regent.

"You changed the color of your hair." My tone was a little too hard. This wasn't supposed to be an accusation, but a conversation to stop anyone from seeing Keltie.

He lifted the dark wisps covering his forehead. "My uncle's make up team couldn't dye my hair blond or shave it short while my scar healed." His lips lifted in a slight smile as if he had enjoyed his slight rebellion. "I decided I liked my natural color. Do you?"

"Um, yeah." I swallowed. So he hadn't been in disguise at the ball.

The guards continued to gawk. Keltie was almost at the top.

"I hope I didn't hurt you, *your majesty*." I flashed what I hoped was a flirtatious smile. A fake flirtatious smile.

Stone growled again.

"You're small." Rye's expression softened and the tease in his tone sent thrills across my skin. "You couldn't injure a fly or a fairy."

I gulped. Did he know?

His friendly face went cold as he spun toward Stone. "She was doing her job. Maybe you should pick someone taller for the task in the future."

"As you wish, your majesty." Stone spoke through gritted teeth.

"Thank you so much, *Prince Zacharye*." My gratefulness was to more than him. Everyone else in the room was too busy watching our drama to notice Keltie at the top of the auraguillotine. "So glad you came to my defense and believe in helping the little people."

"Of course. Are you sure you're not hurt?" Rye's concern caused my stomach to flutter. "I could take you to the royal medic."

I angled away. The last thing I needed was to be taken deeper into the royal palace. "I'm fine."

Keltie had finished the set-up of the device and started climbing down. Stone was ready to gather his team and escape before the explosive device went off in ten minutes. An urge to warn Rye prodded. I didn't want him to suffer any damage.

"You should go see the medic." I wanted him safe, even while my head wanted him dead. Leaning toward him, I placed my palms on his chest.

The closest real guard gasped.

It must be against protocol to touch the prince. Since my hands tingled, it must not be healthy for me either.

"What is the hold up?" Regent Theobald's demand jarred. "The auraguillotine is supposed to be running twenty-four hours a day. We have a schedule."

Nausea rose. A schedule for killing innocent teen majiks. I wanted to believe Rye didn't understand the depth of the persecution. The murder and mayhem. The unfairness of the system the regent had put in place. I hoped the shallow and unconcerned words I'd overheard in the library when he didn't stick up for the majiks had been a cover for his true nature.

Except, he was the prince with real power. Technically, more power than the regent.

"This, um, guard," he faced his uncle with a bland expression. One displaying no depth. And yet, I'd seen the depth of his emotions, seen to the center of his soul—or so I'd thought, "was fixing the machine."

"I don't have time for this." The regent's face scrunched, and bright red spots shone high on his cheeks. He imitated a petulant child. I could picture him stomping his foot and throwing a tantrum. He reminded me of Sybil. "Turn it on."

The job was complete. The explosive would detonate. I took a final glance at Rye. He was close to the machine. If I pushed him closer, I might assassinate him as I was supposed to do. An aching fissure formed in my heart. I'd had difficulty accepting the fact Gardenia wanted me to kill an unknown prince.

This wasn't an unknown royal. This was Rye.

My thoughts seesawed back and forth like the seeds of a dandelion in a strong wind.

Stone must've read my mind because his fingers gripped my arm tighter.

The regent inched closer. "Prince Zacharye wants to be reassured of our processes."

I wished I could push Regent Theobald closer to the machine and the explosion.

Rye scrunched his mouth together in a distasteful puckering pinch. "Questioning the processes."

My bleak outlook lightened. Maybe what he'd learned from me and the other majiks had helped him see how terrible the ruling royal government had treated majiks. Maybe he'd do something to stop this madness.

"It's so technical. Too boring for you, your majesty." Regent Theobald waved away any concern.

My lips flattened, and I wanted to speak up.

Stone tugged on my arm signaling I should stay quiet. As Keltie made slow progress down, she'd moved to the back side of the machine, closer to the line of majiks so she wouldn't be seen. She was about halfway down.

"This is my kingdom. My citizens." Rye spoke strongly, spoke up for himself. "I want to understand."

Pride he at least had the nerve to question the regent's plans filled my lungs. Rye was going to be a better ruler than the regent.

"Turn it on!" Regent Theobald stalked to the control panel. He punched a red button with his fat fist.

The machine chugged starting up. The belching of the tanks filling and emptying caused my stomach to roil. I skimmed between the majiks to Keltie to Stone to Rye.

The majiks in line moved forward again and the first was sucked in. The explosive would go off in nine minutes. How many would be tortured before then? The beginning of the first scream drove a chill up my spine and I sent up a silent prayer. I hoped Stone had a plan. His hard face gave nothing away.

Rye seemed to be holding his breath. His gaze was wide, and his fingers twitched as if ready to throttle the regent. Regent Theobald beamed as the screams got louder.

I skimmed the line of majiks. The next one was sucked inside revealing a small majik behind. A smoke sprite.

My entire body stilled. My eyes grew as wide as a dark knot in a big oak tree. "Arbor!"

Rye's head jerked toward the line. He knew my friend's name.

Stone glowered, then slashed me an antagonistic scowl.

I slapped a hand over my mouth. *Idiot.* I'd given myself away and attracted attention to the line of majiks. And Keltie. My brow started to sweat. This was Arbor. My reason for beginning this quest in the first place. I clasped my mouth shut and controlled my limbs from darting forward.

"Elle?" The small voice didn't sound like my friend. She was confused and dispirited.

I glanced at Stone. His expression was set in, well, stone. Except he didn't understand the depth of my friendship with the smoke sprite. A manic jolt of energy slashed through me. "I've got to save Arbor."

"Our priority is destroying the machine." Stone held on tight to my arm as he whispered. I realized he'd been sent to protect me, not my friend.

Rye's mouth dropped. He'd heard Stone's whispered response. The prince grabbed my other arm. "Who are you?"

I was a wishbone between the two guys.

Keltie climbed faster down the machine. She must've seen the argument and understood our predicament. We didn't have much time before the explosion either.

Yanking both my arms, I tried to get free. When I'd said saving *all majiks,* I'd meant saving *all majiks.*

"An elf is trying to escape." A guard monitoring the majik line raised his weapon and fired at Keltie.

She ducked, and the shot rang off the metal of the machine.

Clenching my fists, I ripped my arms out of both Stone and Rye's grips. I needed to help, to do something to assist both my friends. Arbor was next to be sucked into the machine.

Already spotted, Keltie climbed down toward the entrance with elf speed. She grabbed a lever near the end of the machine. Her sharp gaze connected with mine sending a message.

Images flashed of our short time together. Our first meeting when she confronted Rye and I in the cave. Discussing why she'd been arrested. Her decision to back me up and follow me deeper into the underground portion of the palace. Her leadership. Her bravery. Her friendship.

Keltie swung forward and around.

Around toward the back of the machine.

Around toward the majik vacuuming intake entrance. She kicked out with her feet and connected with Arbor's midsection. The tiny smoke sprite went flying into the air.

Red spots glimmered in front of my vision. Keltie had attacked Arbor. I ran forward trying to get to the sprite before she hit the ground.

I was too late. Her tiny body flopped and hit the concrete with a splat. She landed near the back door.

"Arbor!" I rushed to her side and got to my knees.

The smoke sprite was dazed, but not unconscious. Of course, she'd been dazed standing in line because of the drug she'd been given.

The guards seemed as confused as the drugged majiks. Why would an elf attack a smoke sprite? Stone and Rye both advanced toward me at the same time, bumping their shoulders.

"What is going on here?" Regent Theobald shouted above the noise.

The machine made the terrible sucking cacophony, vacuuming the next majik inside. That should've been Arbor. Keltie hadn't attacked Arbor. The elf had saved her.

My chest expanded and I tipped my head back toward Keltie in gratitude.

Her body got trapped in the suction. Her eyes bugged out and terror flashed on her face. "Aiiea!"

It was her special battle cry, and the roughness sent a glacial chill through me, frosting my insides.

"Keltie!" No worrying about being stealth now. In one swift move, I got to my feet and darted toward the majik intake entrance.

Stone pushed away the other majiks in the line trying to get to Keltie.

"Stop the machine!" Rye dashed toward the control panel.

The guards didn't obey his instructions. Nothing stopped. The machine continued to operate, continued to suck. Continued to kill.

Each of Keltie's fingers lost their grip. She couldn't hold on any longer. Desperation clawed at my lungs with ragged, trembling nails. The suction was too strong.

Her body slipped inside.

The horrible pandemonium of the machine combined with Keltie's scream.

"Aiea! Aieeeeeeeea! Aieeee—"

Chapter 22

"Noooo!"

The immediate denial sprang to my lips. My mouth hardened, stuck in the same position. Like my mind. Stuck with one thought. Keltie was dead.

When my screams faded into nothingness the cold hard truth stabbed. My new friend was gone. Killed by the machine. Killed by this monstrous royal government. Killed by Rye and his uncle.

There'd be no more battles for her.

She'd sacrificed herself for my friend. For me.

Flying across the room, rage throbbed in my veins. I only saw one thing past the wetness in my eyes. My enemy. I pummeled on Rye's chest. "How could you? How could you let this happen when you're the stinking prince?"

Even though I was close, he pulled me in, wrapping his arms around me. "I'm sorry."

I continued to pound out my anger, each hit becoming weaker. How could people be so cruel to each other? How could I stand by and watch?

"Arrest that guard. She's attacking Prince Zacharye."

Regent Theobald gathered his purple robes and swished toward the exit. "I must be protected and taken to safety."

My fists stopped mid-punch from the shock of the regent's words.

He hurried from the room with a couple of royal guards surrounding him. The door banged closed and the lock clicked in place. Coward. He didn't care about the safety of his nephew, only his own royal blood.

Three guards circled us. Stone was the fourth.

His glare could've seared my skin. He was angry, and sad, and some other emotion I couldn't define.

"I'm okay." The prince raised one hand to reassure the guards and patted my back with the other. "I know this guard."

Not really. Except now wasn't the time to point that out. He didn't know my initial task was to kill him while saving Arbor. He didn't know I'd joined forces to destroy the auraguillotine and if I lived, to pursue justice for majiks.

Whether through negotiation or revolution.

"Stop the machine!" Rye ordered for the second time.

The guard at the control panel shook his head. "The regent—"

"Ellery." Stone grabbed my arm and pulled me from the prince's embrace. "We need to go."

Rye didn't resist, although his gaze connected to mine and communicated with me in a silent plea for understanding.

Understanding of what, I didn't know. No matter how I felt, or what I wanted to believe, he was my adversary. He might've ordered them to stop the machine, however the regent clearly held more sway.

"Now." Stone's command caused me to stop staring and survey the area.

The guards had listened to the prince's first command and

hadn't apprehended me. Even so, they stood with their weapons raised ready to attack. They hadn't switched off the machine. Their fierce expressions told me they wouldn't hesitate to kill if I made one wrong move. The prince had given me precious time to attempt escape.

"Elle?" Arbor's soft tone carried over the commotion. She stood on her own two feet near the spot she'd fallen.

I wanted to reach out to her, assure her, tell her everything was going to be all right. But I didn't know for certain. We were surrounded by enemy guards and locked in a room with a bomb set to go off in minutes.

And the machine continued to suck one majik in at a time.

"Ellery?" Rye didn't only question my name. With a single word he questioned my intentions.

I was being pulled in three different directions. I wanted to confront and question the prince. I'd agreed to help Stone destroy the machine and save the majiks. I'd sworn to rescue Arbor. I'd already lost one friend today, and one last night, I refused to lose another.

Rushing toward Arbor, I glanced at the explosive device. The red number glared five minutes.

"Go, now." Rye shoved Stone toward me. "If you can get out, I'll stop them from following."

How? The guards listened to only some of his orders. And why? Whose side was the prince on?

The prince wheeled toward the guards. "The majiks currently in the room will be released under my orders."

The guards grumbled. They kept their weapons pointed at us.

I swooped Arbor into my hands. My best friend was with me again. At least I'd been successful at one thing. Sort of. If we escaped. I didn't have time to celebrate. *We* didn't have time.

A guard stomped toward us following the regent's orders, not the prince's.

"Elle!" Arbor's nervous shout screeched in my ear.

Stone jumped in front and punched the guard in the face. He removed his rifle and pointed it at the next guard. By doing so, he exposed his motives to his guard associates. He was now in danger.

A tremble slid through me and everything started happening at once.

The other guards zeroed in on us.

I placed Arbor on my shoulder and stuck my hand in my bag.

Rye raised his hands in a combative stance and edged toward me. The problem was I didn't know which side he'd be fighting on. I wanted to believe he'd protect me.

Focus. I couldn't think about him. I needed to settle on a weapon from my bag.

"Give me something helpful," I whispered.

Chaos broke out around me. Stone used the butt of his gun to smack a guard in the chest. He swung around and took out two more. A few of the guards hadn't moved, unsure whether to attack.

My hand settled around a slim, malleable object. I tugged it out and discovered a coiled rope in my hand. The silver whip made from tight, cylindrical notches glowed with magic. The tip of the rope spurt fire.

Warmth radiated across my skin. I wouldn't go down without a fight.

"Who are you? And what did you do with my anti-magic Elle?" Arbor's joke sounded almost normal.

"Watch this." Flinging the whip, sparks of color flew off its tip.

Tcha.

I whipped the rope forward. My untrained arms knew what to do. Maybe that was part of the magic.

The rope coiled around a guard's legs like a snake. He tried to run, and his steps faltered. I yanked on the rope and the guard fell.

"Woot!" Arbor cheered.

Stone battled against three guards. Another guard drew a long gun. Its red laser light shown on my torso. I gulped.

"Don't hurt her!" Rye scrambled to block the guard's shot. "Don't hurt her."

I paused in my wind up of the whip. He cared about me. The proof was in his protection. Although, he didn't know I was half-majik or understand the depth of my deception.

"That guy is crushing on you." Arbor whispered in my ear.

I hated to burst her bubble. "That guy is the prince."

My beliefs about Rye went back and forth like my whip. Good or bad?

Stone conked two of the guards together, knocking both of them out. "Arbor! Lead the majiks out of here."

He was fighting for me and the majiks. I could count on him.

Rye? I wasn't so sure.

Arbor listened to the order without question. She flew off and twittered around the majiks waiting in line. Hopefully, she could be persuasive.

Rye left my side and scurried away from the fighting. Was he trying to save himself like his weasel of an uncle?

I used my whip harder to take out two more guards. The whip brought the enemy down and stunned them into submission. I didn't understand the weapon's powers, but I was using it and winning.

While I fought, I kept my gaze on Rye.

Which pissed me off because I shouldn't be interested. I shouldn't care.

He argued with the guard controlling the auraguillotine, both their hands gesticulating. His pointing fingers rolled into fists. I took down another guard and lumbered toward the back. He shoved the guard aside. The guard couldn't attack the prince. Rye reached the control panel and started punching buttons. Did he know what he was doing?

Was he helping or hurting my cause?

I lassoed another guard and pushed a dazed and straggling majik toward the back exit. We needed to get as many majiks out of the room before the explosion.

The screeching of the machine stopped.

My breath hitched and I paused.

Rye had managed to turn off the auraguillotine. My pulse picked up its pace. He must be on my side.

A guard grabbed me around the neck from behind. He pinned my arms to my sides. I couldn't use the magical whip. My nostrils flared, and a scream built inside my lungs. I'd been so close to the exit.

Arbor flew to my side and misted into a puff of smoke, spraying the guard's face. He shook his head but didn't let go. Struggling against my captor, I scanned the room for help.

Three guards held Stone on the ground. A fourth guard pointed a weapon to his head. He had no chance of escaping.

"Fly away, Arbor."

Her wings fluttered against my neck. She stayed put, loyal to the end.

My chest swelled, and calmness spread through my veins. The machine would be dust soon and we would die with it. I tilted my chin to a proud and defiant angle. The prince would die, too. My original mission would be complete.

A heaviness filled my heart weighing it down. I didn't

want Rye or Stone to die. Or Arbor or any of the majiks either. Yet destroying the auraguillotine needed to happen.

Stone glanced at me, then to the countdown clock. We both understood where this would end in…

Two minutes.

Rye stepped around the now-silent machine. His expression gleamed with a light of sympathy, but he didn't say anything. Didn't approach me. Didn't defend.

My heart tightened and pulled, shrinking. He was the prince. If he wanted, he could save me. Although the guards hadn't listened to his earlier order.

The four guards holding Stone dragged him to his feet. Another guard stomped toward us with a majik detector. He raised the long stick to Stone's head and ran it down the length of his large body. My friend fought their hold.

Beeeeeep. Whir-whir-whir-whir.

My body vibrated. Stone was a majik. I spotted the greenish veins by his neck. The unusual color should've been a clue. Plus, his size. He wasn't as big as a regular giant, and yet he was bigger than most humans.

Half giant?

He nodded, understanding my realization.

We had more in common than I'd realized. And, we both were working for Gardenia. The thought dropped in my stomach and wallowed there.

The guard easily reached my head with the detector.

I braced myself for the telling sound. I wasn't embarrassed anymore. I was proud of who I was.

Beeeeeep. Whir-whir-whir-whir.

No surprise on Stone's face. He knew I was majik. He probably knew more about me than I did. I'd force him to tell me everything when, and if, I got the chance.

Rye's skin paled to the unhealthy shade he'd had in all his

princely vids, the pasty color the males at school imitated. "It's the smoke sprite on her shoulder setting the detector off. Remove her friend."

"Go!" I shushed Arbor away.

This time she listened. She flew toward the back door the other majiks had left open.

Hopefully, I'd saved my best friend. She could escape before the bomb exploded.

That's when it hit me. Gardenia had chosen me for this mission so I'd learn the truth, accept my heritage, and realize I needed to fight.

Holding my body still, I tilted my chin higher. The guard wanded me again.

Beeeeeep. Whir-whir-whir-whir.

Steeling myself, I held Rye's gaze as the guard pronounced, "She's an ugly zauber."

I took offense to the ugly part.

"Majik?" At least Rye used the correct term.

I waited for him to defend me. To tell the guards he knew me, and I was a friend.

He didn't. He clamped his lips together and pivoted away. From me. From everything I'd believed we had together.

My shoulders dropped. What did we have together? A stroll beneath the castle, a kiss? He wouldn't even admit to befriending a majik. I'd thought we'd made a connection last night. The kiss had been special. Of course, at that point he'd believed I was one hundred percent human. My body wavered. I'd placed too much faith in a guy I'd just met.

"Rye?" I couldn't stop myself from calling out.

He turned back. His gaze pierced through me, and then to Stone. The silver orbs flashed with hurt. His mouth pursed together in an angry pucker.

"You both are under arrest." A guard advanced with two sets of magnetic cuffs.

What did it matter? I was ready to face my death. I'd succeeded in saving Arbor, ruining the auraguillotine, and possibly killing the prince.

Everyone in this room would die in less than a minute. My friends and I would spark the revolution.

I glanced at the countdown clock and watched the final seconds *tick, tick, tick.*

Chapter 23

*K*ablow.

The room exploded.

The machine fractured and pieces of metal flew like shrapnel. Smoke mushroomed out in large, black billows. Fire sputtered shooting flames into the air like a firework display, similar to the one I'd created which had started this adventure.

Jolting, I ducked and covered my head. The guards holding me followed my actions. Adrenaline burst through my veins. This could be the end of all of us.

A guard near the control panel screamed and yanked a piece of metal out of his arm.

An ogre stomped her large foot on an out of control flame.

A female guard fell to the ground clutching her midsection.

A fairy had a piece of shrapnel stuck in his wing.

People fell left and right. Chunks, and ashes, and other particles hit me, and the majiks still in line, and the guards holding me. I gasped for air and yet still struggled to breathe. The granules choked, clogged my throat, and stuffed my nose.

The guards let go of my arms and dropped to the ground

to protect themselves. I stayed partially standing, hunched, watching and searching for my companions.

Arbor, Stone, and Rye.

The machine toppled to the ground in large fragments. The concrete floor exploded on impact, whizzing more debris into the air. My exposed skin scratched and burned. The smell of dirt, and oil, and chemicals spilled into the room causing me to gag.

Now free, the lasso in my hand whipped out of its own accord and blasted a piece of the machine headed toward me and sent the shards flying in the opposite direction.

My eyes bugged. My arm lashed back and forth. The whip was a shield and a weapon in one. The line of the rope blurred with the speed of its movement stopping shard after shard and chunk after chunk. I didn't control the lasso, only watched in fascination.

A sharp hunk of metal went flying toward the control panel where Rye stood. A guard yanked him to the ground and covered the prince's body with his own. The metal sliced through the guard's uniform. Ugly, dark red stains colored the guard's back. What about the prince?

My pulse raced and stumbled. With my whip protecting, I edged toward the control panel dodging flying sections of the machine.

A new sound rose, the rumbling of metal grating on metal. The closer I got to the control panel, the louder the noise. I waved at the smoke and focused on one thing. The large control panel shook and wavered. It toppled on the edge.

The panel fell and crashed. On top of Rye and the guard.

My heart clutched, and my skin went cold and clammy. Everything inside me quivered. "Rye!" Over the clamor, I could barely hear myself scream. "Rye!"

I tugged on the fallen control panel, trying to lift the heavy piece of machinery. It wouldn't budge. I yanked and pushed and finally kicked the dang thing. Only Stone had the strength to lift it.

Using the lasso to protect myself, I worked my way to the spot Stone had been standing. His three guards were gone. Seeing me, he scrambled to his feet and then stopped.

His gaze widened and his pupils darted around following the action of my whip. "What the heck?"

I was amazed by the whip's magical force, too. But we could *ooh* and *ah* about weapons later.

"Follow me and stay close." Keeping the whip's defensive techniques steered in the opposite direction, I worked my way back to the spot where the prince lay.

On both sides of us, guards were dead or injured. Blood stained the once-spotlessly clean floor. Smoke obscured the other side of the room. My lasso continued to defend, and I stood taller. It felt good to finally be the capable one.

"That's incredible." Stone grinned and then winced.

A large gash marred his non-fighting arm. The blood congealed in a strange mixture of red and green. Infected or giant blood?

"You're injured."

"Just a scratch." Pulling a tattered sleeve down, he covered the wound. "Let's get you out of here before these guards recover or more guards arrive."

"But—" I'd wanted to help Rye.

A loud rumbling from the back exit caught my attention. More guards must be arriving.

"Too late." I hoped the traumatized majiks we'd sent through earlier had gotten away. My shoulders slumped and I stopped moving toward the control panel. Rye would have his own army to help him soon. "Now what?"

"We fight alone." Stone's declaration said more than the words.

It was just the two of us. My eyes burned and my chin trembled. This was it. My life would end here before I had the chance to declare my new intentions. To be recognized as a fairy and to fight on the side of the majiks. Numbness traveled from the top of my head to the tips of my toes. I'd fight until my last breath.

"Not alone." Tos stood in the exit doorway with her hands on her tiny hips.

I flickered my eyelids wondering if I was imagining her. Through the smoke she resembled a conquering hero except she was so small. Who was I to judge by size? Small could be mighty. I'd proven that. My chest expanded, and I took in a few satisfied breaths.

I'd thought palace guards were approaching, not other majiks. Not friends.

Arbor flew over the brownie's head.

Tos marched into the room with a majik brigade in step behind her. "We're here to fight."

Behind her stood Hokima with a fierce expression. And behind him marched other brownies and fairies and trolls and elves. An entire contingent of majiks had arrived. Warmth spread in my bloodstream bringing hope back to life. The numbness disappeared. Tos and Hokima had gotten out of the palace alive and returned with friends to help. Stone and I weren't alone. And it proved a fairy and a giant and a brownie could be friends and work together.

I bent down and gave Tos a big hug. "Thank you."

"You're welcome." She cleared her throat. "Capture or kill any human alive in this room."

Stone drew his weapon prepared to fight if any of the guards struggled. "I can't believe you came back and brought help."

"I told the brownie chief what you planned, and he spoke with leaders of the other majik clans. The fairies especially wanted to be involved. Each sent fighters for me to command."

And they were listening.

A group of brownies and fairies and all sorts of majik creatures ready to fight side by side. A troll forced a captured guard to his feet while an ogre threatened with a weapon. A brownie went from body to body determining whether the guards were alive or dead. A fairy collected human weapons. The mixed majik army worked as a team to clean the battle scene and make sure no humans got away.

I anchored a hand on my hip and the other hand gave a thumbs up.

Stone lowered his weapon because things were under control. "How did you find our location, Tos?"

"We ran into the majiks you saved from the auraguillotine." She high-fived Stone on his calf. "Most of them joined us. Where's Keltie?"

My throat clogged and I couldn't speak.

"She didn't make it." Stone's voice choked.

Tos and Hokima stared at the ground.

"She was a hero. She saved lots of majiks." Including Arbor.

Arbor fluttered overhead shouting warnings and directions. I recognized a few of the majiks Keltic had saved before dying. A sharp sadness filled my lungs and I pushed it aside. The elf would not die for no reason. We'd won this battle, destroyed the machine, and were willing to fight for the cause.

I was willing to fight for the cause.

"Rye." My feet moved on their own as if pulled to him. I needed to make sure he was okay, at the same time my original task banged in my head.

Assassinate the prince.

The injured moaned and the captured complained. I hurried past. Doubt ticked like cricket's legs rubbing together in my mind. My quandary about whether to kill an unknown prince had challenged me. Even though I was now committed to the majik cause, I didn't know if I could kill a known entity.

Kill Rye.

The large, locked front doors on the far side of the room burst open. Palace guards stormed inside. They held innovated weapons and they didn't give orders before shooting. Bursts discharged from their guns.

"Ellery. We need to go." Stone grabbed my arm and tugged.

The guards advanced, taking positions behind what was left of the machine. Their guns never stopped. A majik near me went down.

I held back a cry. "But Rye…"

A bullet whizzed past my ear. Stone ducked and in one smooth move he scooped me up and threw me onto his shoulder.

"Hey." I fisted my hands.

Ignoring me, he signaled to the rest of the majiks and headed for the back exit. "Let's move out."

Arbor rounded everyone else up by flying around, completely comfortable with her new leadership role.

"What." I pounded Stone's back with my fist. "About." I pounded again. "Rye!"

"If he's not dead already, those guards won't give you the chance to kill him." Stone's statement hit like a second explosive device.

"You knew?" My ears pounded. "You knew I was charged with killing the prince?"

Another fact Stone hadn't confessed. Another aspect of his secret mission he didn't explain. He'd been sent to watch me and to make sure I carried out the assassination. As if I was a little kid or an AWOL soldier. Gardenia hadn't trust me.

His large feet stomped on the hard dirt ground as he ran past the cells and into the dark tunnels. My pulsed hammered. Tos darted in front of us and led the way. The other majiks followed.

My rage morphed into sweat and I wasn't even running. I'd decided to disobey Gardenia's orders by avoiding the prince.

Now I didn't know if Rye was alive or dead.

Chapter 24

The rest of the journey happened in a daze. Hokima had memorized the short cut he and Tos had taken from the safe room. At the exit, transport pods waited. We were whisked away. Stone, Arbor, and I arrived at Queens Academy. A place I'd sworn I'd never go, and now couldn't wait to get started on my training.

"It used to be the fairy palace." Stone must've seen me staring out the window at the grounds below.

The palace-turned-academy was built out of stone and marble resembling an ancient fortress. So different than the human palace of crystal and glass. A large wall circled the palace, its ground, and the outbuildings. The gardens had been turned into a sports field and weapons training ground.

The podship landed and the door opened with a silent swish. My stomach tumbled as I emerged onto the lawn in front of a grand stone staircase with gleaming marble pillars. A balcony ran the length of the building.

The palace guards saluted Stone and escorted us into the palace. The grand entryway boasted a large chandelier made from live flowers. The shiny marble floors reflected our dirty and bedraggled images. We probably should've come in through the back door.

Large golden doors with intricately carved wood panels depicting a forest were thrown open. We were led into a large reception area. More marble floors and flowered chandeliers. My gaze was drawn to the stage at the end where a single throne chair sat. The chair floated on a cloud stationed between two large oak trees. The branches of the trees glowed matching the chandelier above. Looking up, the night sky was visible.

Gardenia paced in front of the stage. Her hair had been pulled back in a tight bun, and yet many wisps had escaped as if she'd been fighting a battle of her own.

"Commander Gardenia." Stone saluted smartly, and Arbor followed his action.

Cute, how she imitated the half giant soldier.

Still mad at Gardenia and Stone for their lack of trust, I wasn't going to salute anyone.

"You're safe." Gardenia hugged me. "I'm so glad you made it out alive." She glared at Stone, probably blaming him for the danger I'd been in.

Stiffening, I slipped out of her arms. "You sent me on a mission. Unprepared and untrained."

"Yes, but not a suicide mission to destroy the auraguillotine." Worry lines formed around her lips. She glared again at Stone.

"It was a smart idea to get rid of the machine while we were so close." Stone's even tone didn't show any emotion. Not a muscle moved on his face.

The compliment soothed some of my anger.

"What about the young prince?" Her gaze flashed to me, before zeroing back on Stone.

My heart crushed, remembering Rye's face as he turned

away from me when he'd learned I was a majik. He didn't care about the real me. Just like my stepmother and stepsisters, he was disgusted by my majik half. I shouldn't mourn him.

Stone summarized the events in the torture chamber ending with, "We don't know if the prince is alive or dead."

"Why didn't the dagger force me to kill the prince when I first met him?" I needed to learn everything about the fairy world if I planned to live in it, fight for it. "I thought the dagger was enchanted as part of the Binding Promise."

"Give us a minute." Gardenia pointed to the door with her chin.

The way Stone and Arbor pivoted and left, showed how important my fairy godmother was in this world.

The nerves in my stomach twisted. I was alone with her.

She nibbled on her bottom lip. "The dagger weighs justice over crime. It must've decided that Prince Zacharye was worthy to live."

"Why didn't you tell me that beforehand?" A spike went through my chest. All that worry about how to avoid killing the prince hadn't been necessary. "If you want me fighting on your side, I need to learn everything about being a fairy."

"You're going to fight on our side?" Her surprise should've pleased me because she'd actually had doubts about the final outcome.

"Yes." The surety centered in my chest.

"You do need to learn everything." A trembling edge in her tone scared me.

The silence in the room oppressed or maybe it was the long shadow from the throne chair. The chair hovered like a muted reminder of what was at stake. I wiggled my shoulders trying to get comfortable with the new environment. This palace would be my home until I was ready for battle.

I needed to break the tension. "Why aren't you sitting on your royal throne?"

"Oh." She swirled around. Her white eyebrows shot upwards as if she'd been caught. She smoothed the lines of worry on her face. "It's not my throne to sit on. The Queen is still alive, and the lost princess has been found."

"That never stopped Regent Theobald."

Gardenia held a similar title to regent. Overseeing the fairy realm while the Queen was ill and until the true heir was found. Would Gardenia give up the power and control when the princess returned home?

"True." She tapped her long finger on her chin. "Which is why we're having this conflict now. I knew Prince Zacharye's father. He was a good man who died tragically and mysteriously and way too young."

My heart squeezed. I'd lost my parents, too. "You said the lost princess has been found. Where is she?"

According to Bim, the fairy realm was a matriarch society ruled by queens and passed from mother to daughter.

"For the princess's safety, only a few people know her identity." Gardenia stared at the throne chair as if she could make the lost princess materialize. "The chances of the current princess's mother becoming queen was nearly impossible. She had two older sisters who would take the role before her."

Arbor had once told me the queen had allowed the youngest daughter to leave the fairy world for love. She had two older daughters and their female offspring to inherit.

"Princess Celeste and Princess Daria died before having any female children." Sadness flickered on my fairy godmother's face.

"I'm sorry." With the deaths of the two princesses, Rye's parents, and possibly Rye, being royal sounded dangerous. I'd rather die fighting in a glorious battle than from palace intrigue. I blew out a breath. "I'm ready to attend the fairy academy and train to fight in the upcoming revolution."

That should bring a smile to Gardenia's face. I was giving her everything she wanted. It was what I wanted, too.

"I'm glad you've decided to accept your destiny." She didn't look happy. Her eyes took on a strange gleam. Her mouth compressed. "But you won't be fighting."

"Why not? That's what you've wanted since I turned sixteen." An odd strangled sound came from my throat. "A war is inevitable, and you need every good fairy on your side to fight."

She crossed her arms and her gaze alighted on the throne chair. "Fighting is too dangerous for you."

Stone had said something similar.

My stomach dropped expecting a roadblock. "That's ridiculous. I'm a fast learner. I have this amazing whip."

Gardenia unclasped her arms and grabbed my shoulders. Her bony fingers dug into my skin. "Fighting is too dangerous for you because you're the lost princess, Ellery."

Get a Sneak Peek of the Second Book in the series, releasing summer 2020...

CINDERELLA SOLDIER
A GLASS SLIPPER ADVENTURE

What if you discovered you're a long-lost fairy princess, but instead of taking the throne you want to become a powerful warrior and fight in the war?

The fairy kingdom is in an uproar. The lost heir to the throne has been found and everyone wants to know her identity. Except Ellery wasn't brought up to be royal and doesn't want anyone to learn she's the newly found princess. For several reasons.

Ellery wouldn't be allowed to become a soldier in the war of magic versus technology. She doesn't know or care about etiquette and ancestry. And her life would be in danger from those who want to ensure she never rules.

To keep Ellery safe from court intrigue, her fairy godmother sends her on a secret mission to retrieve an important magical artifact. After a journey fraught with peril, Ellery arrives at her destination to discover the real danger is still ahead. She must compete for the powerful relic against other champions from royal clans including someone she'd once loved and believed lost.

But to save the magical beings, Ellery will fight no matter the cost.

As she battles to claim the precious prize, Ellery finds herself drawn once again to the skilled warrior who had stolen her heart. But he's the enemy, wanting to destroy what she seeks to save, and she must decide: Is their love more powerful than magic?

Excerpt:

Sharp steel pressed against my neck. "This is the way to win, princess."

I sucked in a ragged breath and not from the closeness of the blade. Perry couldn't know the truth, few did. Because princess wasn't just a taunt, it was a title.

My title.

Locking gazes with him, I glared at his attempt to best me. His silver eyes flashed with what looked like hatred, and then went hard and cool. Cute, but a total stranger even if he was one of my new classmates. Did he forget we were on the same side training for a real battle? To be real soldiers in the fight against Regent Theobald and his cronies.

The blade pressed harder against my throat. Perry's long,

dark hair had been braided away from his forehead. His thin, angular face always appeared in a superior pout. "Concede, Ellery."

Why did it sound as if he was asking me to give up more than this fight?

"No." I wrapped my fingers tighter around my coiled carbon lasso, a connection of magical notches that did my bidding. And its own. A weapon that had found me on my first adventure.

My weapon whipped forward and wrapped around the hilt of his blade. The blade clattered onto the weapons training ground in a puff of dry dirt.

Perry scowled and backed away, disgust written across his face. "You're using magic, not skill."

He seemed to feel the need to best me in weapons and in magic class. It was as if he needed to prove his superiority in every aspect of fairy training. Which I didn't doubt. I'd received my fairy magic only a few months ago when I'd turned sixteen. The weapons training was completely new to me. And yet, I held my own. Real battle experience counted for something.

My chin tilted up and power thrummed through my veins. Yanking the whip back, I took a deep breath. I coiled the shiny rope with care and held it at my hip. "We're fairies. Magic is what we do."

I was only half-fairy. A fact that the other students consistently pointed out.

"You need to learn how to fight without magic. That's what weapons class is about." Perry stepped back and snatched his blade off the ground.

I'd known the Queens Academy would be worse than human school. Battle training had been combined with magic training—because I still needed help with my newly-forming powers—and added on were fairy etiquette and history. I didn't need the last two to win a war.

"Weren't you beneath Regent Theobald's royal palace where magic is suppressed?"

"No comment." Turning away, I strolled to the portable arsenal and perused my choices of weapons. He had a point about learning to fight without magic. Not that I'd admit it.

This war would be magic versus technology. Why study the ancient arts when we had power deep inside us? Still, I picked up a sabre and ran my gloved hand over the blade. Perry wanted a fair fight with no magic, so I'd give him one.

I slashed the weapon and a zing traveled through my arm. Turning, I faced my opponent. "En guard."

"Allez." He lunged, his blade glinting with sunlight.

I feinted to the right.

He lunged again, and our swords clashed.

The impact shattered up my arm and shook my spine. The weakness and fear brought me to a different place when I'd been feeble and unsure. I wasn't that person anymore.

I charged forward.

He attacked with intent as if relishing the need to hurt or embarrass me. To make me lose this fight. "Not so confident without your magic."

A guffaw shot out of my mouth. If he had seen my use of magic a week ago, he never would've made that statement. "Fairies have magic. You have magic. We should use it."

A new attitude for me.

"You should learn the hard way." Perry jabbed at my chest and I took a jump back into the shadows formed by the academy's balcony. "Then, when you use magic its easy."

He arced his sword down in a smooth move showing how simple it was for him.

I blocked it with my sabre. The clanging of metal rang in my head. Sweat formed on my upper lip.

He swung at me again and I ducked.

This wasn't a friendly bout or practice. This guy was going for me. I was okay with that. The hard training would exhaust me, and I'd forget…

Don't think about the prince.

I hadn't heard if he'd survived our one night together. My eyes burned at the memory of a huge chunk of metal flying toward Prince Zacharye, one of his guards diving on top of him, and all the blood. Then, the heavy panel had crashed, crushing everything beneath. Including the prince.

And I hadn't had time to check to see if he was alive or dead.

Perry's blade crashed against mine, bringing me back to the present. Blow after blow, the assault continued.

I found it difficult to breathe and I kept moving further and further back. He had me pinned against the balustrade. My opponent conjured a second sword from mid-air.

My heart raced and the sweat on my upper lip formed a thin layer of ice. "You said no magic."

"I said you should learn the hard way. I've learned. Now it's your turn." His wings spread, adding to his strength.

My head spun, and my gaze tried to follow the swirls of his weapons. I pressed against the concrete of the balustrade and my weapons hand fell to my side. Defeat set in. No wings, terrible magic, average fighting skills. Would I ever be good enough to become a soldier in the queen's army?

He pressed against me and in a barely audible whisper he said, "Why did you have to be found?"

Next in the series: *Cinderella Spy*

A Note from Allie Burton

I hope you enjoyed CINDERELLA ASSASSIN and are looking forward to the second book in the series coming out later this year.

Please consider giving this book a rating or review at your place of purchase. In this brave new book world, the only way for a good story to find its way into the hands of other readers is if the people who loved it let others know. We authors appreciate any little bit of help you can give, and reviews encourage me to write faster.

Receive a free book when you sign up for my newsletter. You can join at www.allieburton.com/contact.html and you'll also get the latest book news.

I love to hear from my readers! If you have any questions or comments, or just want to say "hi," please feel free to email me at allie@allieburton.com or connect with me on Twitter @allie_burton and Facebook at AllieBurtonAuthor and Instagram.com at allieburtonauthor.

If you're interested in my other young adult series, below is additional information. Thanks for reading CINDERELLA ASSASSIN!

Allie

ATLANTIS RIPTIDE
LOST DAUGHTERS OF ATLANTIS BOOK ONE

When a girl runs away from the circus...

For all her sixteen years, Pearl Poseidon has been a fish out of water. A freak on display for her adoptive parents' profit. Running away from her horrible life, she craves one thing—anonymity. But when she saves a small boy from drowning, she exposes herself and her mutant abilities to Chase, a budding investigative reporter.

Now, he has questions. And so do the police.

Once Pearl discovers her secret identity, she learns she's part of a larger war between battling Atlanteans. A battle that will decide who rules the oceans. A battle raging between evil and her true family. Will she find a way to use her powers in time to save a kingdom she never knew existed?

This is the start of a young adult fantasy action adventure novel series. "Free sweet summer young adult paranormal with death-defying underwater rescues." — Reviewer

Other books in the Atlantis series: Atlantis Red Tide, Atlantis Rising Tide, Atlantis Tide Breaker, Atlantis Dark Tides, Atlantis Twisting Tides, Atlantis Glacial Tides

WARRIOR'S DESTINY
WARRIOR ACADEMY BOOK ONE

An ancient amulet.
A powerful soul demanding she obey.
A double cross that ends with a curse.

During a heist to steal an ancient amulet, sixteen-year-old Olivia unwittingly receives the soul of King Tut…and the deadly curse that comes with it.

A member of a secret society, Xander believes he is destined to inherit the soul and wield its powers. He is determined to confront the devious thief and claim what is rightfully his.

When he discovers the horrible truth behind the Society's plans, he must join forces with Olivia to find a way to end the curse before it destroys the world. Facing untold dangers, Olivia and Xander must learn to trust each other and, eventually their hearts.

As the mystery surrounding the amulet unfolds, is their love enough to save them and the world from destruction?

"If you are a fan of Rick Riordan books about a quest with love and history thrown in…this is for you!" — Hooked In A Book Review (Originally published as Soul Slam)

Other books in series: Warrior's Chaos, Warrior's Prophecy, Warrior's Curse, Warrior's Rising

ALSO BY ALLIE BURTON

A GLASS SLIPPER ADVENTURE
Young Adult

Cinderella Assassin
Cinderella Soldier
Cinderella Spy

LOST DAUGHTERS OF ATLANTIS SERIES
Young Adult

Atlantis Riptide
Atlantis Red Tide
Atlantis Rising Tide
Atlantis Tide Breaker
Atlantis Dark Tides
Atlantis Twisting Tides
Atlantis Glacial Tides

WARRIOR ACADEMY SERIES
Young Adult

Warrior's Destiny
Warrior's Chaos
Warrior's Prophecy
Warrior's Curse
Warrior's Rising

CASTLE RIDGE SERIES
Contemporary Romance

The Romance Dance
The Christmas Match
The Flirtation Game
The Playboy Switch
The Billionaire's Ploy
The Heartbreak Contract

About the Author

Allie Burton has always been a reader and writer. She wrote her first novel at the age of twelve when she was stranded at a hospital by a snowstorm. Receiving her first romance from her grandmother, she fell in love with the genre. As an adult, she read young adult books with her own teens and was excited to find something fresh and new. Now, she writes both.

Having so many jobs as a teen and adult became great research material for the stories she writes. She has been everything from a bike police officer to a mascot escort to an advertising executive. She has lived on three continents and in four states and has studied art, fashion design, and marine biology.

Allie is a member of several writing organizations. She loves to ski, golf, and run. Currently, she lives in Colorado with her husband and two children.

www.allieburton.com
www.twitter.com/allie_burton
www.facebook.com/AllieBurtonAuthor
www.instagram.com/allieburtonauthor